Shades of Dracula

Shades of Dracula

*The Uncollected Macabre
Stories of Bram Stoker*

Compiled & Introduced
by Peter Haining

the apocryphile press
BERKELEY, CA
www.apocryphile.org

apocryphile press
BERKELEY, CA

Apocryphile Press
1700 Shattuck Ave #81
Berkeley, CA 94709
www.apocryphile.org

First published in London, England
by William Kimber & Co., Ltd.
Copyright 1982 by Peter Haining.
First Apocryphile edition, 2006.

ISBN 1-933993-06-5

In Memory of
BRAM STOKER
Who else?

VAMPIRES IN NEW ENGLAND.

Dead Bodies Dug Up and Their Hearts Burned to Prevent Disease.

STRANGE SUPERSTITION OF LONG AGO.

The Old Belief Was that Ghostly Monsters Sucked the Blood of Their Living Relatives.

RECENT ethnological research has disclosed something very extraordinary in Rhode Island. It appears that the ancient vampire superstition still survives in that State, and within the last few years many people have been digging up the dead bodies of relatives for the purpose of burning their hearts.

Near Newport scores of such exhumations have been made, the purpose being to prevent the dead from preying upon the living. The belief entertained is that a person who has died of consumption is likely to rise from the grave at night and suck the blood of surviving members of his or her family, dooming them to a similar fate.

The discovery of the survival educated New England of a tion dating back to the days of apulus and Nebuchadnezzar made by George R. Stetson, a ogist of repute. He has found pant in a district which incl towns of Exeter, Foster, El East Greenwich and many hamlets. This region, where al farms are numerous, is the t ground of the book agent, the peddler and the patent medic The social isolation is as co it was two centuries ago.

Here Cotton Mather and th medical, clerical and lay bel the uncanny ideas of bygone could still hold high carn merely the out-of-the-way ag folk, but the more intelligent the urban communities are their belief in vampirism. noted was that of an intelli well-to-do head of a family years ago lost several of his by consumption. After they w he dug them up and burned

was driven through the chest, and the heart being taken out was either burned or chopped into small pieces. For in this way only could a vampire be deprived of power to do mischief. In one case a man who was unburied sat up in his coffin, with fresh blood on his lips. The official in charge of the ceremonies held a crucifix before his face and saying, "Do you recognise your Saviour?" chopped the unfortunate's head off. This person presumably had been buried alive in a cataleptic trance.

WERE THEY BURIED ALIVE?

How is the phenomenon to be accounted for? Nobody can say with certainty, but it may be that the fright into which people were thrown by the epidemic had the effect of predisposing nervous persons to catalepsy. In a word, people were buried alive in a condition where, the vital functions being suspended, they remained as it were dead for a while. It is a common thing for a cataleptic to bleed at the mouth just before returning to consciousness. According to the popular superstition, the vampire left his or her body in the grave while engaged in nocturnal prowls.

The epidemic prevailed all over southeastern Europe, being at its worst in Hungary and Servia. It is supposed to have originated in Greece, where a belief was entertained to the effect that Latin Christians buried in that country could not decay in their graves, being under the ban of the Greek Church. The cheerful notion was that they got out of their graves at night and pursued the occupation of ghouls. The superstition as to ghouls is very ancient and undoubtedly of Oriental origin. Generally speaking, however, a ghoul is just the opposite of a vampire, being a living person who preys on dead bodies, while a vampire is a dead person that feeds on the blood of the living. If you had your choice, which would you rather be, a vampire or a ghoul?

One of the most familiar of the stories of the Arabian Nights tells of a woman who annoyed her husband very much by refusing food. Nothing more than a few grains of rice would she eat at meals. He discovered that she was in the habit of stealing away from his side in the night, and, following her on one such occasion, he found her engaged in digging up and devouring a corpse.

Among the numerous folk tales about vampires is one relating to a fiend named Dakanavar, who dwelt in a cave in Armenia. He would not permit anybody to penetrate into the mountains of Ulmish Altotem or to count their valleys.

Contents

		page
	Introduction	9
I	The Crystal Cup	14
II	The Chain of Destiny	29
III	The Castle of the King	74
IV	The Fate of Fenella	91
V	Vampires in New England	101
VI	Walpurgis Night	109
VII	The Seer	123
VIII	Another Dracula?	134
IX	At Last	189
X	In the Valley of the Shadow	198
	Acknowledgements	205

Introduction

'Welcome to my house! Enter freely and of your own will!'
He made no motion of stepping to meet me, but stood like
a statue, as though his gesture of welcome had fixed him
into stone. The instant, however, that I had stepped over
the threshold, he moved impulsively forward, and holding
out his hand grasped mine with a strength that made me
wince, an effect which was not lessened by the fact that it
seemed as cold as ice — more like the hand of a dead than
a living man.

With these words we are introduced to one of the most famous
figures in literature, Count Dracula, as he greets the unsuspecting Jonathan Harker at the door to his eerie, mist-shrouded
castle in Transylvania. *'I am Dracula; and I bid you welcome,*
Mr Harker,' the man whom we later learn to be a vampire
continues, before enveloping his guest — and by proxy ourselves
— into the pages of one of the most enduring classics in the
horror genre, *Dracula* by Abraham 'Bram' Stoker (1847–1912),
published nearly one hundred years ago and still among the
most widely read works of its kind.

It is a sad, but perhaps understandable fact, that Dracula is
today far more famous than his creator: a fate that has also been
shared by many other great writers such as Mary Shelley who
gave us *Frankenstein* and Sir Arthur Conan Doyle who, if
acknowledged at all in Sherlockian circles, is usually referred to
as the 'literary agent' of that remarkable detective Sherlock
Holmes. While Stoker was alive, however, any fame that he had

achieved through the creation of the vampire count was of secondary importance: for his life was almost totally devoted to managing the affairs of the great Victorian actor, Sir Henry Irving (1838–1905). And it is arguable that the comparative paucity of Stoker's contribution to literature in the shape of eighteen books and a single collection of short stories is due in no small measure to his singleminded absorption in this task. Stoker's own career was, in fact, dominated by his association with Irving: prior to becoming his manager in 1878 he had served without distinction or much enthusiasm as a civil servant in Dublin, and after the actor's death in 1905 he lived only six more years in a state of rapidly declining health, adding just a few volumes to the one great success of his writing career, his masterpiece, *Dracula*, published in 1897.

The passage of time has been kinder in its appreciation of Stoker than was his own. Though on his death on 20 April 1912 he merited only a single, brief obituary in *The Times* (and that mostly devoted to his association with Sir Henry Irving), since then his work has been the subject of innumerable films, plays and broadcasts, as well as countless scholarly studies and enough books – be they reprints of *Dracula* or biographies of the man and his work – to fill a small library. In any assessment of the horror genre as a whole, *Dracula* is rightly seen as a landmark, and Christopher Lee, the film star who many people credit with having given the most authentic performance of the vampire on the screen, believes that Stoker's book 'almost single-handedly took the tradition of the Gothic novel and brought it into modern times – at the same stroke arousing an interest in vampires which has remained undiminished to this day.'

Among professional writers of fantasy and horror fiction, Stoker is now accorded great respect and admiration, and Stephen King, the author of *Carrie*, *The Shining* and other enormous best-sellers on both sides of the Atlantic, has confessed recently in his fascinating survey of the genre, *Danse Macabre* (1981) that his own novel, *Salem's Lot*, 'bears an intentional similarity to Bram Stoker's *Dracula*'. He writes: 'The scenes from *Dracula* which I chose to retool for my own book were the ones which impressed me the most deeply, the ones

Stoker seemed to have written at fever pitch.' (I do not think I should spoil the pleasure of potential readers of either book by disclosing which these scenes are!) And in praising *Dracula* as 'a remarkable achievement that reverberates in the mind', he also bemoans the fact that Stoker's other work is so little known, in particular his 'absolutely champion short stories'.

Although it has been pointed out in a good many of the studies of Bram Stoker that he wrote a number of short stories during his lifetime, only one posthumous collection has ever been made, by his wife, almost immediately after his death. This thin volume of just nine stories appeared in 1914 under the title *Dracula's Guest*, and though the tales all made fine reading and showed their author to be a master of the short story form as well as the novel, the book was perhaps most intriguing for its Introduction by Florence Stoker. For in this she wrote: 'A few months before the lamented death of my husband — I might say even as the shadow of death was over him — he planned three series of short stories for publication, and the present volume is one of them.' In the remainder of her brief preamble she declares that the contents were 'based on my husband's original list of stories' but that he 'might have seen fit to revise this work which is mainly from the earlier years of his strenuous life if he had lived longer.' What she makes no mention of here — nor are there any indications to be found elsewhere — is *what* Bram Stoker proposed to include in the other two 'series' of short stories. Death, of course, may well have intervened before he could even bring his mind to bear on making selections from the remaining pile of his short fiction. Or he may have planned to write new stories to be added to those which had already appeared in English and American magazines. The truth is, we just don't know.

It is a mystery that has intrigued me ever since I first discovered the works of Bram Stoker more than a quarter of a century ago — and one that I have tried partly to resolve with this collection. Bram has certainly made it no easy task — for he did not confine his contributions to any one publication, nor any one country, being published during his lifetime in several obscure Irish journals, numerous English periodicals and even a batch of American magazines. He compounded the difficulty in tracing them by keeping no records of their sale and even appeared indifferent about retaining file copies of most. Nonetheless, intensive research in England, Ireland and America has made it possible to reclaim from dusty oblivion enough stories to produce the kind of thematic collection which might have occurred to him and which will hopefully appeal to the army of admirers of *Dracula*. For what I have done here is assemble a group of his stories which all relate in some way or another to that great novel: some pre-dating it and revealing how his love of the weird was leading him inexorably towards its creation, and the rest subsequent works which show how its influence was never far from his mind when he took up his pen again.

The influences on Stoker's life and, in turn, those which he imposed on others, have been discussed fully in other books and need no repetition here. The argument as to what inspired him to write *Dracula* — ranging from his own tongue-in-cheek explanation that he dreamed it after a heavy dinner of dressed crab, to the stories of a bloodthirsty fifteenth-century Transylvanian prince named Vlad Tepes, 'Vlad the Impaler', recounted to him by a mysterious Hungarian named Arminius Vambery — will doubtless go on being debated for many years yet. For my part, the only incontrovertible piece of evidence is an item included in this collection, 'Vampires of New England', a story torn from an American newspaper and found among Bram's working papers for *Dracula*. That this item played a part in the creation of the book is, I believe, beyond dispute, all the more so because of the facts it contains which also reoccur in the story. I have gone into more detail about it in the preface.

Similarly, too, I have included an episode which Stoker wrote originally as an Introduction to *Dracula* — giving a foretaste of what was to come — but which the publishers, Archibald Constable, asked him to delete for reasons of length. It is interesting to speculate on whether, if they had had any idea of the success which was shortly to be on their hands, they would have allowed it to remain. In any event, the story stayed in manuscript until after Stoker's death when it was first published in *The Story Teller* under the title of 'Walpurgis Night'. The background details to this, along with all the other stories in the collection, are given in the accompanying prefaces.

Of other items by Stoker which still remain uncollected, the larger proportion are essays and articles dealing with the theatre, and Sir Henry Irving in particular. They would doubtless deserve a place in any book dealing with the theatrical side of Bram's life and, indeed, students of British theatre history during the closing years of the last century and the first decade of the twentieth, will find much to interest them in his informative contributions to magazines like the *Fortnightly Review*, *vide* 'Americans as Actors' and 'Dead Heads' (both 1909) about the filling of theatres with non-paying guests to drum up business; and the *Nineteenth Century Magazine* which published his controversial essay, 'Censorship of Plays' (1909) and the very last thing he wrote, appropriately about Sir Henry Irving, 'Irving and Stage Lighting' published in June 1911.

As to the stories in this collection which have once again risen, vampire-like, for a new lease of life, I believe they will further enhance their author's reputation and perhaps take us a little closer to solving the mystery as to how the worldly-wise business manager of a famous actor could have created what Stephen King has called 'this fearsome, immortal monster'. For Bram Stoker has given literature one of its truly original and timeless creations — and here, for those who would have more of him, are further *Shades of Dracula* . . .

PETER HAINING

I

The Crystal Cup

Bram Stoker was born on 8 November 1847 at 15 The Crescent, Clontarf in Dublin, the third of seven children of Charlotte and Abraham Stoker, a government clerk employed at Dublin Castle. Bram, named after his father, was a small, sickly child, who nearly died in infancy, but grew into a sturdy and masculine youth thanks to his dedication to physical fitness. Because of this early ill-health, he found much solace in his father's extensive library and read avidly of all kinds of literature. From his father he also inherited a love of the theatre, to which he was to be enthusiastically drawn as he grew from boy into man. Bram was educated at Trinity College in Dublin, distinguishing himself at history and composition, and by the time he was in his late teens he already had the reputation of being a 'scribbler' among his four brothers and two sisters.

Although his mother, who was a devoted social worker and had herself written a number of essays on social reform, encouraged his literary efforts, Bram's father had already decreed for him a career in the Civil Service and in 1870 he started work as a clerk in Dublin Castle. The job proved dull and monotonous, and Bram found some relief by writing stories and essays, but no one would publish them. The boredom of his life was only relieved by visits to the theatre, and it was during one such outing in August 1867 that he saw a fast rising young English actor named Henry Irving and found himself irresistibly attracted to the man. Later, he had an opportunity of meeting the actor and a friendship rapidly developed between them. Then in 1878 Irving invited Stoker to join him as his manager and for the rest of the actor's life (he died in 1905), the two were virtually inseparable, Bram playing a secondary but immensely important role in Irving's rise to stardom.

In the intervening years, however, Bram never lost sight of his desire to write, and as a result of his knowledge of the stage managed to secure the (unpaid) job of theatre critic to one of the local papers, the *Dublin Mail*, in November 1871. This modest success encouraged him to continue writing, and almost a year later, in September 1872, his first story was published. The tale was called 'The Crystal Cup' and because of the many rejections he had already received from Editors in Ireland, Bram spread his net wider and sent the story to London to a popular monthly journal, *The London Society*. To his great joy, it was accepted for publication – yet as in the case of his theatrical critiques, it is highly unlikely that he received any payment for it. Still, such was his delight at seeing his first story in print that the trifling matter of a fee bothered him not at all!

Considered in hindsight, it is perhaps only to be expected that after having tried so many other types of stories (he is believed to have written numerous straightforward tales of love, romance and history), Bram should have scored his first success – albeit a modest one – with a piece of pure fantasy. It was evident even then that he had a talent for this genre in which he would later become so proficient, and in the story itself there are several of the elements of construction and changes in viewpoint that were to be used with such success in *Dracula*. Here, then, in 'The Crystal Cup' we can see the first flowering of Stoker's talent at the age of twenty-five, as well as the first faint shade of the vampire masterpiece to come . . .

The Crystal Cup

1. The Dream-birth

The blue waters touch the walls of the palace; I can hear their soft, lapping wash against the marble whenever I listen. Far out at sea I can see the waves glancing in the sunlight, ever-smiling, ever-glancing, ever-sunny. Happy waves! — happy in your gladness, thrice happy that ye are free!

I rise from my work and spring up the wall till I reach the embrasure. I grasp the corner of the stonework and draw myself up till I crouch in the wide window. Sea, sea, out away as far as my vision extends. There I gaze until my eyes grow dim; and in the dimness of my eyes my spirit finds its sight.

My soul flies on the wings of memory away beyond the blue, smiling sea — away beyond the glancing waves and the gleaming sails, to the land I call my home. As the minutes roll by, my actual eyesight seems to be restored, and I look around me in my old birth-house. The rude simplicity of the dwelling comes back to me as something new. There I see my old books and manuscripts and pictures, and there, away on their old shelves, high up above the door, I see my first rude efforts in art.

How poor they seem to me now! And yet, were I free, I would not give the smallest of them for all I now possess. Possess? How I dream.

The dream calls me back to waking life. I spring down from my window-seat and work away frantically, for every line I draw on paper, every new form that springs on the plaster, brings me nearer freedom. I will make a vase whose beauty will put to shame the glorious works of Greece in her golden prime! Surely a love like mine and a hope like mine must in time make some form of beauty spring to life! When He beholds it he will exclaim with rapture, and will order my instant freedom. I can forget my hate, and the deep debt of revenge which I owe him when I think of liberty — even from his hands. Ah! then on the wings of the morning shall I fly beyond the sea to my home — her home — and clasp her to my arms, never more to be separated.

But, oh Spirit of Day! if she should be — No, no, I cannot think of it, or I shall go mad. Oh Time, Time! maker and destroyer of men's fortunes, why hasten so fast for others whilst thou laggest so slowly for me? Even now my home may have become desolate, and she — my bride of an hour — may sleep calmly in the cold earth. Oh this suspense will drive me mad! Work, work! Freedom is before me; Aurora is the reward of my labour!

So I rush to my work; but to my brain and hand, heated alike, no fire or no strength descends. Half mad with despair, I beat myself against the walls of my prison, and then climb into the embrasure, and once more gaze upon the ocean, but find there no hope. And so I stay till night, casting its pall of blackness over nature, puts the possibility of effort away from me for yet another day.

So my days go on, and grow to weeks and months. So will they grow to years, should life so long remain an unwelcome guest within me; for what is man without hope? and is not hope nigh dead within this weary breast?

Last night, in my dreams, there came, like an inspiration from the Day-Spirit, a design for my vase.

All day my yearning for freedom — for Aurora, or news of her — had increased tenfold, and my heart and brain were on fire. Madly I beat myself, like a caged bird, against my prison-bars. Madly I leaped to my window-seat, and gazed with bursting eyeballs out on the free, open sea. And there I sat till my passion had worn itself out; and then I slept, and dreamed of thee, Aurora — of thee and freedom.

In my ears I heard again the old song we used to sing together when, as children, we wandered on the beach; when, as lovers, we saw the sun sink in the ocean, and I would see its glory doubled as it shone in thine eyes, and was mellowed against thy cheek; and when, as my bride, you clung to me as my arms went round you on that desert tongue of land whence rushed that band of sea-robbers that tore me away.

Oh! how my heart curses those men — not men, but fiends! But one solitary gleam of joy remains from that dread encounter — that my struggle stayed those hellhounds, and that, ere I was stricken down, this right hand sent one of them to his home. My spirit rises as I think of the blow that saved thee from a life worse than death. With the thought I feel my cheeks burning, and my forehead swelling with mighty veins.

My eyes burn, and I rush wildly round my prison-house.

'Oh! for one of my enemies, that I might dash out his brains against these marble walls, and trample his heart out as he lay before me!'

These walls would spare him not. They are pitiless, alas! I know too well. 'Oh, cruel mockery of kindness, to make a palace a prison, and to taunt a captive's aching heart with forms of beauty and sculptured marble!'

Wondrous, indeed, are those sculptured walls! Men call them passing fair; but oh, Aurora! with thy beauty ever before my eyes, what form that men call lovely can be fair to me? Like him who gazes sunwards, and sees no light on earth, from the glory that dyes his iris, so thy beauty or its memory has turned the fairest things of earth to blackness and deformity.

In my dream last night, when in my ears came softly, like music stealing across the waters from afar, the old song we used to sing together, then to my brain, like a ray of light, came an idea whose grandeur for a moment struck me dumb. Before my eyes grew a vase of such beauty that I knew my hope was born to life, and that the Great Spirit had placed my foot on the ladder that leads from this my palace-dungeon to freedom and to thee. Today I have got a block of crystal − for only in such pellucid substance can I body forth my dream − and have commenced my work.

I found at first that my hand had lost its cunning, and I was beginning to despair, when, like the memory of a dream, there came back in my ears the strains of the old song. I sang it softly to myself, and as I did so I grew calmer; but oh! how differently the song sounded to me when thy voice, Aurora, rose not in unison with my own!

But what avails pining? To work! Every touch of my chisel will bring me nearer thee.

My vase is daily growing near to completion. I sing as I work, and my constant song is the one I love so well. I can hear the echo of my voice in the vase; and as I end, the wailing song note is prolonged in sweet, sad music in the crystal cup.

I listen, ear down, and sometimes I weep as I listen, so sadly comes the echo to my song. Imperfect though it may be, my voice makes sweet music, and its echo in the cup guides my hand towards perfection as I work. Would that thy voice rose and fell with mine, Aurora, and then the world would behold a vase of such beauty as never before woke up the slumbering fires of man's love for what is fair; for if I do such work in sadness, imperfect as I am in my solitude and sorrow, what would I do in joy, perfect when with thee?

I know that my work is good as an artist, and I feel that it is as a man; and the cup itself, as it daily grows in beauty, gives back a clearer echo. Oh! if I worked in joy how gladly would it give back our voices! *Then* would we hear an echo and music such as mortals seldom hear; but now the echo like my song, seems imperfect. I grow daily weaker; but still I work on — work my whole soul — for am I not working for freedom and for thee.

My work is nearly done. Day by day, hour by hour, the vase grows more finished. Ever clearer comes the echo whilst I sing; ever softer, ever more sad and heartening comes the echo of the wail at the end of the song. Day by day I grow weaker and weaker; still I work on with all my soul. At night the thought comes to me, whilst I think of thee, that I will never see thee more — that I breathe out my life into the crystal cup, and that it will last there when I am gone.

So beautiful has it become, so much do I love it, that I could gladly die to be the maker of such a work, were it not for thee — for my love for thee, and my hope of thee, and my fear for thee, and my anguish for thy grief when thou knowest I am gone.

My work requires but few more touches. My life is slowly ebbing away, and I feel that with my last touch my life will pass out for ever into the cup. Till that touch is given I must not die — I will not die. My hate has passed away. So great are my wrongs that revenge of mine would be too small a compensation for my woe. I leave revenge to a juster and a mightier than I. Thee, oh Aurora, I will await in the land of flowers, where thou and I will wander, never more to part, never more! Ah, never more!

Farewell, Aurora — Aurora — Aurora!

2. *The Feast of Beauty*

The Feast of Beauty approaches rapidly, yet hardly so fast as my royal master wishes. He seems to have no other thought than to have this feast greater and better than any ever held before. Five summers ago his Feast of Beauty was nobler than all held in his sire's reign together; yet scarcely was it over, and the rewards given to the victors, when he conceived the giant project whose success is to be tested when the moon reaches her full.

It was boldly chosen and boldly done; chosen and done as boldly as the project of a monarch should be. But still I cannot think that it will end well. This yearning after completeness must be unsatisfied in the end — this desire that makes a monarch fling his kingly justice to the winds, and strive to reach his Mecca over a desert of blighted hopes and lost lives. But hush! I must not dare to think ill of my master or his deeds; and besides, walls have ears. I must leave alone these dangerous topics, and confine my thoughts within proper bounds.

The moon is waxing quickly, and with its fullness comes the Feast of Beauty, whose success as a whole rests almost solely on my watchfulness and care; for if the ruler of the feast should fail in his duty, who could fill the void? Let me see what arts are represented, and what works compete. All the arts will have trophies: poetry in its various forms, and prose-writing; sculpture with carving in various metals, and glass, and wood, and ivory, and engraving gems, and setting jewels; painting on canvas, and glass, and wood, and stone and metal; music, vocal and instrumental; and dancing.

If that woman will but sing, we will have a real triumph of music; but she appears sickly too. All our best artists either get ill or die, although we promise them freedom or rewards or both if they succeed.

Surely never yet was a Feast of Beauty so fair or so richly dowered as this which the full moon shall behold and hear; but ah! the crowning glory of the feast will be the crystal cup. Never yet have these eyes beheld such a form of beauty, such a wondrous mingling of substance and light. Surely some magic power must have helped to draw such loveliness from a cold block of crystal. I must be careful that no harm happens to the vase. Today when I touched it, it gave forth such a ringing sound that my heart jumped with fear lest it should sustain any injury. Henceforth, till I deliver it up to my master, no hand but my own shall touch it lest any harm should happen to it.

Strange story has that cup. Born to life in the cell of a captive torn from his artist home beyond the sea, to enhance the splendour of a feast by his labour — seen at work by spies, and traced and followed until a chance — cruel chance for him — gave him into the hands of the emissaries of my master.

He, too, poor moth, fluttered about the flame: the name of freedom spurred him on to exertion till he wore away his life. The beauty of that cup was dearly bought for him. Many a man would forget his captivity whilst he worked at such a piece of loveliness; but he appeared to have some sorrow at his heart, some sorrow so great that it quenched his pride.

How he used to rave at first! How he used to rush about his chamber, and then climb into the embrasure of his window, and gaze out away over the sea! Poor captive! perhaps over the sea someone waited for his coming who was dearer to him than many cups, even many cups as beautiful as this, if such could be on earth. . . .

Well, well, we must all die soon or late, and who dies first escapes the more sorrow, perhaps, who knows?

How, when he had commenced the cup, he used to sing all day long, from the moment the sun shot its first fiery arrow into the retreating hosts of night clouds, till the shades of evening advancing drove the lingering sunbeams into the west — and always the same song!

How he used to sing, all alone! Yet sometimes I could almost imagine I heard not one voice from his chamber, but two. . . . No more will it echo again from the wall of a dungeon or from a hillside in free air. No more will his eyes behold the beauty of his crystal cup.

It was well he lived to finish it. Often and often have I trembled to think of his death, as I saw him day by day grow weaker as he worked at the unfinished vase. Must his eyes never more behold the beauty that was born of his soul? Oh, never more! Oh Death, grim King of Terrors, how mighty is thy sceptre! All-powerful is the wave of thy hand that summons us in turn to thy kingdom away beyond the poles!

Would that thou, poor captive, hadst lived to behold thy triumph, for victory will be thine at the Feast of Beauty such as man never before achieved. Then thou might have heard the shout that hails the victor in the contest, and the plaudits that greet him as he passes out, a free man, through the palace gates. But now thy cup will come to light amid the smiles of beauty and rank and power, whilst thou liest there in thy lonely chamber, cold as the marble of its walls.

And, after that, the feast will be imperfect, since the victors cannot all be crowned. I must ask my master's direction as to how a blank place of a competitor, should he prove a victor, is to be filled up. So late? I must see him ere the noontide hour of rest be past.

Great Spirit! how I trembled as my master answered my question!

I found him in his chamber, as usual in the noontide. He was lying on his couch disrobed, half-sleeping; and the drowsy zephyr, scented with rich odours from the garden, wafted through the windows on either side by the fans, lulled him to complete repose. The darkened chamber was cool and silent. From the vestibule came the murmuring of many fountains, and the pleasant splash of falling waters.

'Oh, happy,' said I, in my heart, 'oh happy great King, that has such pleasures to enjoy.'

The breeze from the fans swept over the strings of the Aeolian harps, and a sweet, confused, happy melody arose like the murmuring of children's voices singing afar off in the valleys, and floating on the wind.

As I entered the chamber softly, with muffled foot-fall and pent-in breath, I felt a kind of awe stealing over me. To me who was born and have dwelt all my life within the precincts of the court − to me who talk daily with my royal master, and take his minutest directions as to the coming feast − to me who had all my life looked up to my king as to a spirit, and had venerated him as more than mortal − came a feeling of almost horror; for my master looked then, in his quiet chamber, half-sleeping amid the drowsy music of the harps and fountains, more like a common man than a God. As the thought came to me I shuddered in afright, for it seemed to me that I had been guilty of sacrilege. So much had my veneration for my royal master become a part of my nature, that but to think of him as another man seemed like the anarchy of my own soul.

I came beside the couch, and watched him in silence. He seemed to be half-listening to the fitful music; and as the melody swelled and died away his chest rose and fell as he breathed in unison with the sound.

After a moment or two he appeared to become conscious of the presence of someone in the room, although by no motion of his face could I see that he heard any sound, and his eyes were shut. He opened his eyes, and, seeing me, asked, 'Was all right about the Feast of Beauty?' for that is the subject ever nearest to his thoughts. I answered that all was well, but that I had come to ask his royal pleasure as to how a vacant place amongst the competitors was to be filled up.

He asked, 'How vacant?' and on my telling him 'From death', he asked again, quickly, 'Was the work finished?'

When I told him that it was, he lay back again on his couch with a sigh of relief, for he had half arisen in his anxiety as he asked the question.

Then he said, after a minute, 'All the competitors must be present at the feast.'

'All?' said I.

'All,' he answered again, 'alive or dead; for the old custom must be preserved, and the victors crowned.'

He stayed still for a minute more, and then said, slowly, 'Victors or martyrs.'

And I could see that the kingly spirit was coming back to him.

Again he went on, 'This will be the last Feast of Beauty; and all the captives shall be set free. Too much sorrow has sprung already from my ambition. Too much injustice has soiled the name of king.'

He said no more, but lay still and closed his eyes. I could see by the working of his hands and the heaving of his chest that some violent emotion troubled him, and the thought arose, 'He is a man, but he is yet a king; and, though a king as he is, still happiness is not for him. Great Spirit of Justice! thou metest out his pleasures and his woes to man, to king and slave alike! Thou lovest best to whom thou givest peace!'

Gradually my master grew more calm, and at length sunk into a gentle slumber; but even in his sleep he breathed in unison with the swelling murmur of the harps.

'To each is given,' said I gently, 'something in common with the world of actual things. Thy life, oh King, is bound by chains of sympathy to the voice of Truth, which is Music! Tremble, lest in the presence of a master-strain thou should feel thy littleness, and die!' and I softly left the room.

3. The Story of the Moonbeam

Slowly I creep along the bosom of the waters.

Sometimes I look back as I rise upon a billow, and see behind me many of my kin sitting each upon a wave-summit as upon a throne. So I go on for long, a power that I wist not forcing me onward, without will or purpose of mine.

At length, as I rise upon a mimic wave, I see afar a hazy light that springs from a vast palace, through whose countless windows flame lamps and torches. But at the first view, as if my coming had been a signal, the lights disappear in an instant.

Impatiently I await what may happen; and as I rise with each heart-beat of the sea, I look forward to where the torches had gleamed. Can it be a deed of darkness that shuns the light?

The time has come when I can behold the palace without waiting to mount upon the waves. It is built of white marble, and rises steep from the brine. Its sea-front is glorious with columns and statues; and from the portals the marble steps sweep down, broad and wide to the waters, and below them, down as deep as I can see.

No sound is heard, no light is seen. A solemn silence abounds, a perfect calm.

Slowly I climb the palace walls, my brethren following as soldiers up a breach. I slide along the roofs, and as I look behind me walls and roofs are glistening as with silver. At length I meet with something hard and smooth and translucent; but through it I pass and enter a vast hall, where for an instant I hang in mid-air and wonder.

My coming has been the signal for such a burst of harmony as brings back to my memory the music of the spheres as they rush through space; and in the full-swelling anthem of welcome I feel that I am indeed a sun-spirit, a child of light, and that this is my homage to my master.

I look upon the face of a great monarch, who sits at the head of a banquet-table. He has turned his head upwards and back-wards, and looks as if he had been awaiting my approach. He rises and fronts me with the ringing out of the welcome-song, and all the others in the great hall turn towards me as well. I can see their eyes gleaming. Down along the immense table, laden with plate and glass and flowers, they stand holding each a cup of ruby wine, with which they pledge the monarch when the song is ended, as they drink success to him and to the 'Feast of Beauty'.

I survey the hall. An immense chamber, with marble walls covered with bas reliefs and frescoes and sculptured figures, and panelled by great columns that rise along the surface and support a dome-ceiling painted wondrously; in its centre the glass lantern by which I entered.

On the walls are hung pictures of various forms and sizes, and down the centre of the table stretches a raised platform on which are placed works of art of various kinds.

At one side of the hall is a dais on which sits persons of both sexes with noble faces and lordly brows, but all wearing the same expression − care tempered by hope. All these hold scrolls in their hands.

At the other side of the hall is a similar dais, on which sit others fairer to earthly view, less spiritual and more marked by surface-passion. They hold music scores. All these look more joyous than those on the other platform, all save one, a woman, who sits with downcast face and dejected mien, as of one without hope. As my light falls at her feet she looks up, and I feel happy. The sympathy between us has called a faint gleam of hope to cheer that poor pale face.

Many are the forms of art that rise above the banquet-table and all are lovely to behold. I look on all with pleasure one by one, till I see the last of them at the end of the table away from the monarch, and then all the others seem as nothing to me.

What is this that makes other forms of beauty seem as nought when compared with it, when brought within the radius of its lustre? A crystal cup, wrought with such wondrous skill that light seems to lose its individual glory as it shines upon it and is merged in its beauty.

'Oh Universal Mother, let me enter there. Let my life be merged in its beauty, and no more will I regret my sun-strength hidden deep in the chasms of my moon-mother. Let me live there and perish there, and I will be joyous whilst it lasts, and content to pass into the great vortex of nothingness to be born again when the glory of the cup has fled.'

Can it be that my wish is granted, that I have entered the cup and become a part of its beauty?

'Great Mother, I thank thee.'

Has the cup life? or is it merely its wondrous perfectness that makes it tremble, like a beating heart, in unison with the ebb and flow, the great wave-pulse of nature. To me it feels as if it had life.

I look through the crystal walls and see at the end of the table, isolated from all others, the figure of a man seated. Are those cords that bind his limbs? How suits that crown of laurel, those wide, dim eyes, and that pallid hue? It is passing strange. The Feast of Beauty holds some dread secrets and sees some wondrous sights.

I hear a voice of strange, rich sweetness, yet wavering − the voice of one *almost* a king by nature. He is standing up; I see him through my palace-wall. He calls a name and sits down again.

Again I hear a voice from the platform of scrolls, the Throne of Brows; and again I look and behold a man who stands trembling yet flushed, as though the morning light shone bright upon his soul. He reads in cadenced measure a song in praise of my moon-mother, the Feast of Beauty, and the king. As he speaks, he trembles no more, but seems inspired, and his voice rises to a tone of power and grandeur, and rings back from walls and dome. I hear his words distinctly, though saddened in tone, in the echo from my crystal home. He concludes and sits down, half-fainting, amid a whirlwind of applause, every note, every beat of which is echoed as the words had been.

Again the monarch rises and calls 'Aurora,' that she may sing for freedom. The name echoes in the cup with a sweet, sad sound. So sad, so despairing seems the echo, that the hall seems to darken and the scene to grow dim.

'Can a sun-spirit mourn, or a crystal vessel weep?'

She, the dejected one, rises from her seat on the Throne of Sound, and all eyes turn upon her save those of the pale one, laurel-crowned. Thrice she essays to begin, and thrice nought comes from her lips but a dry, husky sigh, till an old man who has been moving round the hall settling all things cries out, in fear lest she should fail, 'Freedom!'

The word is re-echoed from the cup. She hears the sound, turns towards it and begins.

Oh, the melody of that voice! And yet it is not perfect alone; for after the first note comes an echo from the cup that swells in unison with the voice, and the two sounds together seem as if one strain came ringing from the lips of the All-Father himself. So sweet it is, that all throughout the hall sit spellbound, and scarcely dare to breathe.

In the pause after the first verses of the song, I hear the voice of the old man speaking to a comrade, but his words are unheard by any other, 'Look at the king. His spirit seems lost in a trance of melody. Ah! I fear me some evil: the nearer the music approaches to perfection the more rapt he becomes. I dread lest a perfect note shall prove his death-call.'

His voice dies away as the singer commences the last verse.

Sad and plaintive is the song; full of feeling and of tender love, but love overshadowed by grief and despair. As it goes on the voice of the singer grows sweeter and more thrilling, more real; and the cup, my crystal time-home, vibrates more and more as it gives back the echo. The monarch looks like one entranced, and no movement is within the hall.

The song dies away in a wild wail that seems to tear the heart of the singer in twain; and the cup vibrates still more as it gives back the echo. As the note, long-swelling, reaches its highest, the cup, the Crystal Cup, my wondrous home, the gift of the All-Father, shivers into millions of atoms, and passes away.

Ere I am lost in the great vortex I see the singer throw up her arms and fall, freed at last, and the king sitting, glory-faced, but pallid with the hue of Death.

II

The Chain of Destiny

While Bram continued to labour over his duties at Dublin Castle by day, he looked forward to immersing himself still more deeply in the world of the press at night. Apart from his theatrical notices for the *Dublin Mail*, he also began contributing commentaries to a weekly journal called *The Warder* and small essays to various local newspapers. Although he still received little if any payment for much of this work, it did bring him into contact with other journals and editors, and finally landed him the job of editor of a new evening paper called the *Irish Echo*. What is astonishing about this appointment is that it was only on a part-time basis, and he could only work on the paper each afternoon after he had finished his duties as a civil servant! Yet Bram gave it everything he had, and it was not his lack of hard work or determined newsgathering that contributed to the paper failing to reach its owner's expectations, overambitious as they doubtless were.

However, he sensed an uneasy situation developing at Dublin Castle where his seniors were becoming unhappy about his association with the newspaper and, reluctantly, he decided to give up the editorship after four months. But he was determined not to give up writing. Instead he contented himself by trying his hand at another kind of composition: a serial story for one of the city's popular weekly journals, *The Shamrock*, which was always in the market for such items. The magazine was a potpourri of news, views, opinions and stories, and also liked to give its readers a weekly dose of thrills. So, having succeeded in finding a market with his fantasy, 'The Crystal Cup', Bram decided on a story of horror, working towards four cliff-hanging moments so that the magazine could publish it in four issues. In this way, he hoped, the magazine would not only be able to encourage its readers to buy next week's issue, but his name would be made with them as well as the editor.

Bram called the serial, 'The Chain of Destiny', and among the most striking elements of his plot was a romance over-shadowed by an evil curse and a strange, mysterious character called 'the phantom of the Fiend'. To Stoker's delight, the serial was accepted by *The Shamrock* and appeared in issues number 466, 447, 448 and 449 in the spring of 1875.

Although the story is to a degree influenced by that classic vampire story 'Carmilla' by another Irish writer, Joseph Sheridan Le Fanu, which had just been published to consider-able acclaim in the *Dublin University Magazine*, and which we know Bram read avidly, it does have a style and treatment of its subject which is peculiarly Stoker's own. As his first attempt at horror, it is also his most positive step in the direction of *Dracula*, while in the shape of 'the phantom of the fiend' we can sense the character of the undead count of Transylvania begin-ning to materialise . . .

The Chain of Destiny

1. A Warning

It was so late in the evening when I arrived at Scarp that I had but little opportunity of observing the external appearance of the house; but, as far as I could judge in the dim twilight, it was a very stately edifice of seemingly great age, built of white stone. When I passed the porch, however, I could observe its internal beauties much more closely, for a large wood fire burned in the hall and all the rooms and passages were lighted. The hall was almost baronial in its size, and opened on to a staircase of dark oak so wide and so generous in its slope that a carriage might almost have been driven up it. The rooms were large and lofty, with their walls, like those of the staircase, panelled with oak black from age. This sombre material would have made the house intensely gloomy but for the enormous width and height of both rooms and passages. As it was, the effect was a homely combination of size and warmth. The windows were set in deep embrasures, and, on the ground story, reached from quite level with the floor to almost the ceiling. The fireplaces were quite in the old style, large and surrounded with massive oak carvings, representing on each some scene from Biblical history, and at the side of each fireplace rose a pair of massive carved iron fire-dogs. It was altogether just such a house as would have delighted the heart of Washington Irving or Nathaniel Hawthorne.

The house had been lately restored; but in effecting the restoration comfort had not been forgotten, and any modern improvement which tended to increase the homelike appearance of the rooms had been added. The old diamond paned casements, which had remained probably from the Elizabethan age, had given place to more useful plate glass; and, in like manner, many other changes had taken place. But so judiciously had every change been effected that nothing of the new clashed with the old, but the harmony of all the parts seemed complete.

I thought it no wonder that Mrs Trevor had fallen in love with Scarp the first time she had seen it. Mrs Trevor's liking the place was tantamount to her husband's buying it, for he was so wealthy that he could get almost anything money could purchase. He was himself a man of good taste, but still he felt his inferiority to his wife in this respect so much that he never dreamt of differing in opinion from her on any matter of choice or judgment. Mrs Trevor had, without exception, the best taste of any one whom I ever knew, and, strange to say, her taste was not confined to any branch of art. She did not write, or paint, or sing; but still her judgment in writing, painting, or music, was unquestioned by her friends. It seemed as if nature had denied to her the power of execution in any separate branch of art, in order to make her perfect in her appreciation of what was beautiful and true in all. She was perfect in *the art of harmonising — the art of every-day life*. Her husband used to say, with a far-fetched joke, that her star must have been in the House of Libra, because everything which she said and did showed such a nicety of balance.

Mr and Mrs Trevor were the most model couple I ever knew
— they really seemed not twain, but one. They appeared to
have adopted something of the French idea of man and wife —
that they should not be the less like *friends* because they were
linked together by indissoluble bonds — that they should share
their pleasures as well as their sorrows. The former outbalanced
the latter, for both husband and wife were of that happy tem-
perament which can take pleasure from everything, and find
consolation even in the chastening rod of affliction.

Still, through their web of peaceful happiness ran a thread of
care. One that cropped up in strange places, and disappeared
again, but which left a quiet tone over the whole fabric — they
had no child.

> They had their share of sorrow, for when time was ripe
> The still affection of the heart became an outward
>   breathing type,
> That into stillness passed again,
> But left a want unknown before.

There was something simple and holy in their patient endur-
ance of their lonely life — for lonely a house must ever be without children to those who love truly. Theirs was not the eager,
disappointed longing of those whose union had proved fruitless.
It was the simple, patient, hopeless resignation of those who
find that a common sorrow draws them more closely together
that many common joys. I myself could note the warmth of their
hearts and their strong philoprogenitive feeling in their manner
towards me.

From the time when I lay sick in college when Mrs Trevor
appeared to my fever-dimmed eyes like an angel of mercy, I felt
myself growing in their hearts. Who can imagine my gratitude
to the lady who, merely because she heard of my sickness and
desolation from a college friend, came and nursed me night and
day till the fever left me. When I was sufficiently strong to be
moved she had me brought away to the country, where good air,
care, and attention soon made me stronger than ever. From
that time I became a constant visitor at the Trevors' house; and
as month after month rolled by I felt that I was growing in their
affections. For four summers I spent my long vacation in their

house, and each year I could feel Mr Trevor's shake of the hand grow heartier, and his wife's kiss on my forehead — for so she always saluted me — grow more tender and motherly.

Their liking for me had now grown so much that in their heart of hearts — and it was a sanctum common to them both — they secretly loved me as a son. Their love was returned manifold by the lonely boy, whose devotion to the kindest friends of his youth and his trouble had increased with his growth into manhood. Even in my own heart I was ashamed to confess how I loved them both — how I worshipped Mrs Trevor as I adored the mother whom I had lost so young, and whose eyes shone sometimes even then upon me, like stars, in my sleep.

It is strange how timorous we are when our affections are concerned. Merely because I had never told her how I loved her as a mother, because she had never told me how she loved me as a son, I used sometimes to think of her with a sort of lurking suspicion that I was trusting too much to my imagination. Sometimes even I would try to avoid thinking of her altogether, till my yearning would grow too strong to be repelled, and then I would think of her long and silently, and would love her more and more. My life was so lonely that I clung to her as the only thing I had to love. Of course I loved her husband, too, but I never thought about him in the same way; for men are less demonstrative about their affections to each other, and even aknowledge them to themselves less.

Mrs Trevor was an excellent hostess. She always let her guests see that they were welcome, and, unless in the case of casual visitors, that they were expected. She was, as may be imagined, very popular with all classes; but what is more rare, she was equally popular with both sexes. To be popular with her own sex is the touchstone of a woman's worth. To the houses of the peasantry she came, they said, like an angel, and brought comfort wherever she came. She knew the proper way to deal with the poor; she always helped them materially, but never offended their feelings in so doing. Young people all adored her.

My curiosity had been aroused as to the sort of place Scarp was; for, in order to give me a surprise, they would not tell me anything about it, but said that I must wait and judge it for myself. I had looked forward to my visit with both expectation and curiosity.

When I entered the hall, Mrs Trevor came out to welcome me and kissed me on the forehead, after her usual manner. Several of the old servants came near, smiling and bowing, and wishing welcome to 'Master Frank.' I shook hands with several of them, whilst their mistress looked on with a pleased smile.

As we went into a snug parlour, where a table was laid out with the materials for a comfortable supper, Mrs Trevor said to me:

'I am glad you came so soon, Frank. We have no one here at present, so you will be quite alone with us for a few days; and you will be quite alone with me this evening, for Charley is gone to a dinner-party at Westholm.'

I told her that I was glad that there was no one else at Scarp, for that I would rather be with her and her husband than any one else in the world. She smiled as she said:

'Frank, if any one else said that, I would put it down as a mere compliment; but I know you always speak the truth. It is all very well to be alone with an old couple like Charley and me for two or three days; but just you wait till Thursday, and you will look on the intervening days as quite wasted.'

'Why?' I inquired.

'Because, Frank, there is a girl coming to stay with me then, with whom I intend you to fall in love.'

I answered jocosely:

'Oh, thank you, Mrs Trevor, very much for your kind intentions — but suppose for a moment that they should be impracticable. "One man may lead a horse to the pond's brink." "The best laid schemes o' mice an' men." Eh?'

'Frank, don't be silly. I do not want to make you fall in love against your inclination; but I hope and I believe that you will.'

'Well, I'm sure I hope you won't be disappointed; but I never yet heard a person praised that I did not experience a disappointment when I came to know him or her.'

'Frank, did I praise any one?'

'Well, I am vain enough to think that your saying that you knew I would fall in love with her was a sort of indirect praise.'

'Dear me, Frank, how modest you have grown. "A sort of indirect praise!" Your humility is quite touching.'

'May I ask who the lady is, as I am supposed to be an interested party?'

'I do not know that I ought to tell you on account of your
having expressed any doubt as to her merits. Besides, I might
weaken the effect of the introduction. If I stimulate your
curiosity it will be a point in my favour.'

'Oh, very well; I suppose I must only wait?'

'Ah, well, Frank, I will tell you. It is not fair to keep you waiting. She is a Miss Fothering.'

'Fothering? Fothering? I think I know that name. I remember
hearing it somewhere, a long time ago, if I do not mistake.
Where does she come from?'

'Her father is a clergyman in Norfolk, but he belongs to the
Warwickshire family. I met her at Winthrop, Sir Harry Blount's
place, a few months ago, and took a great liking for her, which
she returned, and so we became fast friends. I made her
promise to pay me a visit this summer, so she and her sister are
coming here on Thursday to stay for some time.'

'And, may I be bold enough to inquire what she is like?'

'You may inquire if you like, Frank; but you won't get an
answer. I shall not try to describe her. You must wait and judge
for yourself.'

'Wait,' said I, 'three whole days? How can I do that? Do tell
me.'

She remained firm to her determination. I tried several times
in the course of the evening to find out something more about
Miss Fothering, for my curiosity was roused; but all the answer I
could get on the subject was 'Wait, Frank; wait, and judge for
yourself.'

When I was bidding her good night, Mrs Trevor said to
me—

'By-the-bye, Frank, you will have to give up the room which
you will sleep in to-night, after to-morrow. I will have such a full
house that I cannot let you have a double-bedded room all to
yourself; so I will give that room to the Miss Fotherings, and
move you up to the second floor. I just want you to see the room,
as it has a romantic look about it, and has all the old furniture
that was in it when we came here. There are several pictures in it
worth looking at.'

My bedroom was a large chamber — immense for a bedroom — with two windows opening level with the floor, like those of the parlours and drawingrooms. The furniture was old-fashioned, but not old enough to be curious, and on the walls hung many pictures — portraits — the house was full of portraits — and landscapes. I just glanced at these, intending to examine them in the morning, and went to bed. There was a fire in the room, and I lay awake for some time looking dreamily at the shadows of the furniture flitting over the walls and ceiling as the flames of the wood fire leaped and fell, and the red embers dropped whitening on the hearth. I tried to give the rein to my thoughts, but they kept constantly to the one subject — the mysterious Miss Fothering, with whom I was to fall in love. I was sure that I had heard her name somewhere, and I had at times lazy recollections of a child's face. At such times I would start awake from my growing drowsiness, but before I could collect my scattered thoughts the idea had eluded me. I could remember neither when nor where I had heard the name, nor could I recall even the expression of the child's face. It must have been long, long ago, when I was young. When I was young my mother was alive. My mother — mother — mother. I found myself awakening, and repeating the word over and over again. At last I fell asleep.

I thought that I awoke suddenly to that peculiar feeling which we sometimes have on starting from sleep, as if someone had been speaking in the room, and the voice is still echoing through it. All was quite silent, and the fire had gone out. I looked out of the window that lay straight opposite the foot of the bed, and observed a light outside, which gradually grew brighter till the room was almost as light as by day. The window looked like a picture in the framework formed by the cornice over the foot of the bed, and the massive pillars shrouded in curtains which supported it.

With the new accession of light I looked round the room, but nothing was changed. All was as before, except that some of the objects of furniture and ornament were shown in stronger relief than hitherto. Amongst these, those most in relief were the other bed, which was placed across the room, and an old picture that hung on the wall at its foot. As the bed was merely the counterpart of the one in which I lay, my attention became fixed on the picture. I observed it closely and with great interest. it seemed old, and was the portrait of a young girl, whose face, though kindly and merry, bore signs of thought and a capacity for deep feeling — almost for passion. At some moments, as I looked at it, it called up before my mind a vision of Shakespeare's Beatrice, and once I thought of Beatrice Cenci. But this was probably caused by the association of ideas suggested by the similarity of names.

The light in the room continued to grow even brighter, so I looked again out of the window to seek its source, and saw there a lovely sight. It seemed as if there were grouped without the window three lovely children, who seemed to float in mid-air. The light seemed to spring from a point far behind them, and by their side was something dark and shadowy, which served to set off their radiance.

The children seemed to be smiling in upon something in the room, and, following their glances, I saw that their eyes rested upon the other bed. There, strange to say, the head which I had lately seen in the picture rested upon the pillow. I looked at the wall, but the frame was empty, the picture was gone. Then I looked at the bed again, and saw the young girl asleep, with the expression of her face constantly changing, as though she were dreaming.

As I was observing her, a sudden look of terror spread over her face, and she sat up like a sleep-walker, with her eyes wide open, staring out of the window.

Again turning to the window, my gaze became fixed, for a great and weird change had taken place. The figures were still there, but their features and expressions had become woefully different. Instead of the happy innocent look of childhood was one of malignity. With the change the children had grown old, and now three hags, decrepit and deformed, like typical witches, were before me.

But a thousand times worse than this transformation was the change in the dark mass that was near them. From a cloud, misty and undefined, it became a sort of shadow with a form. This gradually, as I looked, grew darker and fuller, till at length it made me shudder. There stood before me the phantom of the Fiend.

There was a long period of dead silence, in which I could hear the beating of my heart; but at length the phantom spoke to the others. His words seemed to issue from his lips mechanically, and without expression — 'To-morrow, and to-morrow, and to-morrow. The fairest and the best.' He looked so awful that the question arose in my mind — 'Would I dare to face him without the window — would any one dare to go amongst those fiends?' A harsh, strident, diabolical laugh from without seemed to answer my unasked question in the negative.

But as well as the laugh I heard another sound — the tones of a sweet sad voice in despair coming across the room.

'Oh, alone, alone! is there no human being near me? No hope — no hope. I shall go mad — or die.'

The last words were spoken with a gasp.

I tried to jump out of bed, but could not stir, my limbs were bound in sleep. The young girl's head fell suddenly back upon the pillow, and the limp-hanging jaw and wide-open, purposeless mouth spoke but too plainly of what had happened.

Again I heard from without the fierce, diabolical laughter, which swelled louder and louder, till at last it grew so strong that in very horror I shook aside my sleep and sat up in bed. I listened and heard a knocking at the door, but in another moment I became more awake, and knew that the sound come from the hall. It was, no doubt, Mr Trevor returning from his party.

The hall-door was opened and shut, and then came a subdued sound of tramping and voices, but this soon died away, and there was silence throughout the house.

I lay awake for long thinking, and looking across the room at the picture and at the empty bed; for the moon now shone brightly, and the night was rendered still brighter by occasional flashes of summer lightning. At times the silence was broken by an owl screeching outside.

As I lay awake, pondering, I was very much troubled by what I had seen; but at length, putting several things together, I came to the conclusion that I had had a dream of a kind that might have been expected. The lightning, the knocking at the hall-door, the screeching of the owl, the empty bed, and the face in the picture, when grouped together, supplied materials for the main facts of the vision. The rest was, of course, the offspring of pure fancy, and the natural consequence of the component elements mentioned acting with each other in the mind.

I got up and looked out of the window, but saw nothing but the broad belt of moonlight glittering on the bosom of the lake, which extended miles and miles away, till its farther shore was lost in the night haze, and the green sward, dotted with shrubs and tall grasses, which lay between the lake and the house.

The vision had utterly faded. However, the dream − for so, I suppose, I should call it − was very powerful, and I slept no more till the sunlight was streaming broadly in at the window, and then I fell into a doze.

2. More Links

Late in the morning I was awakened by Parks, Mr Trevor's man, who always used to attend on me when I visited my friends. He brought me hot water and the local news; and, chatting with him, I forgot for a time my alarm of the night.

Parks was staid and elderly, and a type of a class now rapidly disappearing − the class of old family servants who are as proud of their hereditary loyalty to their masters, as those masters are of name and rank. Like all old servants he had a great love for all sort of traditions. He believed them, and feared them, and had the most profound reverence for anything which had a story.

I asked him if he knew anything of the legendary history of Scarp. He answered with an air of doubt and hesitation, as of one carefully delivering an opinion which was still incomplete.

'Well, you see, Master Frank, Scarp is so old that it must have any number of legends; but it is so long since it was inhabited that no one in the village remembers them. The place seems to have become in a kind of way forgotten, and died out of people's thoughts, and so I am very much afraid, sir, that all the genuine history is lost.'

'What do you mean by the genuine history?' I inquired.

'Well, sir, I mean the true tradition, and not the inventions of the village folk. I heard the sexton tell some stories, but I am quite sure that they were not true, for I could see, Master Frank, that he did not believe them himself, but was only trying to frighten us.'

'And could you not hear of any story that appeared to you to be true?'

'No, sir, and I tried very hard. You see, Master Frank, there is a sort of club held every week in the tavern down in the village, composed of very respectable men, sir — very respectable men, indeed — and they asked me to be their chairman. I spoke to the master about it, and he gave me leave to accept their proposal. I accepted it as they made a point of it; and from my position I have of course a fine opportunity of making inquiries. It was at the club, sir, that I was, last night, so that I was not here to attend on you, which I hope that you will excuse.'

Park's air of mingled pride and condescension, as he made the annoucement of the club, was very fine, and the effect was heightened by the confiding frankness with which he spoke. I asked him if he could find no clue to any of the legends which must have existed about such an old place. He answered with a very slight reluctance—

'Well, sir, there was one woman in the village who was awfully old and doting, and she evidently knew something about Scarp, for when she heard the name she mumbled out something about "awful stories," and "times of horror," and such like things, but I couldn't make her understand what it was I wanted to know, or keep her up to the point.'

'And have you tried often, Parks? Why do you not try again?'

'She is dead, sir!'

I had felt inclined to laugh at Parks when he was telling me of the old woman. The way in which he gloated over the words 'awful stories,' and 'times of horror,' was beyond the power of description; it should have been heard and seen to have been properly appreciated. His voice became deep and mysterious, and he almost smacked his lips at the thought of so much pabulum for nightmares. But when he calmly told me that the woman was dead, a sense of blankness, mingled with awe, came upon me. Here, the last link between myself and the mysterious past was broken, never to be mended. All the rich stores of legend and tradition that had arisen from strange conjunctures of circumstances, and from the belief and imagination of long lines of villagers, loyal to their suzerain lord, were lost forever. I felt quite sad and disappointed; and no attempt was made either by Parks or myself to continue the conversation. Mr Trevor came presently into my room, and having greeted each other warmly we went together to breakfast.

At breakfast Mrs Trevor asked me what I thought of the girl's portrait in my bedroom. We had often had discussions as to characters in faces for we were both physiognomists, and she asked the question as if she were really curious to hear my opinion. I told her that I had only seen it for a short time, and so would rather not attempt to give a final opinion without a more careful study; but from what I had seen of it I had been favourably impressed.

'Well, Frank, after breakfast go and look at it again carefully, and then tell me exactly what you think about it.'

After breakfast I did as directed and returned to the breakfast room, where Mrs Trevor was still sitting.

'Well, Frank, what is your opinion — mind, correctly. I want it for a particular reason?'

I told her what I thought of the girl's character; which, if there be any truth in physiognomy, must have been a very fine one.

'Then you like the face?'

I answered—

'It is a great pity that we have none such now-a-days. They seem to have died out with Sir Joshua and Greuze. If I could meet such a girl as I believe the prototype of that portrait to have been I would never be happy till I had made her my wife.'

To my intense astonishment my hostess jumped up and clapped her hands. I asked her why she did it, and she laughed as she replied in a mocking tone imitating my own voice—

'But suppose for a moment that your kind intentions should be frustrated. "One may lead a horse to the pond's brink." "The best laid schemes o' mice an' men." Eh?'

'Well,' said I, 'there maybe some point in the observation. I suppose there must be since you have made it. But for my part I don't see it.'

'Oh, I forgot to tell you, Frank, that that portrait might have been painted for Diana Fothering.'

I felt a blush stealing over my face. She observed it and took my hand between hers as we sat down on the sofa, and said to me tenderly—

'Frank, my dear boy, I intend to jest with you no more on the subject. I have a conviction that you will like Diana, which has been strengthened by your admiration for her portrait, and from what I know of human nature I am sure that she will like you. Charley and I both wish to see you married, and we would not think of a wife for you who was not in every way eligible. I have never in my life met a girl like Di; and if you and she fancy each other it will be Charley's pleasure and my own to enable you to marry — as far as means are concerned. Now, don't speak. You must know perfectly well how much we both love you. We have always regarded you as our son, and we intend to treat you as our only child when it pleases God to separate us. There now, think the matter over, after you have seen Diana. But, mind me, unless you love each other well and truly, we would far rather not see you married. At all events, whatever may happen you have our best wishes and prayers for your happiness. God bless you, Frank, my dear, dear boy.'

There were tears in her eyes as she spoke. When she had finished she leaned over, drew down my head and kissed my forehead very, very tenderly, and then got up softly and left the room. I felt inclined to cry myself. Her words to me were tender, and sensible, and womanly, but I cannot attempt to describe the infinite tenderness and gentleness of her voice and manner. I prayed for every blessing on her in my secret heart, and the swelling of my throat did not prevent my prayers finding voice. There may have been women in the world like Mrs Trevor, but if there had been I had never met any of them, except herself.

As may be imagined, I was most anxious to see Miss Fothering, and for the remainder of the day she was constantly in my thoughts. That evening a letter came from the younger Miss Fothering apologising for her not being able to keep her promise with reference to her visit, on account of the unexpected arrival of her aunt, with whom she was obliged to go to Paris for some months. That night I slept in my new room, and had neither dream nor vision. I awoke in the morning half ashamed of having ever paid any attention to such a silly circumstance as a strange dream in my first night in an old house.

After breakfast next morning, as I was going along the corridor, I saw the door of my old bedroom open, and went in to have another look at the portrait. Whilst I was looking at it I began to wonder how it could be that it was so like Miss Fothering as Mrs Trevor said it was. The more I thought of this the more it puzzled me, till suddenly the dream came back — the face in the picture, and the figure in the bed, the phantoms out in the night, and the ominous words — 'The fairest and the best.' As I thought of these things all the possibilities of the lost legends of the old house thronged so quickly into my mind that I began to feel a buzzing in my ears and my head began to swim, so that I was obliged to sit down.

'Could it be possible,' I asked myself, 'that some old curse hangs over the race that once dwelt within these walls, and can she be of that race? Such things have been before now!'

The idea was a terrible one for me, for it made to me a reality that which I had come to look upon as merely the dream of a distempered imagination. If the thought had come to me in the darkness and stillness of the night it would have been awful. How happy I was that it had come by daylight, when the sun was shining brightly, and the air was cheerful with the trilling of the song birds, and the lively, strident cawing from the old rookery.

I stayed in the room for some little time longer, thinking over the scene, and, as is natural, when I got over the remnants of my fear, my reason began to question the genuineness — *vraisemblance* of the dream. I began to look for the internal evidence of the untruth to facts; but, after thinking earnestly for some time the only fact that seemed to me of any importance was the confirmatory one of the younger Miss Fothering's apology. In the dream the frightened girl had been alone, and the mere fact of *two* girls coming on a visit had seemed a sort of disproof of its truth. But, just as if things were conspiring to force on the truth of the dream, one of the sisters was not to come, and the other was she who resembled the portrait whose prototype I had seen sleeping in a vision. I could hardly imagine that I had only dreamt.

I determined to ask Mrs Trevor if she could explain in any

way Miss Fothering's resemblance to the portrait, and so went at once to seek her.

I found her in the large drawingroom alone, and, after a few casual remarks, I broached the subject on which I had come to seek for information. She had not said anything further to me about marrying since our conversation on the previous day, but when I mentioned Miss Fothering's name I could see a glad look on her face which gave me great pleasure. She made none of those vulgar commonplace remarks which many women find it necessary to make when talking to a man about a girl for whom he is supposed to have an affection, but by her manner she put me entirely at my ease, as I sat fidgeting on the sofa, pulling purposelessly the woolly tuffs of an antimacassar, painfully conscious that my cheeks were red, and my voice slightly forced and unnatural.

She merely said, 'Of course, Frank, I am ready if you want to talk about Miss Fothering, or any other subject.' She then put a marker in her book and laid it aside, and, folding her arms, looked at me with a grave, kind, expectant smile.

I asked her if she knew anything about the family history of Miss Fothering. She answered—

'Not further than I have already told you. Her father's is a fine old family, although reduced in circumstances.'

'Has it ever been connected with any family in this country? With the former owners of Scarp, for instance?'

'Not that I know of. Why do you ask?'

'I want to find out how she comes to be so like that portrait.'

'I never thought of that. It may be that there was some remote connection between her family and the Kirks who formerly owned Scarp. I will ask her when she comes. Or stay. Let us go and look if there is any old book or tree in the library that will throw a light upon the subject. We have rather a good library now, Frank, for we have all our own books, and all those which belonged to the Scarp library also. They are in great disorder, for we have been waiting till you came to arrange them, for we knew that you delighted in such work.'

'There is nothing I should enjoy more than arranging all these splendid books. What a magnificent library. It is almost a pity to keep it in a private house.'

We proceeded to look for some of those old books of family history which are occasionally to be found in old county houses. The library of Scarp, I saw, was very valuable, and as we presented our search I came across many splendid and rare volumes which I determined to examine at my leisure, for I had come to Scarp for a long visit.

We searched first in the old folio shelves, and, after some few disappointments, found at length a large volume, magnificently printed and bound, which contained views and plans of the house, illuminations of the armorial bearings of the family of Kirk, and all the families with whom it was connected, and having the history of all these families carefully set forth. It was called on the title-page *The Book of Kirk* and was full of anecdotes and legends, and contained a large stock of family tradition. As this was exactly the book which we required, we searched no further, but, having carefully dusted the volume, bore it to Mrs Trevor's boudoir where we could look over it quite undisturbed.

On looking in the index, we found the name of Fothering mentioned, and on turning to the page specified, found the arms of Kirk quartered on those of Fothering. From the text we learned that one of the daughters of Kirk had, in the year 1573, married the son of Fothering against the united wills of her father and brother, and that after a bitter feud of some ten or twelve years, the latter, then master of Scarp, had met the brother of Fothering in a duel and had killed him. Upon receiving the news Fothering had sworn a great oath to revenge his brother, invoking the most fearful curses upon himself and his race if he should fail to cut off the hand that had slain his brother, and to nail it over the gate of Fothering. The feud then became so bitter that Kirk seems to have gone quite mad on the subject. When he heard of Fothering's oath he knew that he had but little chance of escape, since his enemy was his master at every weapon; so he determined upon a mode of revenge which, although costing him his own life, he fondly hoped would accomplish the eternal destruction of his brother-in-law through his violated oath. He sent Fothering a letter cursing him and his race, and praying for the consummation of his own curse invoked in case of failure. He concluded his missive by a prayer for the complete destruction, soul, mind, and body, of the first Fothering who should enter the gate of Scarp, who he hoped would be the fairest and best of the race. Having despatched this letter he cut off his right hand and threw it into the centre of a roaring fire, which he had made for the purpose. When it was entirely consumed he threw himself upon his sword, and so died.

A cold shiver went through me when I read the words 'fairest and best.' All my dream came back in a moment, and I seemed to hear in my ears again the echo of the fiendish laughter. I looked up at Mrs Trevor, and saw that she had become very grave. Her face had a half-frightened look, as if some wild thought had struck her. I was more frightened than ever, for nothing increases our alarms so much as the sympathy of others with regard to them; however, I tried to conceal my fear. We sat silent for some minutes, and then Mrs Trevor rose up saying:

'Come with me, and let us look at the portrait.'

I remember her saying *the* and not *that* portrait, as if some concealed thought of it had been occupying her mind. The same dread had assailed her from a coincidence as had grown in me from a vision. Surely − surely I had good grounds for fear!

We went to the bedroom and stood before the picture, which seemed to gaze upon us with an expression which reflected our own fears. My companion said to me in slightly excited tones: 'Frank, lift down the picture till we see its back.' I did so, and we found written in strange old writing on the grimy canvass a name and a date, which, after a great deal of trouble, we made out to be 'Margaret Kirk, 1572.' It was the name of the lady in the book.

Mrs Trevor turned round and faced me slowly, with a look of horror on her face.

'Frank, I don't like this at all. There is something very strange here.'

I had it on my tongue to tell her my dream, but was ashamed to do so. Besides, I feared that it might frighten her too much, as she was already alarmed.

I continued to look at the picture as a relief from my embarrassment, and was struck with the excessive griminess of the back in comparison to the freshness of the front. I mentioned my difficulty to my companion, who thought for a moment, and then suddenly said—

'I see how it is. It has been turned with its face to the wall.'

I said no word but hung up the picture again; and we went back to the boudoir.

On the way I began to think that my fears were too wildly improbable to bear to be spoken about. It was so hard to believe in the horrors of darkness when the sunlight was falling brightly around me. The same idea seemed to have struck Mrs Trevor, for she said, when we entered the room:

'Frank, it strikes me that we are both rather silly to let our imaginations carry us away so. The story is merely a tradition, and we know how report distorts even the most innocent facts. It is true that the Fothering family was formerly connected with the Kirks, and that the picture is that of the Miss Kirk who married against her father's will; it is likely that he quarrelled with her for so doing, and had her picture turned to the wall − a common trick of angry fathers at all times − but that is all. There can be nothing beyond that. Let us not think any more upon the subject, as it is one likely to lead us into absurdities. However, the picture is a really beautiful one − independent of its being such a likeness of Diana, and I will have it placed in the dining room.'

The change was effected that afternoon, but she did not again allude to the subject. She appeared, when talking to me, to be a little constrained in manner − a very unusual thing with her, and seemed to fear that I would renew the forbidden topic. I think that she did not wish to let her imagination lead her astray, and was distrustful of herself. However, the feeling of constraint wore off before night − but she did not renew the subject.

I slept well that night, without dreams of any kind; and next morning − the third to-morrow promised in the dream − when I came down to breakfast, I was told that I would see Miss Fothering before that evening.

I could not help blushing, and stammered out some commonplace remark, and then glancing up, feeling very sheepish, I saw my hostess looking at me with her kindly smile intensified. She said:

'Do you know, Frank, I felt quite frightened yesterday when

we were looking at the picture; but I have been thinking the matter over since, and have come to the conclusion that my folly was perfectly unfounded. I am sure you agree with me. In fact, I look now upon our fright as a good joke, and will tell it to Diana when she arrives.'

Once again I was about to tell my dream; but again was re-strained by shame. I knew, of course, that Mrs Trevor would not laugh at me or even think little of me for my fears, for she was too well-bred, and kind-hearted, and sympathetic to do any-thing of the kind, and, besides, the fear was one which we had shared in common.

But how could I confess my fright at what might appear to others to be a ridiculous dream, when she had conquered the fear that had been common to us both, and which had arisen from a really strange conjuncture of facts. She appeared to look on the matter so lightly that I could not do otherwise. And I did it honestly for the time.

3. The Third To-morrow

In the afternoon I was out in the garden lying in the shadow of an immense beech, when I saw Mrs Trevor approaching. I had been reading Shelley's 'Stanzas Written in Dejection', and my heart was full of melancholy and a vague yearning after human sympathy. I had thought of Mrs Trevor's love for me, but even that did not seem sufficient. I wanted the love of someone more nearly of my own level, some equal spirit, for I looked on her, of course, as I would have regarded my mother. Somehow my thoughts kept returning to Miss Fothering till I could almost see her before me in my memory of the portrait. I had begun to ask myself the question: 'Are you in love?' when I heard the voice of my hostess as she drew near.

'Ha! Frank, I thought I would find you here. I want you to come to my boudoir.'

'What for?' I inquired, as I rose from the grass and picked up my volume of Shelley.

'Di has come ever so long ago; and I want to introduce you and have a chat before dinner,' said she, as we went towards the house.

'But won't you let me change my dress. I am not in correct costume for the afternoon?'

I felt somewhat afraid of the unknown beauty when the introduction was imminent. Perhaps it was because I had come to believe too firmly in Mrs Trevor's prediction.

'Nonsense, Frank, just as if any woman worth thinking about cares how a man is dressed.'

We entered the boudoir and found a young lady seated by a window that overlooked the croquet ground. She turned round as we came in, so Mrs Trevor introduced us, and we were soon engaged in a lively conversation. I observed her, as may be supposed, with more than curiosity, and shortly found that she was worth looking at. She was very beautiful, and her beauty lay not only in her features but in her expression. At first her appearance did not seem to me so perfect as it afterwards did, on account of her wonderful resemblance to the portrait with whose beauty I was already acquainted. But it was not long before I came to experience the difference between the portrait and the reality. No matter how well it may be painted a picture falls far short of its prototype. There is something in a real face which cannot exist on canvas − some difference far greater than that contained in the contrast between the one expression, however beautiful of the picture, and the moving features and varying expression of the reality. There is something living and lovable in a real face that no art can represent.

When we had been talking for a while in the usual conventional style, Mrs Trevor said, 'Di, my love, I want to tell you of a discovery Frank and I have made. You must know that I always call Mr Stanford, Frank − he is more like my own son than my friend, and that I am very fond of him.'

She then put her arms round Miss Fothering's waist, as they sat on the sofa together, and kissed her, and then, turning towards me, said, 'I don't approve of kissing girls in the presence of gentlemen, but you know that Frank is not supposed to be here. This is my sanctum, and who invades it must take the consequences. But I must tell you about the discovery.'

She then proceeded to tell the legend, and about her finding the name of Margaret Kirk on the back of the picture.

Miss Fothering laughed gleefully as she heard the story, and then said, suddenly,

'Oh, I had forgotten to tell you, dear Mrs Trevor, that I had such a fright the other day. I thought I was going to be prevented coming here. Aunt Deborah came to us last week for a few days, and when she heard that I was about to go on a visit to Scarp she seemed quite frightened, and went straight off to papa and asked him to forbid me to go. Papa asked her why she made the request, so she told a long family legend about any of us coming to Scarp — just the same story that you have been telling me. She said she was sure that some misfortune would happen if I came; so you see that the tradition exists in our branch of the family, too. Oh, you can't fancy the scene there was between papa and Aunt Deborah. I *must* laugh whenever I think of it, although I did not laugh then, for I was greatly afraid that aunty would prevent me coming. Papa got very grave, and aunty thought she had carried her point when he said, in his dear, old, pompous manner,

'"Deborah, Diana has promised to pay Mrs Trevor, of Scarp, a visit, and, of course, must keep her engagement. And if it were for no other reason than the one you have just alleged, I would strain a point of convenience to have her go to Scarp. I have always educated my children in such a manner that they ought not to be influenced by such vain superstitions; and with my will their practice shall never be at variance with the precepts which I have instilled into them."

'Poor aunty was quite overcome. She seemed almost speechless for a time at the thought that her wishes had been neglected, for you know that Aunt Deborah's wishes are commands to all our family.'

Mrs Trevor said —

'I hope Mrs Howard was not offended?'

'Oh, no. Papa talked to her seriously, and at length — with a great deal of difficulty I must say — succeeded in convincing her that her fears were groundless — at least, he forced her to confess that such things as she was afraid of could not be.'

I thought of the couplet —

> A man convinced against his will
> Is of the same opinion still,

but said nothing.

Miss Fothering finished her story by saying—

"Aunty ended by hoping that I might enjoy myself, which I am sure, my dear Mrs Trevor, that I will do.'

'I hope you will, my love.'

I had been struck during the above conversation by the mention of Mrs Howard. I was trying to think of where I had heard the name, Deborah Howard, when suddenly it all came back to me. Mrs Howard had been Miss Fothering, and was an old friend of my mother's. It was thus that I had been accustomed to her name when I was a child. I remembered now that once she had brought a nice little girl, almost a baby, with her to visit. The child was her niece, and it was thus that I now accounted for my half-recollection of the name and the circumstance on the first night of my arrival at Scarp. The thought of my dream here recalled me to Mrs Trevor's object in bringing Miss Fothering to her boudoir, so I said to the latter—

'Do you believe those legends?'

'Indeed I do not, Mr Stanford; I do not believe in anything half so silly.'

'Then you do not believe in ghosts or visions?'

'Most certainly not.'

How could I tell my dream to a girl who had such profound disbelief? And yet I felt something whispering to me that I ought to tell it to her. It was, no doubt, foolish of me to have this fear of a dream, but I could not help it. I was just going to risk being laughed at, and unburden my mind, when Mrs Trevor started up, after looking at her watch, saying—

'Dear me, I never thought it was so late. I must go and see if any others have come. It will not do for me to neglect my guests.'

We all left the boudoir, and as we did so the gong sounded for dressing for dinner, and so we each sought our rooms.

When I came down to the drawing room I found assembled a number of persons who had arrived during the course of the afternoon. I was introduced to them all, and chatted with them till dinner was announced. I was given Miss Fothering to take into dinner, and when it was over I found that we had improved our acquaintance very much. She was a delightful girl, and as I looked at her I thought with a glow of pleasure of Mrs Trevor's prediction. Occasionally I saw our hostess observing us, and as she saw us chatting pleasantly together as though we enjoyed it a more than happy look came into her face. It was one of her most fascinating points that in the midst of gaiety, while she never neglected anyone, she specially remembered her particular friends. No matter what position she might be placed in she would still remember that there were some persons who would treasure up her recognition at such moments.

After dinner, as I did not feel inclined to enter the drawing-room with the other gentlemen, I strolled out into the garden by myself, and thought over things in general, and Miss Fothering in particular. The subject was such a pleasant one that I quite lost myself in it, and strayed off farther than I had intended. Suddenly I remembered myself and looked around. I was far away from the house, and in the midst of a dark, gloomy walk between old yew trees. I could not see through them on either side on account of their thickness, and as the walk was curved I could see but a short distance either before or behind me. I looked up and saw a yellowish, luminous sky with heavy clouds passing sluggishly across it. The moon had not yet risen, and the general gloom reminded me forcibly of some of the weird pictures which William Blake so loved to paint. There was a sort of vague melancholy and ghostliness in the place that made me shiver, and I hurried on.

At length the walk opened and I came out on a large sloping lawn, dotted here and there with yew trees and tufts of pampass grass of immense height, whose stalks were crowned with large flowers. To the right lay the house, grim and gigantic in the gloom, and to the left the lake which stretched away so far that it was lost in the evening shadow. The lawn sloped from the terrace round the house down to the water's edge, and was only broken by the walk which continued to run on round the house in a wide sweep.

As I came near the house a light appeared in one of the windows which lay before me, and as I looked into the room I saw that it was the chamber of my dream.

Unconsciously I approached nearer and ascended the terrace from the top of which I could see across the deep trench which surrounded the house, and looked earnestly into the room. I shivered as I looked. My spirits had been damped by the gloom and desolation of the yew walk, and now the dream and all the subsequent revelations came before my mind with such vividness that the horror of the thing again seized me, but more forcibly than before. I looked at the sleeping arrangements, and groaned as I saw that the bed where the dying woman had seemed to lie was alone prepared, while the other bed, that in which I had slept, had its curtains drawn all round. This was but another link in the chain of doom. Whilst I stood looking, the servant who was in the room came and pulled down one of the blinds, but, as she was about to do the same with the other, Miss Fothering entered the room, and, seeing what she was about, evidently gave her contrary directions, for she let go the window string, and then went and pulled up again the blind which she had let down. Having done so she followed her mistress out of the room. So wrapped up was I in all that took place with reference to that chamber, that it never even struck me that I was guilty of any impropriety in watching what took place.

I stayed there for some little time longer purposeless and terrified. The horror grew so great to me as I thought of the events of the last few days, that I determined to tell Miss Fothering of my dream, in order that she might not be frightened in case she should see anything like it, or at least that she might be prepared for anything that might happen. As soon as I had come to this determination the inevitable question 'when?' presented itself. The means of making the communication was a subject most disagreeable to contemplate, but as I had made up my mind to do it, I thought that there was no time like the present. Accordingly I was determined to seek the drawing-room, where I knew I should find Miss Fothering and Mrs Trevor, for, of course, I had determined to take the latter into our confidence. As I was really afraid to go through the awful yew walk again, I completed the half circle of the house and entered the backdoor, from which I easily found my way to the drawingroom.

When I entered Mrs Trevor, who was sitting near the door, said to me, 'Good gracious, Frank, where have you been to make you look so pale? One would think you had seen a ghost!'

I answered that I had been strolling in the garden, but made no other remark, as I did not wish to say anything about my dream before the persons to whom she was talking, as they were strangers to me. I waited for some time for an opportunity of speaking to her alone, but her duties, as hostess, kept her so constantly occupied that I waited in vain. Accordingly I determined to tell Miss Fothering at all events, at once, and then to tell Mrs Trevor as soon as an opportunity for doing so presented itself.

With a good deal of difficulty — for I did not wish to do anything marked — I succeeded in getting Miss Fothering away from the persons by whom she was surrounded, and took her to one of the embrasures, under the pretence of looking out at the night view. Here we were quite removed from observation, as the heavy window curtains completely covered the recess, and almost isolated us from the rest of the company as perfectly as if we were in a separate chamber. I proceeded at once to broach the subject for which I had sought the interview; for I feared lest contact with the lively company of the drawing-room would do away with my present fears, and so break down the only barrier that stood between her and Fate.

'Miss Fothering, do you ever dream?'

'Oh, yes, often. But I generally find that my dreams are most ridiculous.'

'How so?'

'Well, you see, that no matter whether they are good or bad they appear real and coherent whilst I am dreaming them; but when I wake I find them unreal and incoherent, when I remember them at all. They are, in fact, mere disconnected nonsense.'

'Are you fond of dreams?'

'Of course I am. I delight in them, for whether they are sense or gibberish when you wake, they are real whilst you are asleep.'

'Do you believe in dreams?'

'Indeed, Mr Stanford, I do not.'

'Do you like hearing them told?'

'I do, very much, when they are worth telling. Have you been dreaming anything? If you have, do tell it to me.'

'I will be glad to do so. It is about a dream which I had that concerns you, that I came here to tell you.'

'About me. Oh, how nice. Do, go on.'

I told her all my dream, after calling her attention to our conversation in the boudoir as a means of introducing the subject. I did not attempt to heighten the effect in any way or to draw any inferences. I tried to suppress my own emotion and merely to let the facts speak for themselves. She listened with great eagerness, but, as far as I could see, without a particle of either fear or belief in the dream as a warning. When I had finished she laughed a quiet, soft laugh, and said—

'That is delicious. And was I really the girl that you saw afraid of ghosts? If papa heard of such a thing as that even in a dream what a lecture he would give me! I wish I could dream anything like that.'

'Take care,' said I, 'you might find it too awful. It might indeed prove the fulfilling of the ban which we saw in the legend in the old book, and which you heard from your aunt.'

She laughed musically again, and shook her head at me wisely and warningly.

'Oh, pray do not talk nonsense and try to frighten me − for I warn you that you will not succeed.'

'I assure you on my honour, Miss Fothering, that I was never more in earnest in my whole life.'

'Do you not think that we had better go into the room?' said she, after a few moment's pause.

'Stay just a moment, I entreat you,' said I. 'What I say is true. I am really in earnest.'

'Oh, pray forgive me if what I said led you to believe that I doubted your word. It was merely your interference which I disagreed with. I thought you had been jesting to try and frighten me.'

'Miss Fothering, I would not presume to take such a liberty. But I am glad that you trust me. May I venture to ask you a favour? Will you promise me one thing?'

Her answer was characteristic—

'No. What is it?'

'That you will not be frightened at anything which may take place to-night?'

She laughed softly again.

'I do not intend to be. But is that all?'

'Yes, Miss Fothering, that is all; but I want to be assured that you will not be alarmed — that you will be prepared for *any-thing* which may happen. I have a horrid foreboding of evil — some evil that I dread to think of — and it will be a great comfort to me if you will do one thing.'

'Oh, nonsense. Oh, well, if you really wish it I will tell you if I will do it when I hear what it is.'

Her levity was all gone when she saw how terribly in earnest I was. She looked at me boldly and fearlessly, but with a tender, half-pitying glance as if conscious of the possession of strength superior to mine. Her fearlessness was in her free, independent attitude, but her pity was in her eyes. I went on —

'Miss Fothering, the worst part of my dream was seeing the look of agony on the face of the girl when she looked round and found herself alone. Will you take some token and keep it with you till morning to remind you, in case anything should happen, that you are not alone — that there is one thinking of you, and one human intelligence awake for you, though all the rest of the world should be asleep or dead?'

In my excitement I spoke with fervour, for the possibility of her enduring the horror which had assailed me seemed to be growing more and more each instant. At times since that awful night I had disbelieved the existence of the warning, but when I thought of it by night I could not but believe, for the very air in the darkness seemed to be peopled by phantoms to my fevered imagination. My belief had been perfected to-night by the horror of the yew walk, and all the sombre, ghostly thoughts that had arisen amid its gloom.

There was a short pause. Miss Fothering leaned on the edge of the window, looking out at the dark, moonless sky. At length she turned and said to me, with some hesitation, 'But really, Mr Stanford, I do not like doing anything from fear of supernatural things, or from a belief in them. What you want me to do is so simple a thing in itself that I would not hesitate a moment to do it, but that papa has always taught me to believe that such occurrences as you seem to dread are quite impossible, and I know that he would be very much displeased if any act of mine showed a belief in them.'

'Miss Fothering, I honestly think that there is not a man living

who would wish less than I would to see you or anyone else dis-
obeying a father either in word or spirit, and more particularly when that father is a cleryman; but I entreat you to
gratify me on this one point. It cannot do you any harm; and
I assure you that if you do not I will be inexpressibly
miserable. I have endured the greatest tortures of suspense for
the last three days, and to-night I feel a nervous horror of
which words can give you no conception. I know that I have
not the smallest right to make the request, and no reason for
doing it except that I was fortunate, or unfortunate, enough
to get the warning. I apologise most sincerely for the great
liberty which I have taken, but believe me that I act with the
best intentions.'

My excitement was so great that my knees were trembling,
and large drops of perspiration were rolling down my face.

There was a long pause, and I had almost made up my mind
for a refusal of my request when my companion spoke again.

'Mr Stanford, on that plea alone I will grant your request. I
can see that for some reason which I cannot quite comprehend
you are deeply moved; and that I may be the means of saving
pain to any one, I will do what you ask. Just please to state what
you wish me to do.'

I thought from her manner that she was offended with me;
however I explained my purpose:

'I want you to keep about you, when you go to bed, some
token which will remind you in an instant of what has passed
between us, so that you may not feel lonely or frightened – no
matter what may happen.'

'I will do it. What shall I take?'

She had her handkerchief in her hand as she spoke. So I put
my hand upon it and blessed it in the name of the Father, Son,
and Holy Ghost. I did this to fix its existence in her memory by
awing her slightly about it. 'This,' said I, 'shall be a token that
you are not alone.' My object in blessing the handkerchief was
fully achieved, for she did seem somewhat awed, but still she
thanked me with a sweet smile. 'I feel that you act from your
heart,' said she, 'and my heart thanks you.' She gave me her
hand as she spoke, in an honest, straightforward manner, with
more the independence of a man than the timorousness of a

woman. As I grasped it I felt the blood rushing to my face, but before I let it go an impulse seized me and I bent down and touched it with my lips. She drew it quickly away, and said more coldly than she had yet spoken: 'I did not mean you to do that.'

'Believe me I did not mean to take a liberty – it was merely the natural expression of my gratitude. I feel as if you had done me some great personal service. You do not know how much lighter my heart is now than it was an hour ago, or you would forgive me for having so offended.'

As I made my apologetic excuse, I looked at her wistfully. She returned my glance fearlessly, but with a bright, forgiving smile. She then shook her head slightly, as if to banish the subject.

There was a short pause, and then she said:

'I am glad to be of any service to you; but if there be any possibility of what you fear happening it is I who will be benefited. But mind, I will depend upon you not to say a word of this to *anybody*. I am afraid that we are both very foolish.'

'No, no, Miss Fothering. *I* may be foolish, but you are acting nobly in doing what seems to you to be foolish in order that you may save me from pain. But may I not even tell Mrs Trevor?'

'No, not even her. I should be ashamed of myself if I thought that anyone except ourselves knew about it.'

'You may depend upon me. I will keep it secret if you wish.'

'Do so, until morning at all events. Mind, if I laugh at you then I will expect you to join in my laugh.'

'I will,' said I. 'I will be only too glad to be able to laugh at it.' And we joined the rest of the company.

When I retired to my bedroom that night I was too much excited to sleep – even had my promise not forbidden me to do so. I paced up and down the room for some time, thinking and doubting. I could not believe completely in what I expected to happen, and yet my heart was filled with a vague dread. I thought over the events of the evening – particularly my stroll after dinner through that awful yew walk and my looking into the bedroom where I had dreamed. From these my thoughts wandered to the deep embrasure of the window where I had given Miss Fothering the token. I could hardly realise that whole interview as a fact. I knew that it had taken place, but that was all. It was so strange to recall a scene that, now that it was enacted, seemed half comedy and half tragedy, and to re-member that it was played in this practical nineteenth century, in secret, within earshot of a room full of people, and only hidden from them by a curtain, I felt myself blushing, half from excitement, half from shame, when I thought of it. But then my thoughts turned to the way in which Miss Fothering had acceded to my request, strange as it was; and as I thought of her my blundering shame changed to a deeper glow of hope. I remembered Mrs Trevor's prediction − 'from what I know of human nature I think that she will like you' − and as I did so I felt how dear to me Miss Fothering was already becoming. But my joy was turned to anger on thinking what she might be called on to endure; and the thought of her suffering pain or fright caused me greater distress than any suffered myself. Again my thoughts flew back to the time of my own fright and my dream, with all the subsequent revelations concerning it, rushed across my mind. I felt again the feeling of extreme terror − as if some-thing was about to happen − as if the tragedy was approaching its climax. Naturally I thought of the time of night and so I looked at my watch. It was within a few minutes of one o'clock. I remembered that the clock had struck twelve after Mrs Trevor had come home on the night of my dream. There was a large clock at Scarp which tolled the hours so loudly that for a long way round the estate the country people all regulated their affairs by it. The next few minutes passed so slowly that each moment seemed an age.

I was standing, with my watch in my hand, counting the moments when suddenly a light came into the room that made the candle on the table appear quite dim, and my shadow was reflected on the wall by some brilliant light which streamed in through the window. My heart for an instant ceased to beat, and then the blood rushed so violently to my temples that my eyes grew dim and my brain began to reel. However, I shortly became more composed, and then went to the window expect-ing to see my dream again repeated.

The light was there as formerly, but there were no figures of children, or witches, or fiends. The moon had just risen, and I could see its reflection upon the far end of the lake. I turned my head in trembling expectation to the ground below where I had seen the children and the hags, but saw merely the dark yew trees and the tall crested pampass tufts gently moving in the night wind. The light caught the edges of the flowers of the grass, and made them most conspicuous.

As I looked a sudden thought flashed like a flame of fire through my brain. I saw in one second of time all the folly of my wild fancies. The moonlight and its reflection on the water shining into the room was the light of my dream, or phantasm as I now understood it to be. Those three tufts of pampass grass clumped together were in turn the fair young children and the withered leaves and the dark foliage of the yew beside them gave substance to the semblance of the fiend. For the rest, the empty bed and the face of the picture, my half recollection of the name of Fothering, and the long-forgotten legend of the curse. Oh, fool! fool that I had been! How I had been the victim of circumstances, and of my own wild imagination! Then came the bitter reflection of the agony of mind which Miss Fothering might be compelled to suffer. Might not the recital of my dream, and my strange request regarding the token, combined with the natural causes of night and scene, produce the very effect which I so dreaded? It was only at that bitter, bitter moment that I realised how foolish I had been. But what was *my* anguish of mind to hers? For an instant I conceived the idea of rousing Mrs Trevor and telling her all the facts of the case so that she might go to Miss Fothering and tell her not to be alarmed. But I had no time to act upon my thought. As I was hastening to the door the clock struck one and a moment later I heard from the room below me a sharp scream — a cry of surprise rather than fear. Miss Fothering had no doubt been awakened by the striking of the clock, and had seen outside the window the very figures which I had described to her.

I rushed madly down the stairs and arrived at the door of her bedroom, which was directly under the one which I now occupied. As I was about to rush in I was instinctively restrained from so doing by the thoughts of propriety; and so for a few moments I stood silent, trembling, with my hand upon the door-handle.

Within I heard a voice − her voice − exclaiming, in tones of stupefied surprise −

'Has it come then? Am I *alone?*' She then continued joyously, 'No, I am *not* alone. His token! Oh, thank God for that. Thank God for that.'

Through my heart at her words came a rush of wild delight. I felt my bosom swell and the tears of gladness spring to my eyes. In that moment I knew that I had strength and courage to face the world, alone, for her sake. But before my hopes had well time to manifest themselves they were destroyed, for again the voice came wailing from the room of blank despair that made me cold from head to foot.

'Ah-h-h! still there? Oh! God, preserve my reason. Oh! for some human thing near me.' Then her voice changed slightly to a tone of entreaty: 'You will not leave me alone? Your token. Remember your token. Help me. Help me *now*.' Then her voice became more wild, and rose to an inarticulate, wailing scream of horror.

As I heard that agonised cry, I realised the idea that it was madness to delay − that I had hesitated too long already − I must cast aside the shackles of conventionality if I wished to repair my fatal error. Nothing could save her from some serious injury − perhaps madness − perhaps death; save a shock which would break the spell which was over her from fear and her excited imagination. I flung open the door and rushed in, shouting loudly:

'Courage, courage. You are not alone. I am here. Remember the token.'

She grasped the handkerchief instinctively, but she hardly comprehended my words, and did not seem to heed my presence. She was sitting up in bed, her face being distorted with terror, and was gazing out upon the scene. I heard from without the hooting of an owl as it flew across the border of the lake. She heard it also, and screamed −

'The laugh, too! Oh, there is no hope. Even he will not dare to go amongst them.'

Then she gave vent to a scream, so wild, so appalling that, as I heard it, I trembled, and the hair on the back of my head bristled up. Throughout the house I could hear screams of affright, and the ringing of bells, and the banging of doors, and the rush of hurried feet; but the poor sufferer comprehended not these sounds; she still continued gazing out of the window awaiting the consummation of the dream.

I saw that the time for action and self-sacrifice was come. There was but one way now to repair my fatal error. To burst through the window and try by the shock to wake her from her trance of fear.

I said no word but rushed across the room and hurled myself, back foremost, against the massive plate glass. As I turned I saw Mrs Trevor rushing into the room, her face wild with excitement. She was calling out —

'Diana, Diana, what is it?'

The glass crashed and shivered into a thousand pieces, and I could feel its sharp edges cutting me like so many knives. But I heeded not the pain, for above the rushing of feet and crashing of glass and the shouting both within and without the room I heard her voice ring forth in a joyous, fervent cry, 'Saved. He *has* dared,' as she sank down in the arms of Mrs Trevor, who had thrown herself upon the bed.

Then I felt a mighty shock, and all the universe seemed filled with sparks of fire that whirled around me with lightning speed, till I seemed to be in the centre of a world of flame, and then came in my ears the rushing of a mighty wind, swelling ever louder, and then came a blackness over all things and a deadness of sound as if all the earth had passed away, and I remembered no more.

4. Afterwards

When I next became conscious I was lying in bed in a dark room. I wondered what this was for, and tried to look around me, but could hardly stir my head. I attempted to speak, but my voice was without power — it was like a whisper from another world. The effort to speak made me feel faint, and again I felt a darkness gathering round me.

I became gradually conscious of something cool on my forehead.

I wondered what it was. All sorts of things I conjectured, but could not fix my mind on any of them. I lay thus for some time, and at length opened my eyes and saw my mother bending over me — it was her hand which was so deliciously cool on my brow. I felt amazed somehow. I expected to see her; and yet I was surprised, for I had not seen her for a long time — a long, long time. I knew that she was dead — could I be dead, too? I looked at her again more carefully, and as I looked, the old features died away, but the expression remained the same. And then the dear, well-known face of Mrs Trevor grew slowly before me. She smiled as she saw the look of recognition in my eyes, and, bending down, kissed me very tenderly. As she drew back her head something warm fell on my face. I wondered what this could be, and after thinking for a long time, to do which I closed my eyes, I came to the conclusion that it was a tear. After some more thinking I opened my eyes to see why she was crying; but she was gone, and I could see that although the window-blinds were pulled up the room was almost dark. I felt much more awake and much stronger than I had been before, and tried to call Mrs Trevor. A woman got up from a chair behind the bed-curtains and went to the door, said something, and came back and settled my pillows.

'Where is Mrs Trevor?' I asked feebly. 'She was here just now.'

The woman smiled at me cheerfully, and answered:

'She will be here in a moment. Dear heart! but she will be glad to see you so strong and sensible.'

After a few minutes she came into the room, and, bending over me, asked me how I felt. I said that I was all right — and then a thought struck me, so I asked,

'What was the matter with me?'

I was told that I had been ill, very ill, but that I was now much better. Something, I know not what, suddenly recalled to my memory all the scene of the bedroom, and the fright which my folly had caused, and I grew quite dizzy with the rush of blood to my head. But Mrs Trevor's arm supported me, and after a time the faintness passed away, and my memory was completely restored. I started violently from the arm that held me up, and called out:

'Is she all right?' I heard her say, "saved." 'Is she all right?'

'Hush, dear boy, hush — she's all right. Do not excite your-self.'

'Are you deceiving me?' I inquired. 'Tell me all — I can bear it. Is she well or no?'

'She has been very ill, but she is now getting strong and well, thank God.'

I began to cry, half from weakness and half from joy, and Mrs Trevor seeing this, and knowing with the sweet instinct of womanhood that I would rather be alone, quickly left the room, after making a sign to the nurse, who sank again to her old place behind the bed-curtain.

I thought for long; and all the time from my first coming to Scarp to the moment of unconsciousness after I sprung through the window came back to me as in a dream. Gradually the room became darker and darker, and my thoughts began to give sem-blance to the objects around me, till at length the visible world passed away from my wearied eyes, and in my dreams I con-tinued to think of all that had been. I have a hazy recollection of taking some food and then relapsing into sleep; but remember no more distinctly until I woke in the morning and found Mrs Trevor again in the room. She came over to my bedside, and sitting down said gaily—

'Ah, Frank, you look bright and strong this morning, dear boy. You will soon be well now I trust.'

Her cool deft fingers settled my pillow and brushed back the hair from my forehead. I took her hand and kissed it, and the doing so made me very happy. By-and-by I asked her how was Miss Fothering.

'Better, much better this morning. She has been asking after you ever since she has been able; and to-day when I told her how much better you were she brightened up at once.'

I felt a flush painfully strong rushing over my face as she spoke, but she went on—

'She has asked me to let her see you as soon as both of you are able. She wants to thank you for your conduct on that awful night. But there, I won't tell any more tales — let her tell you what she likes herself.'

'To thank me — me — for what? For having brought her to the verge of madness or perhaps death through my silly fears and imagination. Oh, Mrs Trevor, I know that you never mock anyone — but to me that sounds like mockery.'

She leaned over me as she sat on my bedside and said, oh, so sweetly, yet so firmly that a sense of the truth of her words came at once upon me—

'If I had a son I would wish him to think as you have thought, and to act as you have acted. I would pray for it night and day, and if he suffered as you have done, I would lean over him as I lean over you now and feel glad, as I feel now, that he had thought and acted as a true-hearted man should think and act. I would rejoice that God had given me such a son; and if he should die — as I feared at first that you should — I would be a prouder and happier woman kneeling by his dead body than I would in clasping a different son, living, in my arms.'

Oh, how my weak fluttering heart did beat as she spoke. With pity for her blighted maternal instincts, with gladness that a true-hearted woman had approved of my conduct toward a woman whom I loved, and with joy for the deep love for myself. There was no mistaking the honesty of her words — her face was perfectly radiant as she spoke them.

I put up my arms — it took all my strength to do it — round her neck, and whispered softly in her ear one word, 'mother.'

She did not expect it, for it seemed to startle her; but her arms tightened around me convulsively. I could feel a perfect rain of tears falling on my upturned face as I looked into her eyes, full of love and long-sought joy. As I looked I felt stronger and better; my sympathy for her joy did much to restore my strength.

For some little time she was silent, and then she spoke as if to herself — 'God *has* given me a son at last. I thank thee, O Father; forgive me if I have at any time repined. The son I prayed for might have been different from what I would wish. Thou doest best in all things.'

For some time after this she stayed quite silent, still supporting me in her arms. I felt inexpressibly happy. There was an atmosphere of love around me, for which I had longed all my life. The love of a mother, for which I had pined since my orphan childhood, I had got at last, and the love of a woman to become far dearer to me than a mother I felt was close at hand.

At length I began to feel tired, and Mrs Trevor laid me back on my pillow. It pleased me inexpressibly to observe her kind motherly manner with me now. The ice between us had at last been broken, we had declared our mutual love, and the white-haired woman was as happy in the declaration as the young man.

The next day I felt a shade stronger, and a similar improve-ment was manifested on the next. Mrs Trevor always attended me herself, and her good reports of Miss Fothering's progress helped to cheer me not a little. And so the days wore on, and many passed away before I was allowed to rise from bed.

One day Mrs Trevor came into the room in a state of sup-pressed delight. By this time I had been allowed to sit up a little while each day, and was beginning to get strong, or rather less weak, for I was still very helpless.

'Frank, the doctor says that you may be moved into another room to-morrow for a change, and that you may see Di.'

As may be supposed I was anxious to see Miss Fothering. Whilst I had been able to think during my illness, I had thought about her all day long, and sometimes all night long. I had been in love with her even before that fatal night. My heart told me that secret whilst I was waiting to hear the clock strike, and saw all my folly about the dream; but now I not only loved the woman but I almost worshipped my own bright ideal which was merged in her. The constant series of kind messages that passed between us tended not a little to increase my attach-ment, and now I eagerly looked forward to a meeting with her face to face.

I awoke earlier than usual next morning, and grew rather feverish as the time for our interview approached. However, I soon cooled down upon a vague threat being held out, that if I did not become more composed I must defer my visit.

The expected time at length arrived, and I was wheeled in my chair into Mrs Trevor's boudoir. As I entered the door I looked eagerly round and saw, seated in another chair near one of the windows, a girl, who, turning her head round languidly, dis-closed the features of Miss Fothering. She was very pale and ethereal looking, and seemed extremely delicate; but in my opinion this only heightened her natural beauty. As she caught sight of me a beautiful blush rushed over her poor, pale face, and even tinged her alabaster forehead. This passed quickly, and she became calm again, and paler than before. My chair was wheeled over to her, and Mrs Trevor's said, as she bent over and kissed her, after soothing the pillow in her chair—

'Di, my love, I have brought Frank to see you. You may talk together for a little while: but, mind, the doctor's orders are very strict, and if either of you excite yourselves about anything I must forbid you to meet again until you are both much stronger.'

She said the last words as she was leaving the room.

I felt red and pale, hot and cold by turns. I looked at Miss Fothering and faltered. However, in a moment or two I summoned up courage to address her.

'Miss Fothering, I hope you forgive me for the pain and danger I caused you by that foolish fear of mine. I assure you that nothing I ever did—'

Here she interrupted me.

'Mr Stanford, I beg you will not talk like that. I must thank you for the care you thought me worthy of. I will not say how proud I feel of it, and for the generous courage and wisdom you displayed in rescuing me from the terror of that awful scene.'

She grew pale, even paler than she had been before, as she spoke the last words, and trembled all over. I feared for her, and said as cheerfully as I could:

'Don't be alarmed. Do calm yourself. That is all over now and past. Don't let its horror disturb you ever again.'

My speaking, although it calmed her somewhat, was not sufficient to banish her fear, and, seeing that she was really excited, I called to Mrs Trevor, who came in from the next room and talked to us for a little while. She gradually did away with Miss Fothering's fear by her pleasant cheery conversation. She, poor girl, had received a sad shock, and the thought that I had been the cause of it gave me great anguish. After a little quiet chat, however, I grew more cheerful, but presently feeling fatigued, was wheeled back to my own room and put to bed.

For many long days I continued very weak, and hardly made any advance. I saw Miss Fothering every day, and each day I loved her more and more. She got stronger as the days advanced, and after a few weeks was comparatively in good health, but still I continued weak. Her illness had been merely the result of the fright she had sustained on that unhappy night; but mine was the nervous prostration consequent on the long period of anxiety between the dream and its seeming fulfilment, united with the physical weakness resulting from my wounds caused by jumping through the window. During all this time of weakness Mrs Trevor was, indeed, a mother to me. She watched me day and night, and as far as a woman could, made my life a dream of happiness. But the crowning glory of that time was the thought that sometimes forced itself upon me — that Diana cared for me. She continued to remain at Scarp by Mrs Trevor's request, as her father had gone to the Continent for the winter, and with my adopted mother she shared the attendance on me. Day after day her care for my every want grew greater, till I came to fancy her like a guardian angel keeping watch over me. With the peculiar delicate sense that accompanies extreme physical prostration I could see that the growth of her pity kept pace with the growth of her strength. My love kept pace with both. I often wondered if it could be sympathy and not pity that so forestalled my wants and wishes; or if it could be love that answered in her heart when mine beat for her. She only showed pity and tenderness in her acts and words, but still I hoped and longed for something more.

Those days of my long-continued weakness were to me sweet, sweet days. I used to watch her for hours as she sat opposite to me reading or working, and my eyes would fill with tears as I thought how hard it would be to die and leave her behind me. So strong was the flame of my love that I believed, in spite of my religious teaching, that, should I die, I would leave the better part of my being behind me. I used to think in a vague imaginative way, that was no less powerful because it was undefined, of what speeches I would make to her — if I were well. How I would talk to her in nobler language than that in which I would now allow my thoughts to mould themselves. How, as I talked, my passion, and honesty, and purity would make me so eloquent that she would love to hear me speak. How I would wander with her through the sunny-gladed woods that stretched away before me through the open window, and sit by her feet on a mossy bank beside some purling brook that rippled gaily over the stones, gazing into the depths of her eyes, where my future life was pictured in one long sheen of light. How I would whisper in her ear sweet words that would make me tremble to speak them, and her tremble to hear. How she would bend to me and show me her love by letting me tell her mine without reproof. And then would come, like the shadow of a sudden rain-cloud over an April landscape, the bitter, bitter thought that all this long-ing was but a dream, and that when the time had come when such things might have been, I would, most likely, be sleeping under the green turf. And she might, perhaps, be weeping in the silence of her chamber sad, sad tears for her blighted love and for me. Then my thoughts would become less selfish, and I would try to imagine the bitter blow of my death − if she loved me − for I knew that a woman loves not by the value of what she loves, but by the strength of her affection and admiration for her own ideal, which she thinks she sees bodied forth in some man. But these thoughts had always the proviso that the dreams of happiness were prophetic. Alas! I had altogether lost faith in dreams. Still, I could not but feel that even if I had never frightened Miss Fothering by telling my vision, she might, nevertheless, have been terrified by the effect of the moonlight upon the flowers of the Pampass tufts, and that, under Provi-dence, I was the instrument of saving her from a shock even greater than that which she did experience, for help might not have come to her so soon. This thought always gave me hope. Whenever I thought of her sorrow for my death, I would find my eyes filled with a sudden rush of tears which would shut out from my waking vision the object of my thoughts and fears. Then she would come over to me and place her cool hand on my forehead, and whisper sweet words of comfort and hope in my ears. As I would feel her warm breath upon my cheek and wafting my hair from my brow, I would lose all sense of pain and sorrow and care, and live only in the brightness of the present. At such times I would cry silently from very happiness, for I was sadly weak, and even trifling things touched me deeply. Many a stray memory of some tender word heard or some gentle deed done, or of some sorrow or distress, would set me thinking for hours and stir all the tender feelings of my nature.

Slowly — very slowly — I began to get stronger, but for many days more I was almost completely helpless. With returning strength came the strengthening of my passion — for passion my love for Diana had become. She had been so woven into my thoughts that my love for her was a part of my being, and I felt that away from her my future life would be but a bare existence and no more. But strange to say, with increasing strength and passion came increasing diffidence. I felt in her presence so bashful and timorous that I hardly dared to look at her, and could not speak save to answer an occasional question. I had ceased to dream entirely, for such day-dreams as I used to have seemed now wild and almost sacrilegious to my sur-excited imagination. But when she was not looking at me I would be happy in merely seeing her or hearing her speak. I could tell the moment she left the house or entered it, and her footfall was the music sweetest to my ears — except her voice. Sometimes she would catch sight of my bashful looks at her, and then, at my conscious blushing, a bright smile would flit over her face. It was sweet and womanly, but sometimes I would think that it was no more than her pity finding expression. She was always in my thoughts, and these doubts and fears constantly assailed me, so that I could feel that the brooding over the subject — a matter which I was powerless to prevent — was doing me an injury; perhaps seriously retarding my recovery.

One day I felt very sad. There had a bitter sense of loneliness come over me which was unusual. It was a good sign of returning health, for it was like the waking from a dream to a world of fact, with all its troubles and cares. There was a sense of coldness and loneliness in the world, and I felt that I had lost something without gaining anything in return — I had, in fact, lost somewhat of my sense of dependence, which is a consequence of prostration, but had not yet regained my strength. I sat opposite a window, itself in shade, but looking over a garden that in the summer had been bright with flowers, and sweet with their odours, but which, now, was lit up only in patches by the quiet mellow gleams of the autumn sun, and brightened by a few stray flowers that had survived the first frosts.

As I sat I could not help thinking of what my future would be. I felt that I was getting strong, and the possibilities of my life seemed very real to me. How I longed for courage to ask Diana to be my wife! Any certainty would be better than the suspense I now constantly endured. I had but little hope that she would accept me, for she seemed to care less for me now than in the early days of my illness. As I grew stronger she seemed to hold somewhat aloof from me; and as my fears and doubts grew more and more, I could hardly bear to think of my joy should she accept me, or of my despair should she refuse. Either emotion seemed too great to be borne.

To-day when she entered the room my fears were vastly increased. She seemed much stronger than usual, for a glow, as of health, ruddied her cheeks, and she seemed so lovely that I could not conceive that such a woman would ever condescend to be my wife. There was an unusual constraint in her manner as she came and spoke to me, and flitted round me, doing in her own graceful way all the thousand little offices that only a woman's hand can do for an invalid. She turned to me two or three times, as if she was about to speak; but turned away again, each time silent, and with a blush. I could see that her heart was beating violently. At length she spoke.

'Frank.'

Oh! what a wild throb went through me as I heard my name from her lips for the first time. The blood rushed to my head, so that for a moment I was quite faint. Her cool hand on my forehead revived me.

'Frank, will you let me speak to you for a few minutes as honestly as I would wish to speak, and as freely?'

'Go on.'

'You will promise me not to think me unwomanly or forward, for indeed I act from the best motives − promise me?'

This was said slowly with much hestitation, and a convulsive heaving of the chest.

'I promise.'

'We can see that you are not getting as strong as you ought, and the doctor says that there is some idea too much in your mind – that you brood over it, and that it is retarding your recovery. Mrs Trevor and I have been talking about it. We have been comparing notes, and I think we have found out what your idea is. Now, Frank, you must not pale and red like that, or I will have to leave off.'

'I will be calm – indeed, I will. Go on.'

'We both thought that it might do you good to talk to you freely, and we want to know if our idea is correct. Mrs Trevor thought it better that I should speak to you than she should.'

'What is the idea?'

Hitherto, although she had manifested considerable emotion, her voice had been full and clear, but she answered this last question very faintly, and with much hesitation.

'You are attached to me, and you are afraid I – I don't love you.'

Her voice was checked by a rush of tears, and she turned her head away.

'Diana,' said I, 'dear Diana,' and I held out my arms with what strength I had.

The colour rushed over her face and neck, and then she turned, and with a convulsive sigh laid her head upon my shoulder. One weak arm fell round her waist, and my other hand rested on her head. I said nothing. I could not speak, but I felt the beating of her heart against mine, and thought that if I died then I must be happy for ever, if there be memory in the other world.

For a long, long, blissful time she kept her place, and gradually our hearts ceased to beat so violently, and we became calm.

Such was the confession of our love. No plighted faith, no passionate vows, but the silence and the thrill of sympathy through our hearts were sweeter than words could be.

Diana raised her head and looked fearlessly but appealingly into my eyes as she asked me—

'Oh, Frank, did I do right to speak? Could it have been better if I had waited?'

She saw my wishes in my eyes, and bent down her head to me. I kissed her on the forehead and fervently prayed, 'Thank God that all was as it has been. May He bless my own darling wife for ever and ever.'

'Amen,' said a sweet, tender voice.

We both looked up without shame, for we knew the tones of my second mother. Her face, streaming with tears of joy, was lit up by a sudden ray of sunlight throught the casement.

III

The Castle of the King

Publication of 'The Chain of Destiny' by 'A. Stoker Esq' in *The Shamrock* undoubtedly increased Bram's literary standing in Dublin, and he was able to place other articles and essays with local publications with rather more ease than previously. Having successfully written a serial, he now began to think about a full length book, and was attracted to the idea of a 'grim novel' based on the cholera outbreak which had decimated the population of Sligo in 1832. The facts of this terrible plague were well known to him, as his mother, Charlotte, had actually lived through the events and they had left an indelible impression on her mind. Indeed, she had recounted the details to Bram on more than one occasion, and had even written a letter to him in which she summarised the awful months during which three quarters of the people in Sligo had died. Even the most cursory reading of this remarkable document leaves the reader in no doubt that it was from his mother that Bram inherited his literary prowess.

In any event, Bram toyed with this idea, but pressure of work at the Castle plus his journalistic commitments made him shelve it for the time being. Instead, he returned to short stories and began a tale which was ultimately to form part of his first book of fiction. He called the story 'The Castle of the King' and again we can find in it images that were to recur later in *Dracula*. The tale centres on the journey of a young poet searching for his loved one who has apparently died in a mysterious castle. His journey takes him across a hostile terrain alive with snakes which constantly menace him with their fangs until he arrives before the gates of the King's towering, mist-shrouded castle. The whole place seems dead, and the reader experiences the same chilling sensations as he does when approaching Castle Dracula. Stoker published the story in *The Warder* in 1876, and although it was later to be linked with other stories about the strange kingdom, these were only written spasmodically over the next five years and the resulting book — by then his second — did not appear until 1882 when it was published under the title of *Under The Sunset* by the London firm of Sampson Low, Marston, Searle & Rivington.

Bram's first book had actually appeared in 1879 and bore the ponderous title, *Duties of Clerks of Petty Sessions in Ireland*. He had been set to write this by his seniors in Dublin Castle who evidently thought that anyone who used his pen outside office hours with such facility might just as well be employed in a similar capacity while at his desk! The book is precisely the kind of tome its title suggests, and although it was 'strongly recommended' in an Introduction by the Chief Registrar at the Castle, and in time came to be regarded as a standard reference book, Bram constantly joked about it, and said its contents were 'as dry as dust'. Keen though he was to be published, his ambitions lay rather more strongly towards being a storyteller than a writer of text books!

The Castle of the King

When they told the poor Poet that the One he loved best was lying sick in the shadow of danger, he was nigh distraught.

For weeks past he had been alone; she, his Wife, having gone afar to her old home to see an aged grandsire ere he died.

The Poet's heart had for some days been oppressed with a strange sorrow. He did not know the cause of it; he only knew with the deep sympathy which is the poet's gift, that the One he loved was sick. Anxiously had he awaited tidings. When the news came, the shock, although he expected a sad message, was too much for him, and he became nigh distraught.

In his sadness and anxiety he went out into the garden which long years he had cultured for Her. There, amongst the bright flowers, where the old statues stood softly white against the hedges of yew, he lay down in the long uncut summer grass, and wept with his head buried low.

He thought of all the past — of how he had won his Wife and how they loved each other; and to him it seemed a sad and cruel thing that she was afar and in danger, and he not near to comfort her or even to share her pain.

Many many thoughts came back to him, telling the story of the weary years whose gloom and solitude he had forgotten in the brightness of his lovely home.

How in youth they twain had met and in a moment loved. How his poverty and her greatness had kept them apart. How he had struggled and toiled in the steep and rugged road to fame and fortune.

How all through the weary years he had striven with the single idea of winning such a place in the history of his time, that he should be able to come and to her say, 'I love you,' and to her proud relations, 'I am worthy, for I too have become great.'

How amid all this dreaming of a happy time which might come, he had kept silent as to his love. How he had never seen her or heard her voice, or even known her habitation, lest, knowing, he should fail in the purpose of his life.

How time — as it ever does to those who work with honesty and singleness of purpose — crowned the labours and the patience of his life.

How the world had come to know his name and reverence and love it as of one who had helped the weak and weary by his example; who had purified the thoughts of all who listened to his words; and who had swept away baseness before the grandeur and simpleness of his noble thoughts.

How success had followed in the wake of fame.

How at length even to his heart, timorous with the doubt of love, had been borne the thought that he had at last achieved the greatness which justified him in seeking the hand of her he loved.

How he had come back to his native place, and there found her still free.

How when he had dared to tell her of his love she had whispered to him that she, too, had waited all the years, for that she knew that he would come to claim her at the end.

How she had come with him as his bride into the home which he had been making for her all these years. How, there, they had lived happily; and had dared to look into the long years to come for joy and content without a bar.

How he thought that even then, when though somewhat enfeebled in strength by the ceaseless toil of years and the care of hoping, he might look to the happy time to come.

But, alas! for hope; for who knoweth what a day may bring forth? Only a little while ago his Dear One had left him hale, departing in the cause of duty; and now she lay sick and he not nigh to help her.

All the sunshine of his life seemed passing away. All the long years of waiting and the patient continuance in well-doing which had crowned their years with love, seemed as but a passing dream, and was all in vain − all, all in vain.

Now with the shadow hovering over his Beloved One, the cloud seemed to be above and around them, and to hold in its dim recesses the doom of them both.

'Why, oh why,' asked the poor Poet to the viewless air, 'did love come to us? Why came peace and joy and happiness, if the darkening wings of peril shadow the air around her, and leave me to weep alone?'

Thus he moaned, and raved, and wept; and the bitter hours went by him in his solitude.

As he lay in the garden with his face buried in the long grass, they came to him and told him with weeping, that tidings − sad, indeed − had come.

As they spoke he lifted his poor head and gazed at them; and they saw in the great, dark, tender eyes that now he was quite distraught. He smiled at them sadly, as though not quite understanding the import of their words. As tenderly as they could they tried to tell him that the One he loved best was dead.

They said:

'She has walked in the Valley of the Shadow,' but he seemed to understand them not.

They whispered,

'She has heard the Music of the Spheres,' but still he comprehended not.

Then they spoke to him sorrowfully and said:

'She now abides in the Castle of the King.'

He looked at them eagerly, as if to ask:

'What castle? What king?'

They bowed their heads; and as they turned away weeping they murmured to him soft —

'The Castle of the King of Death.'

He spoke no word; so they turned their weeping faces to him again. They found that he had risen and stood with a set purpose on his face. Then he said sweetly:

'I go to find her, that where she abideth, I too may there abide.'

They said to him:

'You cannot go. Beyond the Portal she is, and in the Land of Death.'

Set purpose shone in the Poet's earnest, loving eyes as he answered them for the last time:

'Where she has gone, there go I too. Through the Valley of the Shadow shall I wend my way. In these ears also shall ring the Music of the Spheres. I shall seek, and I shall find my Beloved in the Halls of the Castle of the King. I shall clasp her close — even before the dread face of the King of Death.'

As they heard these words they bowed their heads again and wept, and said:

'Alas! alas!'

The poet turned and left them; and passed away. They fain would have followed; but he motioned them that they should not stir. So, alone, in his grief he went.

As he passed on he turned and waved his hand to them in farewell. Then for a while with uplifted hand he stood, and turned him slowly all around.

Suddenly his outstretched hand stopped and pointed. His friends looking with him saw, where, away beyond the Portal, the idle wilderness spread. There in the midst of desolation the mist from the marshes hung like a pall of gloom on the far off horizon.

As the Poet pointed there was a gleam of happiness — very very faint it was — in his poor sad eyes, distraught with loss, as if afar he beheld some sign or hope of the Lost One.

Swiftly and sadly the Poet fared on through the burning day.

The Rest Time came; but on he journeyed. He paused not for shade or rest. Never, even for an instant did he stop to cool his parched lips with an icy draught from the crystal springs.

The weary wayfarers resting in the cool shadows beside the fountains raised their tired heads and looked at him with sleepy eyes as he hurried. He heeded them not; but went ever onward with set purpose in his eyes, as though some gleam of hope bursting through the mists of the distant marshes urged him on.

So he fared on through all the burning day, and all the silent night. In the earliest dawn, when the promise of the still unrisen sun quickened the eastern sky into a pale light, he drew nigh the Portal. The horizon stood out blackly in the cold morning light.

There, as ever, stood the Angels who kept watch and ward, and oh, wondrous! although invisible to human eyes, they were seen of him.

As he drew nigh they gazed at him pityingly and swept their great wings out wide, as if to shelter him. He spake; and from his troubled heart the sad words came sweetly through the pale lips:

'Say, Ye who guard the Land, has my Beloved One passed hither on the journey to the Valley of the Shadow, to hear the Music of the Spheres, and to abide in the Castle of the King?'

The Angels at the Portal bowed their heads in token of assent; and they turned and looked outward from the Land to where, far off in the idle wilderness, the dank mists crept from the lifeless bosom of the marsh.

They knew well that the poor lonely Poet was in quest of his Beloved One; so they hindered him not, neither urged they him to stay. They pitied him much for that much he loved.

They parted wide, that through the Portal he might pass without let.

So, the Poet went onwards into the idle desert to look for his Beloved One in the Castle of the King.

For a time he went through gardens whose beauty was riper than the gardens of the Land. The sweetness of all things stole on the senses like the odours from the Isles of the Blest.

The subtlety of the King of Death, who rules in the Realms of

Evil, is great. He has ordered that the way beyond the Portal be made full of charm. Thus those straying from the paths ordained for good see around them such beauty that in its joy the gloom and cruelty and guilt of the desert are forgotten.

But as the Poet passed onwards the beauty began to fade away.

The fair gardens looked as gardens do when the hand of care is taken off, and when the weeds in their hideous luxuriance choke, as they spring up, the choicer life of the flowers.

From cool alleys under spreading branches, and from crisp sward which touched as soft as velvet the Wanderer's aching feet, the way became a rugged stony path, full open to the burning glare. The flowers began to lose their odour, and to dwarf to stunted growth. Tall hemlocks rose on every side, infecting the air with their noisome odour.

Great fungi grew in the dark hollows where the pools of dank water lay. Tall trees, with branches like skeletons, rose − trees which had no leaves, and under whose shadow to pause were to die.

Then huge rocks barred the way. These were only passed by narrow, winding passages, overhung by the ponderous cliffs above, which ever threatened to fall and engulph the Sojourner.

Here the night began to fall; and the dim mist rising from the far-off marshes, took weird shapes of gloom. In the distant fastnesses of the mountains the wild beasts began to roar in their cavern lairs. The air became hideous with the fell sounds of the night season.

But the poor Poet heeded not ill sights or sounds of dread. Onward he went ever − unthinking of the terrors of the night. To him there was no dread of darkness − no fear of death − no consciousness of horror. He sought his Beloved One in the Castle of the King; and in that eager quest all natural terrors were forgot.

So fared he onward through the livelong night. Up the steep defiles he trod. Through the shadows of the huge rocks he passed unscathed. The wild animals came around him roaring fiercely − their great eyes flaming like fiery stars through the blackness of the night.

From the high rocks great pythons crawled and hung to seize

their prey. From the crevices of the mountain steeps, and from cavernous rifts in the rocky way poisonous serpents glided and rose to strike.

But close though the noxious things came, they all refrained to attack; for they knew that the lonely Sojourner was bound for the Castle of their King.

Onward still, onward he went — unceasing — pausing not in his course — but pressing ever forward in his quest.

When daylight broke at last, the sun rose on a sorry sight. There toiling on the rocky way, the poor lonely Poet went ever onwards, unheeding of cold or hunger or pain.

His feet were bare, and his footsteps on the rockstrewn way were marked by blood. Around and behind him, and afar off keeping equal pace on the summits of the rocky ridges, came the wild beasts that looked on him as their prey, but that refrained from touching him because he sought the Castle of their King.

In the air wheeled the obscene birds who follow ever on the track of the dying and the lost. Hovered the bare-necked vultures with eager eyes, and hungry beaks. Their great wings flapped lazily in the idle air as they followed in the Wanderer's track. The vulture are a patient folk, and they await the falling of the prey.

From the cavernous recesses in the black mountain gorges crept, with silent speed, the serpents that there lurk. Came the python, with his colossal folds and endless coils, whence looked forth cunningly the small flat head. Came the boa and all his tribe, which seize their prey by force and crush it with the dread strictness of their embrace. Came the hooded snakes and all those which with their venom destroy their prey. Here, too, came those serpents most terrible of all to their quarry — which fascinate with eyes of weird magic and by the slow gracefulness of their approach.

Here came or lay in wait, subtle snakes, which take the colour of herb, or leaf, or dead branch, or slimy pool, amongst which they lurk, and so strike their prey unsuspecting.

Great serpents there were, nimble of body, which hang from rock or branch. These griping tight to their distant hold, strike downward with the rapidity of light as they hurl their whip-like bodies from afar upon their prey.

Thus came forth all these noxious things to meet the Questing Man, and to assail him. But when they knew he was bound for the dread Castle of their King, and saw how he went onward without fear, they abstained from attack.

The deadly python and the boa towering aloft, with colossal folds, were passive, and for the nonce, became as stone. The hooded serpents drew in again their venomous fangs. The mild, deep earnest eyes of the fascinating snake became lurid with baffled spleen, as he felt his power to charm was without avail. In its deadly descent the hanging snake arrested its course, and hung a limp line from rock or branch.

Many followed the Wanderer onwards into the desert wilds, waiting and hoping for a chance to destroy.

Many other perils also were there for the poor Wanderer in the desert idleness. As he went onward the rocky way got steeper and darker. Lurid fogs and deadly chill mists arose.

Then in this path along the trackless wilderness were strange and terrible things.

Mandrakes — half plant, half man — shrieked at him with despairing cry, as, helpless for evil, they stretched out their ghastly arms in vain.

Giant thorns arose in the path; they pierced his suffering feet and tore his flesh as onward he trod. He felt the pain, but he heeded it not.

In all the long, terrible journey he had but one idea other than his eager search for his Beloved One. He thought that the children of men might learn much from the journey towards the Castle of the King, which began so fair, amidst the odorous gardens and under the cool shadow of the spreading trees. In his heart the Poet spake to the multitude of the children of men; and from his lips the words flowed like music, for he sang of the Golden Gate which the Angels call TRUTH.

> 'Pass not the Portal of the Sunset Land!
> Pause where the Angels at their vigil stand.
> Be warned! and press not though the gates lie wide,
> But rest securely on the hither side.
>
> Though odorous gardens and cool ways invite,
> Beyond are darkest valleys of the night.

Rest! Rest contented. – Pause whilst undefiled,
Nor seek the horrors of the desert wild.'

Thus treading down all obstacles with his bleeding feet, passed ever onwards, the poor distraught Poet, to seek his Beloved One in the Castle of the King.

Even as onward he went the life that is of the animals seemed to die away behind him. The jackals and the more cowardly savage animals slunk away. The lions and tigers, and bears, and wolves, and all the braver of the fierce beasts of prey which followed on his track even after the others had stopped, now began to halt in their career.

They growled low and then roared loudly with uplifted heads; the bristles of their mouths quivered with passion, and the great white teeth champed angrily together in baffled rage. They went on a little further; and stopped again roaring and growling as before. Then one by one they ceased, and the poor Poet went on alone.

In the air the vultures wheeled and screamed, pausing and halting in their flight, as did the savage beasts. These too ceased at length to follow the Wanderer in his constant onward course.

Longest of all kept up the snakes. With many a writhe and stealthy onward glide, they followed hard upon the footsteps of the Questing Man. In the blood marks of his feet upon the flinty rocks they found a joy and hope, and they followed ever.

But time came when the awful aspect of the places where the Poet passed checked even the serpents in their track – the gloomy defiles whence issue the poisonous winds that sweep with desolation even the dens of the beasts of prey – the sterile fastnesses which march upon the valleys of desolation. Here even the stealthy serpents paused in their course; and they too fell away. They glided back, smiling with deadliest rancour, to their obscene clefts.

Then came places where plants and verdure began to cease. The very weeds became more and more stunted and inane. Farther on they declined into the sterility of lifeless rock. Then the most noxious herbs that grew in ghastly shapes of gloom and terror lost even the power to harm, which outlives their living growth. Dwarfed and stunted even of evil, they were compact of the dead rock. Here even the deadly Upas tree could strike no root into the pestiferous earth.

Then came places where, in the entrance to the Valley of the Shadow, even solid things lost their substance, and melted in the dank and cold mists which swept along.

As he passed, the distraught Poet could feel not solid earth under his bleeding feet. On shadows he walked, and amid them, onward through the Valley of the Shadow to seek his Beloved One in the Castle of the King.

The Valley of the Shadow seemed of endless expanse. Circled by the teeming mist, no eye could pierce to where rose the great mountains between which the Valley lay.

Yet they stood there − Mount Despair on the one hand, and the Hill of Fear upon the other.

Hitherto the poor bewildered brain of the Poet had taken no note of all the dangers, and horrors, and pains which surrounded him − save only for the lesson which they taught. But now, lost as he was in the shrouding vapour of the Valley of the Shadow, he could not but think of the terrors of the way. He was surrounded by grisly phantoms that ever and anon arose silent in the mist, and were lost again before he could catch to the full their dread import.

Then there flashed across his soul a terrible thought—

Could it be possible that hither his Beloved One had travelled? Had there come to her the pains which shook his own form with agony? Was it indeed necessary that she should have been appalled by all these surrounding horrors?

At the thought of her, his Beloved One, suffering such pain and dread, he gave forth one bitter cry that rang through the solitude − that cleft the vapour of the Valley, and echoed in the caverns of the mountains of Despair and Fear.

The wild cry prolonged with the agony of the Poet's soul rang through the Valley, till the shadows that peopled it woke for the moment into life-in-death. They flitted dimly along, now melting away and anon springing again into life − till all the Valley of the Shadow was for once peopled with quickened ghosts.

Oh, in that hour there was agony to the poor distraught Poet's soul.

But presently there came a calm. When the rush of his first agony passed, the Poet knew that to the Dead came not the horrors of the journey that he undertook. To the Quick alone is the horror of the passage to the Castle of the King. With the thought came to him such peace that even there — in the dark Valley of the Shadow — stole soft music that sounded in the desert gloom like the Music of the Spheres.

Then the poor Poet remembered what they had told him; that his Beloved One had walked through the Valley of the Shadow, that she had known the Music of the Spheres, and that she abode in the Castle of the King. So he thought that as he was now in the Valley of the Shadow, and as he heard the Music of the Spheres, that soon he should see the Castle of the King where his Beloved One abode. Thus he went on in hope.

But alas! that very hope was a new pain that ere this he wot not of.

Hitherto he had gone on blindly, recking not of where he went or what came a-nigh him, so long as he pressed onward on his quest; but now the darkness and the peril of the way had new terrors, for he thought of how they might arrest his course. Such thoughts made the way long indeed, for the moments seemed an age with hoping. Eagerly he sought for the end to come, when, beyond the Valley of the Shadow through which he fared, he should see rising the turrets of the Castle of the King.

Despair seemed to grow upon him; and as it grew there rang out, ever louder, the Music of the Spheres.

Onward, ever onward, hurried in mad haste the poor distraught Poet. The dim shadows that peopled the mist shrank back as he passed, extending towards him warning hands with long gloomy fingers of deadly cold. In the bitter silence of the moment, they seemed to say:

'Go back! Go back!'

Louder and louder rang now the Music of the Spheres. Faster and faster in mad, feverish haste rushed the Poet, amid the shrinking Shadows of the gloomy valley. The peopling shadows as they faded away before him, seemed to wail in sorrowful warning:

'Go back! Go back!'

Still in his ears rang ever the swelling tumult of the music.

Faster and faster he rushed onward; till, at last, wearied nature gave way and he fell prone to earth, senseless, bleeding, and alone.

After a time — how long he could not even guess — he awoke from his swoon.

For awhile he could not think where he was; and his scattered senses could not help him.

All was gloom and cold and sadness. A solitude reigned around him, more deadly than aught he had ever dreamt of. No breeze was in the air; no movement of a passing cloud. No voice or stir of living thing in earth, or water, or air. No rustle of leaf or sway of branch — all was silent, dead, and deserted. Amid the eternal hills of gloom around, lay the valley devoid of aught that lived or grew.

The sweeping mists with their multitude of peopling shadows had gone by. The fearsome terrors of the desert even were not there. The Poet, as he gazed around him, in his utter loneliness, longed for the sweep of the storm or the roar of the avalanche to break the dread horror of the silent gloom.

Then the Poet knew that through the Valley of the Shadow had he come; that scared and maddened though he had been, he had heard the Music of the Spheres. He thought that now hard by the desolate Kingdom of Death he trod.

He gazed all around him, fearing lest he should see anywhere the dread Castle of the King, where his Beloved One abode; and he groaned as the fear of his heart found voice:

'Not here! oh not here, amid this awful solitude.'

Then amid the silence around, upon distant hills his words echoed:

'Not here! oh not here,' till with the echoing and reechoing rock, the idle wilderness was peopled with voices.

Suddenly the echo voices ceased.

From the lurid sky broke the terrible sound of the thunder peal. Along the distant skies it rolled. Far away over the endless ring of the grey horizon it swept — going and returning — pealing — swelling — dying away. It reversed the aether, muttering now in ominous sound as of threats, and anon crashing with the voice of dread command.

In its roar came a sound as of a word:

'Onward.'

To his knees the Poet sank and welcomed with tears of joy the sound of the thunder. It swept away as a Power from Above the silent desolation of the wilderness. It told him that in and above the Valley of the Shadow rolled the mighty tones of Heaven's command.

Then the Poet rose to his feet, and with new heart went onwards into the wilderness.

As he went the roll of the thunder died away, and again the silence of desolation reigned alone.

So time wore on; but never came rest to the weary feet. Onwards, still onwards he went, with but one memory to cheer him — the echo of the thunder roll in his ears, as it pealed out in the Valley of Desolation:

'Onward! Onward!'

Now the road became less and less rocky, as on his way he passed. The great cliffs sank and dwindled away, and the ooze of the fens crept upward to the mountain's feet.

At length the hills and hollows of the mountain fastnesses disappeared. The Wanderer took his way amid mere trackless wastes, where was nothing but quaking marsh and slime.

On, on he wandered; stumbling blindly with weary feet on the endless road.

Over his soul crept ever closer the blackness of despair. Whilst amid the mountain gorges he had been wandering, some small cheer came from the hope that at any moment some turn in the path might show him his journey's end. Some entry from a dark defile might expose to him, looming great in the distance — or even anigh him — the dread Castle of the King. But now with the flat desolation of the silent marsh around him, he knew that the Castle could not exist without his seeing it.

He stood for a while erect, and turned him slowly round, so that the complete circuit of the horizon was swept by his eager eyes. Alas! never a sight did he see. Nought was there but the black line of the horizon, where the sad earth lay against the level sky. All, all was compact of a silent gloom.

Still on he tottered. His breath came fast and laboured. His

weary limbs quivered as they bore him feebly up. His strength
— his life — was ebbing fast.

On, on, he hurried, ever on, with one idea desperately fixed
in his poor distraught mind — that in the Castle of the King he
should find his Beloved One.

He stumbled and fell. There was no obstacle to arrest his feet;
only from his own weakness he declined.

Quickly he arose and went onward with flying feet. He
dreaded that should he fall he might not be able to arise
again.

Again he fell. Again he rose and went on his way desperately,
with blind purpose.

So for a while went he onwards, stumbling and falling; but
arising ever and pausing not on his way. His quest he followed,
of his Beloved One abiding in the Castle of the King.

At last so weak he grew that when he sank he was unable to
rise again.

Feebler and feebler he grew as he lay prone; and over his
eager eyes came the film of death.

But even then came comfort; for he knew that his race was
run, and that soon he would meet his Beloved One in the Halls
of the Castle of the King.

To the wilderness his thoughts he spoke. His voice came forth
with a feeble sound, like the moaning before a storm of the wind
as it passes through reeds in the grey autumn:

'A little longer. Soon I shall meet her in the Halls of the King;
and we shall part no more. For this it is worth to pass through
the Valley of the Shadow and to listen to the Music of the
Spheres with their painful hope. What boots it though the
Castle be afar? Quickly speed the feet of the dead. To the fleet-
ing spirit all distance is but a span. I fear not now to see the
Castle of the King; for there, within its chiefest Hall, soon shall I
meet my Beloved — to part no more.'

Even as he spoke he felt that the end was nigh.

Forth from the marsh before him crept a still, spreading mist.
It rose silently, higher — higher — enveloping the wilderness
for far around. It took deeper and darker shades as it arose. It
was as though the Spirit of Gloom were hid within, and grew
mightier with the spreading vapour.

To the eyes of the dying Poet the creeping mist was as a shadowy castle. Arose the tall turrets and the frowning keep. The gateway with its cavernous recesses and its beetling towers took shape as a skull. The distant battlements towered aloft into the silent air. From the very ground whereon the stricken Poet lay, grew, dim and dark, a vast causeway leading into the gloom of the Castle gate.

The dying Poet raised his head and looked. His fast failing eyes, quickened by the love and hope of his spirit, pierced through the dark walls of the keep and the gloomy terrors of the gateway.

There, within the great Hall where the grim King of Terrors himself holds his court, he saw her whom he sought. She was standing in the ranks of those who wait in patience for their Beloved to follow them into the Land of Death.

The Poet knew that he had but a little while to wait, and he was patient — stricken though he lay, amongst the Eternal Solitudes.

Afar off, beyond the distant horizon, came a faint light as of the dawn of a coming day.

As it grew brighter the Castle stood out more and more clearly; till in the quickening dawn it stood revealed in all its cold expanse.

The dying Poet knew that the end was at hand. With a last effort he raised himself to his feet, that standing erect and bold, as is the right of manhood, he might so meet face to face the grim King of Death before the eyes of his Beloved One.

The distant sun of the coming day rose over the horizon's edge.

A ray of light shot upward.

As it struck the summit of the Castle keep the Poet's Spirit in an instant of time swept along the causeway. Through the ghostly portal of the Castle it swept, and met with joy the kindred Spirit that it loved before the very face of the King of Death.

Quicker then than the lightning's flash the whole Castle melted into nothingness; and the sun of the coming day shone calmly down upon the Eternal Solitudes.

In the Land within the Portal rose the sun of the coming day.

It shone calmly and brightly on a fair garden, where, among the long summer grass lay the Poet, colder than the marble statues around him.

IV

The Fate of Fenella

In 1878, as I mentioned in the Introduction, the friendship of the young civil servant, Bram Stoker, and the much acclaimed actor Henry Irving, became a business association as well. When Irving asked Bram to become his Acting Manager, he did not think twice about giving up his secure job at the Castle in return for all the vagaries of fortune inherent in the theatrical profession. 'I accepted at once,' he said later, 'I had then had some thirteen years in the public service, a term entitling me to a pension in case of retirement . . . but I was content to throw in my lot with his.'

Bram soon found that his duties entailed virtually everything from controlling the actor's finances to serving as a buffer between Irving and his adoring public. But as with his writing, he threw himself into the task with gusto, and it comes as no surprise to find that he had few opportunities to put pen to paper — in the literary sense — for several years. Another important event in his life was meeting Florence Balcome, a dark-haired, attractive young girl who shortly thereafter became his wife.

In 1883, Henry Irving undertook his first visit to America, and naturally Bram went with him. The change of scenery and the general delights of the tour inspired Bram on his return to write a brief, and now very rare, booklet which he called *A Glimpse of America* (1885). During the next few years, Bram published little, only one novel, *The Snake's Pass* (1889), which was nevertheless highly praised by the critics, one of whom compared him to Le Fanu. However, there can be little doubt that

by this time his literary ability was being widely recognised, and
we have evidence of this in 1892 when the enormously successful
Cassell's Magazine invited him to contribute to a totally new
concept in serial storytelling they were launching. It was to be a
continuing mystery story, each chapter written by a different
author, and published month by month in the magazine.
Despite the pressure of work, Bram was obviously attracted to
the idea, and as he was being asked to follow guidelines that
would have been firmly established by the time the story
reached him (at Chapter Ten), he doubtless thought the commission would not tax his ingenuity too much. But typically of
Bram, he produced a chapter that was skilfully, ingenious and
arguably the best of all the twenty-four episodes.

In announcing the start of 'The Fate of Fenella', the Editor of
Cassell's wrote: 'The publishers claim with no little satisfaction
that in this serial they are offering the reading public a genuine
novelty. The idea of a novel written by twenty-four popular
writers is certainly an original one. The ladies and gentlemen
who have written "The Fate of Fenella" have done their work
quite independently of each other. There has been collabora-
tion but not consultation.'

The list of the contributors is almost a Who's Who of the con-
temporary literary world, and included such names as the
romantic novelists Helen Mathers and Florence Marryat;
G. Manville Fenn the writer of high adventure stories; the great
humourist F. Anstey, and Arthur Conan Doyle, then busy giving the world the first adventures of Sherlock Holmes. In Bram's
episode which follows we can once again anticipate the spectre
of Dracula in the form of Frank Onslow with his 'gaunt cheeks'
and 'deadly pallor' and the intriguing reference to 'someone
. . . who made those marks on the dead man's throat'.

The Fate of Fenella

Lord Francis Onslow lifted his cap. The action was an instinctive one, for he was face to face with a lady; but he was half
dazed with the unexpected meeting, and could not collect his
thoughts. He only remembered that when he had last seen his

wife she was opening the door of her chamber to De Mürger.
For weeks he had been schooling himself for such a meeting, for
he knew that on his return such might at any time occur; but
now, when the moment had come, and unexpectedly, the old
pain of his shame overwhelmed him anew. His face grew white
— white till it seemed to Fenella that it was of the pallor of
death. She knew that she had been so far guilty of what had
happened that the murder had been the outcome of her previous acts. She knew also that her husband was ignorant of his
part in the deed — and her horror of the man, blood-guilty in
such a way, was fined down by the sense of her own partial guilt.
The trial, with all its consequent pain to a proud and sensitive
woman, had softened her, and she grasped at any hope. The
sight of Frank, his gaunt cheeks, which told their tale of suffering, and now the deadly pallor, awoke all the protective feeling
which is a part of a woman's love. It was with her whole soul in
her voice that she said again:

'Frank!' His voice was stern as well as sad as he answered her:

'What is it?' Her heart went cold, but she persevered.

'Frank, I must have a word with you — I must. For God's
sake, for Ronny's sake, do not deny me.' She did not know that
as yet Frank Onslow was in ignorance of De Mürger's death; and
when his answer came it seemed more hard than even he
intended:

'Do you wish to speak of that night?' In a faint voice she
answered:

'I do.' Then looking in his eyes and seeing the hard look
becoming harder still — for a man is seldom generous with a
woman where his honour is concerned, she added:

'O Heaven! Frank! You do not think me guilty! No, no, not
you! not you! That would be too cruel!'

Frank Onslow paused and said:

'Fenella, God help me! but I do,' and he turned away his
head. His wife, of course, thought that he alluded to the
murder, and not to her sin against him as he saw it, and with a
low moan she turned away and hid her face in her hands. Then
with an effort she drew herself up, and without a word or a
single movement to show that she even recognized his presence,
she passed on up the street.

Frank Onslow stood for a few moments watching her retreating figure, and then went across the street and turned the next corner on his way to the post-office, for which he had been inquiring when he met his wife. At the door he was stopped by a cheery voice and an outstretched hand:

'Onslow!'

'Castleton!' The two men shook hands warmly.

'I see you did not get my telegram,' said Lord Castleton. 'It is waiting for you at the post-office.'

'What telegram?'

'To tell you that I was on my way here from London. I went in your interest, old fellow. I thought you would like full particulars — the newspapers are so vague.'

'What papers? My interest? Tell me all. I am ignorant of all that has passed for the last six weeks.' A vague, shadowy fear began to creep over his spirits. Castleton's voice was full of sympathy as he answered:

'Then you have not heard of — but stay. It is a long story. Come back to the yacht. I was just going to join you there. We shall be all alone, and I can tell you all. I have the newspapers here for you.' He motioned to a roll under his arm.

The two went down to the harbour, and finding the sailor waiting with the boat at the steps, were rowed to the yacht and got on board. Here the two men were all alone. Then, with a preliminary clearing of his voice, Castleton began his story:

'Frank Onslow — better get the worst over at once — just after you went away from Harrogate your wife was tried for murder and acquitted.'

'My God! Fenella tried for murder? Whose murder?'

'That scoundrel De Mürger. It seems he went into her room in the night and attempted violence, so she stabbed him —'

Castleton stopped in amazement, for a look of radiance came over Frank Onslow's face, as he murmured 'Thank God!' Recalled to himself by Castleton's silence, for he was too amazed to go on, Frank said. 'I have a reason, old fellow; I shall tell it to you later, but go on. Tell me all the facts, or let me read the papers. Remember I am as yet quite ignorant of it all and I am full of anxiety!'

Without a word Castleton handed him the papers, and, lighting a fresh cigar, sat down with his back to him, and presently yielded to the sun and fresh air and fell into a doze.

Frank Onslow took the papers, and read carefully from end to end the account of the trial of his wife for the murder of De Mürger. When he had finished he sat with the folded paper in his hand, and his eyes had the same far-away look in them which they had had on that fatal night. The hypnotic trance was on him again.

Presently he rose, and with stealthy steps approached his sleeping friend. Murmuring 'Why did I not kill him?' he struck with the folded paper, as though with a dagger, the form before him. Castleton, who had sunk into a pleasant sleep and whose fat face was wreathed with a smile, was annoyed at the rude awakening. 'What the devil!' he began angrily, and then stopped as his eyes met the face of his friend and he realized that he was in some sort of trance. He grew very pale as he saw Frank Onslow stab, and stab, and stab again. There was a certain grotesqueness in the affair — the man in such terrible earnest, in his mind committing murder, while his real weapon was but a folded paper. As he stabbed he hissed, 'Why did I not kill him? Why did I not kill him?' Then he went through a series of movements as though he were softly pulling an imaginary door shut behind him, and so back to his own chair, where he sat down hiding his face in his hands.

Castleton sat looking at him in amazement, and then murmured to himself:

'They thought it was someone stronger than Fenella whose grasp made those marks on the dead man's throat.' He suddenly looked round to see that no one but himself had observed what had happened, and then, being satisfied on this point, murmured again:

'A noble woman, by Jove! A noble woman!' He called out:

'Frank — Frank Onslow! Wake up, man.' Onslow raised his head as a man does when suddenly awakened, and smiled as he said:

'What is it, old man? Have I been asleep?' It was quite evident that he had no recollection of what had just passed. Castleton came and sat down beside him, and his kindly face was grave as he asked:

'You have read the papers?'

'I have.'

'Now tell me — you offered to do so — why you said 'Thank God!' when I told you that your wife had killed De Mürger?'

Frank Onslow paused. Although the memory of what he had thought to be his shame had been with him daily and nightly until he had become familiarized with it, it was another thing to speak of it, even to such a friend as Castleton. Even now, when it was apparent from the issue of the trial that his wife had avenged so dreadfully the attempt upon her honour, he felt it hard to speak on the subject. Castleton saw the doubt and struggle in his mind which was reflected in his face, and said earnestly, as he laid his hand upon his shoulder:

'Do not hesitate to tell me, Frank. I do not ask out of mere curiosity. I am perhaps a better friend than you think in helping to clear up a certain doubt which I see before me. I think you know I am a friend.'

'One of the best a man ever had!' said Frank impulsively, as he took the other's hand. Then turning away his head, he said slowly:

'You were surprised because I was glad Fenella killed that scoundrel. I can tell you, Castleton, but I would not tell anyone else. It was because I saw him enter her room, and, God forgive me! I thought at the time that it was by her wish. That is why I came away from Harrogate that night. That is what kept me away. How could I go back and face my friends with such a shame fresh upon me? It was your lending me your yacht, old man, that made life possible. When I was by myself through the wildness of the Bay of Biscay and among the great billows of the Atlantic I began to be able to bear. I had steeled myself, I thought, and when I heard that so far from my wife being guilty of such a shame, she actually killed the man that attempted her honour, is it any wonder that I felt joyful?'

After a pause Castleton asked:

'How did you come to see — to see it. Why did you take no step to prevent it? Forgive me, old fellow, but I want to understand.'

Frank Onslow went to the rail, and leaned over. When he came back Castleton saw that his eyes were wet. With what cheerfulness he could assume, he answered:

'On that very night I had made up my mind to try to win back my wife's love. I wrote a letter to her, a letter in which I poured out my whole soul, and I left my room to put it under her door, so that she would get it in the morning. But' − here he paused, and then said, slowly, 'but when in the corridor, I saw her door open, and at the same moment De Mürger appeared.'

'Did she seem surprised?'

'Not at first. But a moment after a look of amazement crossed her face, and she stepped back into the room, he following her.' As he said this he put his head between his hands and groaned.

'And then?' added his friend.

'And then I hardly know what happened. My mind seems full of a dim memory of a blank existence, and then a series of wild whirling thoughts, something like that last moment after death in Wiertz's picture. I think I must have slept, for it was two o'clock when I saw Fenella, and the clock was striking five when I crossed the bridge after I had left the hotel.'

'And the letter? What became of it?'

Frank started. 'The letter? I never thought of it. Stay! I must have left it on the table in my room. I remember seeing it there a little while before I came away.'

'How was it addressed? Do not think me inquisitive, but I cannot help thinking that that letter may yet be of some great importance.'

Frank smiled, a sad smile enough, as he answered: 'By the pet name I had for Fennella − Mrs Right. I used to chaff her because she always defended her position when we argued, and so, when I wanted to tease her, I called her Mrs Right.'

'Was it written on hotel paper?'

'No. I was going to write on some, but I thought it would be better to use the sort we had when − when we were first married. There were a few sheets in my writing case, so I took one.'

'That was headed somewhere in Surrey, was it not?'

'Yes; Chiddingford, near Haslemere. It was a pretty place,

too, called The Grange. Fenella fell in love with it, and made me buy it right away.'

'Is anyone living there now?'

'It is let to someone. I don't think that I heard the name. The agent knows. When the trouble came I told him to do what he could with it, and not to bother me with it any more. After a while he wrote and asked if I would mind it being let to a foreigner? I told him he might let it to a devil so long as he did not worry me.'

Lord Castleton paused awhile, and asked the next question in a hesitating way. He felt embarrassed, and showed it:

'Tell me one thing more, old fellow − if − if you don't mind.'

'My dear Castleton, I'll tell you anything you like.'

'How did you sign the letter?' Onslow's face looked sad as he answered:

'I signed it by another old pet name we both understood. We had pet names − people always have when they are first married,' he added with embarrassment.

'Of course,' murmured the sympathetic Castleton.

'One such name lasted a long time. An old friend of my father's came to see us, and in a playful moment he said I was a "sad dog". Fenella took it up and used to call me "Doggie," and I often signed myself "Frank Doggie" − as men usually do.'

'Of course,' again murmured Castleton, as if such a signature was a customary thing. Then he added, 'And on this occasion?'

'On this occasion I used the name that seemed full of happiest memories. "Frank Doggie" may seem idiotic to an outsider, but to Fenella and myself it might mean much.'

The two men sat silent awhile, and then Castleton asked softly:

'I suppose it may be taken for granted that Lady Francis never got the letter?'

'I take it, it is so; but it is no matter now, I refused to speak with her just before I met you. I did not know then what I know now − and she will never speak to me again.' He sighed as he spoke, and turned away. Then he went to the rail of the yacht and leaned over with his head down, looking into the still blue water beneath him.

'Poor old Frank!' said Castleton to himself. 'I can't but think that this matter may come right yet. I must find out what became of that letter, in case Lady Francis never got it. It would prove to her that Frank—'

His train of thought suddenly stopped. A new idea seemed to strike him so forcibly that it quite upset him. Onslow, who had come over from the rail, noticed it. 'I say, Castleton, what is wrong with you? You have got quite white about the gills.'

'Nothing — nothing,' he answered hastily. 'I am subject to it. They call it heart. Pardon me for a bit, I'll go to my bunk and lie down,' and he went below.

In truth, he was overwhelmed by the thought which had just struck him. If his surmise were true, that Onslow, in a hypnotic trance, as he had almost proved by its recurrence, had killed De Mürger, where, then, was Fenella's heroism after all? True that she had taken the blame on herself; but might it not have been that she was morally guilty all the same? Why, then, had she taken the blame? Was it not because she feared that her husband might have refused to screen her shame; or because she feared that if any less heroic aspect of the tragedy was presented to the public, her own fair fame might suffer in greater degree? Could it indeed be that Fenella Onslow was not a heroine, but only a calculating woman of exceeding smartness? Then, again, if Frank Onslow believed that his wife had avenged her honour, was it wise to disturb such belief? He might think, if once the suggestion were made to him, that his honour was preserved only by his own unconscious act.

Was it then wise to disturb existing relations between the husband and wife, sad though they were? Did they come together again, they might in mutual confidence arrive at a real knowledge of the facts, and then — and then, what would be the result? And besides, might there not be some danger in any suggestion made as to his suspicion of who struck the blow? It was true that Lady Francis had been acquitted of the crime, although she confessed to the killing; but her husband might still be tried — and if tried? What then would be the result of the discovery of the missing letter on which he had been building such hopes?

The problem was too much for Lord Castleton. His life had

been too sunny and easy-going to allow of familiarity with great emotions, and such a problem as this was to him overwhelming. The issue was too big for him; and revolving in his own mind all that belonged to it, he glided into sleep.

V

Vampires in New England

It was early in the year 1896 that one of the most significant events occurred in the life of Bram Stoker, and in the creation of *Dracula* in particular. All that winter Henry Irving's company had been in North America tracking from one theatre to another, across Canada, through the heart of America, and ending in New York in February 1896. Irving was now a major attraction in America and he was regarded as a celebrity wherever he went − and the fact that he had been knighted the previous year by Queen Victoria added still further to his prestige. Bram, too, was now quite well-known through his books, and in New York he had the honour of being introduced to Theodore Roosevelt, then the city's Commissioner of Police. He was immediately attracted to the man and wrote in his diary, 'Must be President some day. A man you can't cajole, can't frighten, can't buy.'

On this evidence, Bram was clearly in a prophetic frame of mind, and it is interesting to wonder if he had any idea of *how* important an article which caught his eye in a newspaper was to ultimately prove to him. He came across the item while reading in his New York hotel room on the morning of 2 February 1896. What we can be sure of is that the article, headed 'Vampires in New England' in the *New York World* that Sunday morning so intrigued him that he tore it from the page and tucked it into his writing case. Later it was to be placed with the working papers for his next book − and there it was to remain forgotten until long after that story had been published and earned him undying fame. Long, indeed, after he was dead. The book was, of course, *Dracula*.

It is a curious fact to note that in all the discussion that has
gone on about the origins of Bram's idea for his vampire novel,
little regard has been paid to this one piece of undeniable
evidence that exists – the newspaper cutting found in the early
1970's among his papers. There can, in my estimation, be little
doubt that it helped fire his imagination and we can see from
the internal evidence that it also influenced his notions about
what vampires could do. Why, there is even one vampire mentioned with a name not unlike that of Dracula! I believe it
played the role of a catalyst to the ideas that had been swim-
ming around in his imagination – the ideas already expressed
in the earlier stories included in this book – and thereby
directly helped him create the immortal story of *Dracula*. When
Bram returned to England, the theme for his new book was
evidently racing around in his brain – certainly he was to write
it during the coure of 1896, at 'a fever pitch' to quote his bio-
graphers – but as there was no possibility of his being able to
visit Transylvania, the traditional home of vampires where he
planned to set the story, he needed expert evidence on the
country and its traditions. This he was soon able to obtain from
one of Sir Henry Irving's acquaintances, a Hungarian Professor
Arminius Vambery, who proved himself a mine of information
on supernatural lore, much of it gained from personal research
in the deepest reaches of Europe. He filled Bram's head with
tales and legends, and the story grew in its author's mind with
increasing pace.

Only the physical characteristics of the Count himself
remained to be settled. And, once more, I believe Bram Stoker
found these close to home – in the aristocratic figure of his
'Chief', Sir Henry Irving. One needs only compare portraits of
Irving at this time to see an almost uncanny resemblance to the
descriptions which Bram gives us of Dracula: the tall, spare
figure, the imposing, aquiline profile and the dark, haunting
eyes. Irving, too, favoured black as a colour for his clothes and
frequently wore a swirling cape. What could be more natural
than for Bram to use him as a model for the character which
now so gripped his imagination? To these personal contacts, he
augmented further research in the British Museum – and by
the following winter the book which was to earn him a place in

literary history was complete. Here, then, is this enormously crucial newspaper report from the *New York World*: the life-blood, as it were, from which the vampire took his *genus* . . .

Vampires in New England

VAMPIRES IN NEW ENGLAND

Dead Bodies Dug Up and
Their Hearts Burned to
Prevent Disease

Strange Superstitions of
Long Ago

The Old Belief Was That
Ghostly Monsters Sucked
the Blood of Their
Living Relatives!

Recent ethnological research has disclosed something very extraordinary in Rhode Island. It appears that the ancient vampire superstition still survives in that State, and within the last few years many people have been digging up the dead bodies of relatives for the purpose of burning their hearts.

Near Newport scores of such exhumations have been made, the purpose being to prevent the dead from preying upon the living. The belief entertained is that a person who has died of consumption is likely to rise from the grave at night and suck the blood of surviving members of his or her family, thus dooming them to a similar fate.

The discovery of the survival in highly educated New England of a superstition dating back to the days of Sardanapalus and Nebuchadnezzar has been made by George R. Stetson, an ethnologist of repute. He has found it rampant in a district which includes the towns of Exeter, Foster, Kingstown, East Greenwich and many scattered hamlets. This region, where abandoned farms are numerous, is the tramping-ground of the book agent, the chromo peddler and the patent medicine man. The social isolation is as complete as it was two centuries ago.

Here Cotton Mather and the host of medical, clerical and lay believers in the uncanny ideas of bygone centuries could still hold high carnival. Not merely the out-of-the-way agricultural folk, but the more intelligent people of the urban communities are strong in their belief in vampirism.

One case noted was that of an intelligent and well-to-do head of a family who some years ago lost several of his children by consumption. After they were buried he dug them up and burned them in order to save the lives of their surviving brothers and sisters.

There is one small village distant fifteen miles from Newport where within the last few years there have been at least half a dozen resurrections on this account. The most recent was made two years ago in a family where the mother and four children had already succumbed to consumption. The last of these children was exhumed and the heart was burned.

Another instance was noted in a sea-shore town, not far from Newport, possessing a summer hotel and a few cottages of hot-weather residents. An intelligent man, by trade a mason, informed Mr Stetson that he had lost two brothers by consumption. On the death of his second brother, his father was advised to take up the body and burn the heart. He refused to do so, and consequently he was attacked by the disease. Finally, he died of it. His heart was burned, and in this way the rest of the family escaped.

This frightful superstition is said to prevail in all of the isolated districts of Southern Rhode Island, and it survives to some extent in the large centres of population. Sometimes the body is burned, not merely the heart, and the ashes are scattered.

In some parts of Europe the belief still has a hold on the popular mind. On the Continent from 1727 to 1735 there prevailed an epidemic of vampires. Thousands of people died, as was supposed, from having their blood sucked by creatures that came to their bedsides at night with goggling eyes and lips eager for the life blood of the victim. In Servia it was understood that the demon might be destroyed by digging up the body and piercing it through with a sharp instrument, after which it was decapitated and burned. Relief was found in eating the earth of the vampire's grave. In the Levant the corpse was cut to pieces and boiled in wine.

There was no hope for a person once chosen as a prey by a vampire. Slowly but surely he or she was destined to fade and sicken, receiving meanwhile nightly visits from the monster. Even death was no relief, for − and here was the most horrible part of the superstition − the victim, once dead and laid in the grave, was compelled to become a vampire and in his turn to take up the business of preying on the living. Thus vampirism was indefinitely propagated.

Realise, if you please, that at that period, when science was hardly born and no knowledge had been spread among the people to fight off superstition, belief in the reality of this fearful thing was absolute. Its existence was officially recognised, and military commissions were appointed for the purpose of opening the graves of suspected vampires and taking such measures as were necessary for destroying the latter.

Vampirism became a plague more dreaded than any form of disease. Everywhere people were dying from the attacks of the blood-sucking monsters, each victim becoming in turn a night-prowler in pursuit of human prey. Terror of the mysterious and unearthly peril filled all hearts.

Evidence enough as to the provenance of the mischief was afforded by the condition of many of the bodies that were dug up by the commissioners appointed for the purpose. In many instances corpses which had been buried for weeks and even months were found fresh and lifelike. Sometimes fresh blood was actually discovered on their lips. What proof could be more convincing, inasmuch as was well known, the buried body of the vampire is preserved and nourished by its nightly repasts? The blood on the lips, of course, was that of the victim of the night before.

The faith in vampirism entertained by the public at large was as complete as that which is felt in a discovery of modern science. It was an actual epidemic that threatened the people, spreading rapidly and only to be checked by the adoption of the most drastic measures.

The contents of every suspected grave were investigated, and many corpses found in such a condition as that described were promptly subjected to 'treatment'. This meant that a stake was driven through the chest, and the heart, being taken out, was either burned or chopped into small pieces. For in this way only could a vampire be deprived of power to do mischief.

In one case a man who was unburied sat up in his coffin, with fresh blood on his lips. The official in charge of the ceremonies held a crucifix before his face and saying, 'Do you recognise your Saviour?' chopped the unfortunate's head off. This person presumably had been buried alive in a cataleptic trance.

How is the phenomenon to be accounted for? Nobody can say with certainty, but it may be that the fright into which people were thrown by the epidemic had the effect of predisposing nervous persons to catalepsy. In a word, people were buried alive in a condition where the vital functions being suspended, they remained as it were dead for a while. It is a common thing for a cataleptic to bleed at the mouth just before returning to consciousness. According to the popular superstition, the vampire left his or her body in the grave while engaged in nocturnal prowls.

The epidemic prevailed all over south-eastern Europe, being at its worst in Hungary and Servia. It is supposed to have originated in Greece where a belief was entertained to the effect that Latin Christians buried in that country could not decay in their graves, being under the ban of the Greek Church. The cheerful notion was that they got out of their graves at night and pursued the occupation of ghouls.

The superstition as to ghouls is very ancient and undoubtedly of Oriental origin. Generally speaking, however, a ghoul is just the opposite of a vampire, being a living person who preys on dead bodies, while a vampire is a dead person that feeds on the blood of the living. If you had your choice, which would you rather be, a vampire or a ghoul?

One of the most familiar of the stories of the *Arabian Nights* tells of a woman who annoyed her husband very much by refusing food. Nothing more than a few grains of rice would she eat at meals. He discovered that she was in the habit of stealing away from his side in the night, and, following her on one such occasion, he found her engaged in digging up and devouring a corpse.

Among the numerous folk tales about vampires is one relating to a fiend named Dekanavar, who dwelt in a cave in Armenia. He would not permit anybody to penetrate into the mountains of Ulmish Altotem or to count their valleys. Every one who attempted this had in the night the blood sucked by the monster from the soles of his feet until he died.

At last, however, he was outwitted by two cunning fellows. They began to count the valleys, and when night came they lay down to sleep, taking care to place themselves with the feet of each under the head of the other. In the night the monster came, felt as usual and found a head. Then he felt at the other end and found a head there also.

'Well!' cried he. 'I have gone through all of the three hundred and sixty-six valleys of these mountains and have sucked the blood of people without end, but never yet did I find one with two heads and no feet!' So saying he ran away, and never more was seen in that country, but ever since people have known that the mountains have three hundred and sixty-six valleys.

Belief in the vampire bat is more modern. For a long time it was ridiculed by science as a delusion, but it has been proved to be founded correctly upon fact. It was the famous naturalist Darwin who settled this question.

One night he was camping with a party near Coquimbo in Chile, and it happened that a servant noticed the restlessness of one of the horses. The man went up to the horse and actually caught a bat in the act of sucking blood from the flank of the animal.

While many kinds of bats have been ignorantly accused of this blood-sucking habit, only one species is really a vampire. It constitutes a *genus* all by itself. Just as a man is the only species of the *genus homo*, so the vampire bat is the only species of the *genus dismodus*. Fortunately, it is not very large, having a spread of only two feet. This is not much for a bat. The so-called 'Flying Foxes' of the old world, which go about in flocks and ravage orchards, are of much greater size, and there is a bat of

Java, known as the 'Kalong' that has a spread of five feet from wing tip to wing tip. The body of the true vampire bat weighs only a few ounces.

VI

Walpurgis Night

Dracula was published in May 1897 and the enthusiastic recep-
tion it received from the public and the press more than justified
the high hopes that Bram Stoker had been quietly nurturing for
it. His instincts told him it *was* a good story, perhaps even a
unique one, and if any book was going to make his name, this
was it. The national newspapers raved about the book, the
Daily Mail comparing it to classics of horror fiction like *The
Mysteries of Udolpho* and *Frankenstein*, and the *Pall Mall
Gazette* declared it to be 'horrid and creepy to the last degree'.

Bram himself was most delighted with the praise he received
from his mother who wrote to him from Ireland, 'It is splendid,
a thousand miles beyond anything you have written before, and
I feel certain it will place you very high in the writers of the day
— the story and style being deeply sensational, exciting and
interesting. . . . No book since Mrs Shelley's *Frankenstein* or
indeed any other at all has come near yours in originality or
terror — Poe is nowhere!'

Although Sir Henry Irving was also among the early readers
of *Dracula*, he did not share quite the same ecstatic enthusiasm
shown by everyone else — perhaps he recognised something of
himself in the enigmatic central character who drains the
energies of those around him, I wonder? — and when the story
was dramatised shortly afterwards he was not present at the performance. Indeed, this first stage presentation went generally
unnoticed — a remarkable fact for a story that has since been
dramatised, filmed, broadcast and utilised in all the various
mediums of entertainment times without number.

Another fact which went unrecorded at the time was that Bram had actually cut a whole scene from his original manuscript before the book was printed. His publishers, Constable, had asked him to delete a section so that they might publish it in the financially more attractive size of 390 pages. (The extra words would have apparently taken the page extent beyond 400 pages and necessitated another sixpence on the book's price: something Constable, in their uncertainty about the novel's prospects, were not prepared to risk!) So Bram, as always pressured with work on Irving's behalf, took the easiest course of action – deleting what he had intended to be the first chapter of the book, a foretaste of what is to come in the shape of an encounter on Walpurgis Night between the hero, Jonathan Harker, and one of Count Dracula's terrible emissaries. The episode thereafter lay forgotten among Bram's papers until his death, when Mrs Stoker rediscovered it and allowed its publication, initially, in *The Story Teller* magazine of May 1914, under Bram's title, 'Walpurgis Night'. Later, it was to become known as 'Dracula's Guest' . . .

Walpurgis Night

When we started for our drive the sun was shining brightly on Munich, and the air was full of the joyousness of early summer. Just as we were about to depart, Herr Delbrück (the maître d'hôtel of the Quatre Saisons, where I was staying) came down, bareheaded, to the carriage and, after wishing me a pleasant drive, said to the coachman, still holding his hand on the handle of the carriage door:

'Remember you are back by nightfall. The sky looks bright but there is a shiver in the north wind that says there may be a sudden storm. But I am sure you will not be late.' Here he smiled, and added, 'for you know what night it is.'

Johann answered with an emphatic, 'Ja mein Herr,' and, touching his hat, drove off quickly. When we had cleared the town, I said, after signalling to him to stop:

'Tell me, Johann, what is to-night?'

He crossed himself, as he answered laconically: 'Walpurgis

Nacht.' Then he took out his watch, a great, old-fashioned German silver thing as big as a turnip, and looked at it, with his eyebrows gathered together and a little impatient shrug of his shoulders. I realised that this was his way of respectfully protesting against the unnecessary delay, and sank back in the carriage, merely motioning him to proceed. He started off rapidly, as if to make up for lost time. Every now and then the horses seemed to throw up their heads and sniffed the air suspiciously. On such occasions I often looked round in alarm. The road was pretty bleak, for we were traversing a sort of high, wind-swept plateau. As we drove, I saw a road that looked but little used, and which seemed to dip through a little, winding valley. It looked so inviting that, even at the risk of offending him, I called Johann to stop – and when he had pulled up, I told him I would like to drive down that road. He made all sorts of excuses, and frequently crossed himself as he spoke. This somewhat piqued my curiosity, so I asked him various questions. He answered fencingly, and repeatedly looked at his watch in protest. Finally I said:

'Well, Johann, I want to go down this road. I shall not ask you to come unless you like; but tell me why you do not like to go, that is all I ask.'

For answer he seemed to throw himself off the box, so quickly did he reach the ground. Then he stretched out his hands appealingly to me, and implored me not to go. There was just enough of English mixed with the German for me to understand the drift of his talk. He seemed always just about to tell me something – the very idea of which evidently frightened him; but each time he pulled himself up, saying, as he crossed himself: 'Walpurgis Nacht!'

I tried to argue with him, but it was difficult to argue with a man when I did not know his language. The advantage certainly rested with him, for although he began to speak in English, of a very crude and broken kind, he always got excited and broke into his native tongue – and every time he did so, he looked at his watch. Then the horses became restless and sniffed the air. At this he grew very pale, and, looking around in a frightened way, he suddenly jumped forward, took them by the bridles and led them on some twenty feet. I followed, and asked why he had done this. For answer he crossed himself, pointed to the spot we had left and drew his carriage in the direction of the other road, indicating a cross, and said, first in German, then in English: 'Buried him − him what killed themselves.'

I remembered the old custom of burying suicides at cross-roads: 'Ah! I see, a suicide. How interesting!' But for the life of me I could not make out why the horses were frightened.

Whilst we were talking, we heard a sort of sound between a yelp and a bark. It was far away; but the horses got very restless, and it took Johann all his time to quiet them. He was pale, and said: 'It sounds like a wolf − but yet there are no wolves here now.'

'No?' I said, questioning him; 'Isn't it long since the wolves were so near the city?'

'Long, long,' he answered, 'in the spring and summer; but with the snow the wolves have been here not so long.'

Whilst he was petting the horses and trying to quiet them, dark clouds drifted rapidly across the sky. The sunshine passed away, and a breath of cold wind seemed to drift past us. It was only a breath, however, and more in the nature of a warning than a fact, for the sun came out brightly again. Johann looked under his lifted hand at the horizon and said:

'The storm of snow, he comes before long time.' Then he looked at his watch again, and, straightaway holding his reins firmly − for the horses were still pawing the ground restlessly and shaking their heads − he climbed to his box as though the time had come for proceeding on our journey.

I felt a little obstinate and did not at once get into the carriage.

'Tell me,' I said, 'about this place where the road leads,' and I pointed down.

Again he crossed himself and mumbled a prayer, before he answered: 'It is unholy.'

'What is unholy?' I enquired.

'The village.'

'Then there is a village?'

'No, no. No one lives there hundreds of years.' My curiosity was piqued: 'But you said there was a village.'

'There was.'

'Where is it now?'

Whereupon he burst out into a long story in German and English, so mixed up that I could not quite understand exactly what he said, but roughly I gathered that long ago, hundreds of years, men had died there and been buried in their graves; and sounds were heard under the clay, and when the graves were opened, men and women were found rosy with life, and their mouths red with blood. And so, in haste to save their lives (aye, and their souls! − and here he crossed himself) those who were left fled away to other places, where the living lived, and the dead were dead and not − not something. He was evidently afraid to speak the last words. As he proceeded with his narration, he grew more and more excited. It seemed as if his imagination had got hold of him, and he ended in a perfect paroxysm of fear − white-faced, perspiring, trembling and looking round him, as if expecting that some dreadful presence would manifest itself there in the bright sunshine on the open plain. Finally, in an agony of desperation, he cried:

'Walpurgis Nacht!' and pointed to the carriage for me to get in. All my English blood rose at this, and, standing back, I said:

'You are afraid, Johann − you are afraid. Go home; I shall return alone; the walk will do me good.' The carriage door was open. I took from the seat my oak walking-stick − which I always carry on my holiday excursions − and closed the door, pointing back to Munich, and said, 'Go home, Johann − Walpurgis Nacht doesn't concern Englishmen.'

The horses were now more restive than ever, and Johann was trying to hold them in, while excitedly imploring me not to do anything so foolish. I pitied the poor fellow, he was so deeply in earnest; but all the same I could not help laughing. His English was quite gone now. In his anxiety he had forgotten that his only means of making me understand was to talk my language, so he jabbered away in his native German. It began to be a little tedious. After giving the direction, 'Home!' I turned to go down the cross-road into the valley.

With a despairing gesture, Johann turned his horses towards Munich. I leaned on my stick and looked after him. He went slowly along the road for a while: then there came over the crest of the hill a man tall and thin. I could see so much in the distance.

When he drew near the horses, they began to jump and kick about, then to scream with terror. Johann could not hold them in; they bolted down the road, running away madly. I watched them out of sight, then looked for the stranger, but I found that he, too, was gone.

With a light heart I turned down the side road through the deepening valley to which Johann had objected. There was not the slightest reason, that I could see, for his objection; and I daresay I tramped for a couple of hours without thinking of time or distance, and certainly without seeing a person or a house. So far as the place was concerned, it was desolation itself. But I did not notice this particularly till, on turning a bend in the road, I came upon a scattered fringe of wood; then I recognised that I had been impressed unconsciously by the desolation of the region through which I had passed.

I sat down to rest myself, and began to look around. It struck me that it was considerably colder than it had been at the commencement of my walk − a sort of sighing sound seemed to be around me, with, now and then, high overhead, a sort of muffled roar. Looking upwards I noticed that great thick clouds were drifting rapidly across the sky from north to south at a great height. There were signs of coming storm in some lofty stratum of the air. I was a little chilly, and, thinking that it was the sitting still after the exercise of walking, I resumed my journey.

The ground I passed over was now much more picturesque. There were no striking objects that the eye might single out; but in all there was a charm of beauty. I took little heed of time and it was only when the deepening twilight forced itself upon me that I began to think of how I should find my way home. The brightness of the day had gone. The air was cold, and the drifting of clouds high overhead was more marked. They were accompanied by a sort of far-away rushing sound, through which seemed to come at intervals that mysterious cry which the driver had said came from a wolf. For a while I hesitated. I had said I would see the deserted village, so on I went, and presently came on a wide stretch of open country, shut in by hills all around. Their sides were covered with trees which spread down to the plain, dotting, in clumps, the gentler slopes and hollows which showed here and there. I followed with my eye the winding of the road, and saw that it curved close to one of the densest of these clumps and was lost behind it.

As I looked there came a cold shiver in the air, and the snow began to fall. I thought of the miles and miles of bleak country I had passed, and then hurried on to seek the shelter of the wood in front. Darker and darker grew the sky, and faster and heavier fell the snow, till the earth before and around me was a glistening white carpet, the further edge of which was lost in misty vagueness. The road was here but crude, and when on the level its boundaries were not so marked, as when it passed through the cuttings; and in a little while I found that I must have strayed from it, for I missed underfoot the hard surface, and my feet sank deeper in the grass and moss. Then the wind grew stronger and blew with ever increasing force, till I was fain to run before it. The air became icy-cold, and in spite of my exercise I began to suffer. The snow was now falling so thickly and whirling around me in such rapid eddies that I could hardly keep my eyes open. Every now and then the heavens were torn asunder by vivid lightning, and in the flashes I could see ahead of me a great mass of trees, chiefly yew and cypress all heavily coated with snow.

I was soon amongst the shelter of the trees, and there, in comparative silence, I could hear the rush of the wind high overhead. Presently the blackness of the storm had become merged in the darkness of the night. By-and-by the storm seemed to be passing away: it now only came in fierce puffs or blasts. At such moments the weird sound of the wolf appeared to be echoed by many similar sounds around me.

Now and again, through the black mass of drifting cloud, came a straggling ray of moonlight, which lit up the expanse, and showed me that I was at the edge of a dense mass of cypress and yew trees. As the snow had ceased to fall, I walked out from the shelter and began to investigate more closely. It appeared to me that, amongst so many old foundations as I had passed, there might be still standing a house in which, though in ruins, I could find some sort of shelter for a while. As I skirted the edge of the copse, I found that a low wall encircled it, and following this I presently found an opening. Here the cypresses formed an alley leading up to a square mass of some kind of building. Just as I caught sight of this, however, the drifting clouds obscured the moon, and I passed up the path in darkness. The wind must have grown colder, for I felt myself shiver as I walked; but there was hope of shelter, and I groped my way blindly on.

I stopped, for there was a sudden stillness. The storm had passed; and, perhaps in sympathy with nature's silence, my heart seemed to cease to beat. But this was only momentarily; for suddenly the moonlight broke through the clouds, showing me that I was in a graveyard, and that the square object before me was a great massive tomb of marble, as white as the snow that lay on and all around it. With the moonlight there came a fierce sigh of the storm, which appeared to resume its course with a long, low howl, as of many dogs or wolves. I was awed and shocked, and felt the cold perceptibly grow upon me till it seemed to grip me by the heart. Then while the flood of moonlight still fell on the marble tomb, the storm gave further evidence of renewing, as though it was returning on its track. Impelled by some sort of fascination, I approached the sepulchre to see what it was, and why such a thing stood alone in such a place. I walked around it, and read, over the Doric door, in German —

COUNTESS DOLINGEN OF GRATZ
IN STYRIA
SOUGHT AND FOUND DEATH.
1801.

On the top of the tomb, seemingly driven through the solid marble — for the structure was composed of a few vast blocks of stone — was a great iron spike or stake. On going to the back I saw, graven in great Russian letters: 'The dead travel fast.'

There was something so weird and uncanny about the whole thing that it gave me a turn and made me feel quite faint. I began to wish, for the first time, that I had taken Johann's advice. Here a thought struck me, which came under almost mysterious circumstances and with a terrible shock. This was Walpurgis Night!

Walpurgis Night, when, according to the belief of millions of people, the devil was abroad — when the graves were opened and the dead came forth and walked. When all evil things of earth and air and water held revel. This very place the driver had specially shunned. This was the depopulated village of centuries ago. This was where the suicide lay; and this was the place where I was alone — unmanned, shivering with cold in a shroud of snow with a wild storm gathering again upon me! It took all my philosophy, all the religion I had been taught, all my courage, not to collapse in a paroxysm of fright.

And now a perfect tornado burst upon me. The ground shook as though thousands of horses thundered across it; and this time the storm bore on its icy wings, not snow, but great hailstones which drove with such violence that they might have come from the thongs of Balearic slingers — hailstones that beat down leaf and branch and made the shelter of the cypresses of no more avail than though their stems were standing-corn. At the first I had rushed to the nearest tree; but I was soon fain to leave it and seek the only spot that seemed to afford refuge, the deep Doric doorway of the marble tomb. There, crouching against the massive bronze-door, I gained a certain amount of protection from the beating of the hail-stones, for now they only drove against me as they ricocheted from the ground and the side of the marble.

As I leaned against the door, it moved slightly and opened inwards. The shelter of even a tomb was welcome in that pitiless tempest, and I was about to enter it when there came a flash of forked-lightning that lit up the whole expanse of the heavens. In the instant, as I am a living man, I saw, as my eyes were turned into the darkness of the tomb, a beautiful woman, with rounded cheeks and red lips, seemingly sleeping on a bier. As the thunder broke overhead, I was grasped as by the hand of a giant and hurled out into the storm. The whole thing was so sudden that, before I could realise the shock, moral as well as physical, I found the hailstones beating me down. At the same time I had a strange, dominating feeling that I was not alone. I looked towards the tomb. Just then there came another blinding flash, which seemed to strike the iron stake that surmounted the tomb and to pour through to the earth, blasting and crumbling the marble, as in a burst of flame. The dead woman rose for a moment of agony, while she was lapped in the flame, and her bitter scream of pain was drowned in the thundercrash. The last thing I heard was this mingling of dreadful sound, as again I

was seized in the giant-grasp and dragged away, while the hailstones beat on me, and the air around seemed reverberant with
the howling of wolves. The last sight that I remembered was a
vague, white, moving mass, as if all the graves around me had
sent out the phantoms of their sheeted-dead, and that they were
closing in on me through the white cloudiness of the driving
hail.

Gradually. there came a sort of vague beginning of consciousness; then a sense of weariness that was dreadful. For a time I
remembered nothing; but slowly my senses returned. My feet
seemed positively racked with pain, yet I could not move them.
They seemed to be numbed. There was an icy feeling at the
back of my neck and all down my spine, and my ears, like my
feet, were dead, yet in torment; but there was in my breast a
sense of warmth which was, by comparison, delicious. It was as
a nightmare − a physical nightmare, if one may use such an
expression; for some heavy weight on my chest made it difficult
for me to breathe.

This period of semi-lethargy seemed to remain a long time,
and as it faded away I must have slept or swooned. Then came a
sort of loathing, like the first stage of sea-sickness, and a wild
desire to be free from something − I knew not what. A vast stillness enveloped me, as though all the world were asleep or dead
− only broken by the low panting as of some animal close to
me. I felt a warm rasping at my throat, then came a consciousness of the awful truth, which chilled me to the heart and sent
the blood surging up through my brain. Some great animal was
lying on me and now licking my throat. I feared to stir, for some
instinct of prudence bade me lie still; but the brute seemed to
realise that there was now some change in me, for it raised its
head. Through my eyelashes I saw above me the two great flaming eyes of a gigantic wolf. Its sharp white teeth gleamed in the
gaping red mouth, and I could feel its hot breath fierce and
acrid upon me.

For another spell of time I remembered no more. Then I
became conscious of a low growl, followed by a yelp, renewed
again and again. Then, seemingly very far away, I heard a
'Holloa! holloa!' as of many voices calling in unison. Cautiously I

raised my head and looked in the direction whence the sound came; but the cemetery blocked my view. The wolf still continued to yelp in a strange way, and a red glare began to move round the grove of cypresses, as though following the sound. As the voices drew closer, the wolf yelped faster and louder. I feared to make either sound or motion. Nearer came the red glow, over the white pall which stretched into the darkness around me. Then all at once from beyond the trees there came at a trot a troop of horsemen bearing torches. The wolf rose from my breast and made for the cemetery. I saw one of the horsemen (soldiers by their caps and their long military cloaks) raise his carbine and take aim. A companion knocked up his arm, and I heard the ball whizz over my head. He had evidently taken my body for that of the wolf. Another sighted the animal as it slunk away, and a shot followed. Then, at a gallop, the troop rode forward – some towards me, others following the wolf as it disappeared amongst the snow-clad cypresses.

As they drew nearer I tried to move, but was powerless, although I could see and hear all that went on around me. Two or three of the soldiers jumped from their horses and knelt beside me. One of them raised my head, and placed his hand over my heart.

'Good news, comrades!' he cried. 'His heart still beats!'

Then some brandy was poured down my throat; it put vigour into me, and I was able to open my eyes fully and look around. Light and shadows were moving among the trees, and I heard men call to one another. They drew together, uttering frightened exclamations; and the lights flashed as the others came pouring out of the cemetery pell-mell, like men possessed. When the further ones came close to us, those who were around me asked them eagerly:

'Well, have you found him?'

The reply rang out hurriedly:

'No! no! Come away quick – quick! This is no place to stay, and on this of all nights!'

'What was it?' was the question, asked in all manner of keys. The answer came variously and all indefinitely as though the men were moved by some common impulse to speak, yet were restrained by some common fear from giving their thoughts.

'It — it — indeed!' gibbered one, whose wits had plainly given out for the moment.

'A wolf — and yet not a wolf!' another put in shudderingly.

'No use trying for him without the sacred bullet,' a third remarked in a more ordinary manner.

'Serve us right for coming out on this night! Truly we have earned our thousand marks!' were the ejaculations of a fourth.

'There was blood on the broken marble,' another said after a pause — 'the lightning never brought that there. And for him — is he safe? Look at his throat! See, comrades, the wolf has been lying on him and keeping his blood warm.'

The officer looked at my throat and replied:

'He is all right; the skin is not pierced. What does it all mean? We should never have found him but for the yelping of the wolf.'

'What became of it?' asked the man who was holding up my head, and who seemed the least panic-stricken of the party, for his hands were steady and without tremor. On his sleeve was the chevron of a petty officer.

'It went to its home,' answered the man, whose long face was pallid, and who actually shook with terror as he glanced around him fearfully. 'There are graves enough there in which it may lie. Come, comrades — come quickly! Let us leave this cursed spot.'

The officer raised me to a sitting posture, as he uttered a word of command; then several men placed me upon a horse. He sprang to the saddle behind me, took me in his arms, gave the word to advance; and, turning our faces away from the cypresses, we rode away in swift, military order.

As yet my tongue refused its office, and I was perforce silent. I must have fallen asleep; for the next thing I remembered was finding myself standing up, supported by a soldier on each side of me. It was almost broad daylight, and to the north a red streak of sunlight was reflected, like a path of blood, over the waste of snow. The officer was telling the men to say nothing of what they had seen, except that they found an English stranger, guarded by a large dog.

'Dog! that was no dog,' cut in the man who had exhibited such fear. 'I think I know a wolf when I see one.'

The young officer answered calmly: 'I said a dog.'

'Dog!' reiterated the other ironically. It was evident that his courage was rising with the sun; and, pointing to me, he said, 'Look at his throat. Is that the work of a dog, master?'

Instinctively I raised my hand to my throat, and as I touched it I cried out in pain. The men crowded round to look, some stooping down from their saddles; and again there came the calm voice of the young officer:

'A dog, as I said. If aught else were said we should only be laughed at.'

I was then mounted behind a trooper, and we rode on into the suburbs of Munich. Here we came across a stray carriage, into which I was lifted, and it was driven off to the Quatre Saisons — the young officer accompanying me, whilst a trooper followed with his horse, and the others rode off to their barracks.

When we arrived, Herr Delbrück rushed so quickly down the steps to meet me, that it was apparent he had been watching within. Taking me by both hands he solicitously led me in. The officer saluted me and was turning to withdraw, when I recognised his purpose, and insisted that he should come to my rooms. Over a glass of wine I warmly thanked him and his brave comrades for saving me. He replied simply that he was more than glad, and that Herr Delbrück had at the first taken steps to make all the searching party pleased; at which ambiguous utterance the maître d'hotel smiled, while the officer pleaded duty and withdrew.

'But Herr Delbrück,' I enquired, 'how and why was it that the soldiers searched for me?'

He shrugged his shoulders, as if in depreciation of his own deed, as he replied:

'I was so fortunate as to obtain leave from the commander of the regiment in which I served, to ask for volunteers.'

'But how did you know I was lost?' I asked.

'The driver came hither with the remains of his carriage, which had been upset when the horses ran away.'

'But surely you would not send a search-party of soldiers merely on this account?'

'Oh, no!' he answered; 'but even before the coachman arrived,

I had this telegram from the Boyar whose guest you are,' and he took from his pocket a telegram which he handed to me, and I read:

BISTRITZ.

Be careful of my guest — his safety is most precious to me. Should aught happen to him, or if he be missed, spare nothing to find him and ensure his safety. He is English and therefore adventurous. There are often dangers from snow and wolves and night. Lose not a moment if you suspect harm to him. I answer your zeal with my fortune. — Dracula.

As I held the telegram in my hand, the room seemed to whirl around me; and, if the attentive maître d'hotel had not caught me, I think I should have fallen. There was something so strange in all this, something so weird and impossible to imagine, that there grew on me a sense of my being in some way the sport of opposite forces — the mere vague idea of which seemed in a way to paralyse me. I was certainly under some form of mysterious protection. From a distant country had come, in the very nick of time, a message that took me out of the danger of the snow-sleep and the jaws of the wolf.

VII

The Seer

The success that *Dracula* enjoyed in the years that followed its publication was considerable — indeed the book has never been out of print to this day — and yet while it marked the high-point of Bram's literary career, it also saw the beginning of the decline in his health. The intense demands that working for Irving had made on him, coupled with his family affairs and the matter of finding time for his writing, all began to undermine his strength. In an attempt to stay this decline, he took regular holidays in Scotland at a place he had discovered on the east coast called Cruden Bay near Peterhead. A remote yet picturesque spot by day, with small fishermen's cottages grouped around the bay and towering formations of jagged red rocks to the rear, Cruden could change at night into a demonic place lashed by howling winds and crashing waves. Darkness also gave a particularly eerie and mysterious appearance to the strangely named Slains Castle on the northern cliff above the bay. Perhaps not surprisingly, when we remember his inclinations, Cruden Bay immediately fascinated Bram and its influence is to be found in several of his works.

It was during one of these holidays in 1901 that he had a strange encounter with an old woman on the seashore. The woman was believed by the local people to have supernatural powers and was generally avoided. As a result of their meeting, Bram created a story, 'The Seer', which appeared in *The London Magazine* of November 1901. Doubtless Bram augmented the scraps of supernatural lore which he learned in Cruden Bay with further research in London, but it did make for an evocative story about the ancient belief in 'Second Sight'.

The tale also proved to be the genesis of Bram's next book, *The Mystery of the Sea*, a story of high adventure set in the same locality which appeared in 1902. Though the novel was generally well received — Sir Arthur Conan Doyle, Bram's former collaborator, declaring, 'It has not the fearsomeness of *Dracula*, but it is beautifully handled' — the book did not sell anywhere near as well as the great vampire book. The same fate awaited *The Jewel of the Seven Stars*, a tale of detection which he published in 1904. In truth, neither work showed the same striking originality of concept and imagination that had made *Dracula* so popular with readers, and a lesser man might well at this point have taken these facts as an excuse to stop writing. After all, he had a great many other commitments and he could well rest on his laurels. But Bram Stoker was not such a man, and still felt as compelled to go on with his writing as he had been when a young man. Only his failing health was to thwart his ambitions.

The Seer

I had just arrived at Cruden Bay on my annual visit, and after a late breakfast was sitting on the low wall which was a continuation of the escarpment of the bridge over the Water of Cruden. Opposite to me, across the road and standing under the only little clump of trees in the place was a tall, gaunt old woman, who kept looking at me intently. As I sat, a little group, consisting of a man and two women, went by. I found my eyes follow them, for it seemed to me after they had passed me that the two women walked together and the man alone in front carrying on his shoulder a little black box — a coffin. I shuddered as I thought, but a moment later I saw all three abreast as they had been. The old woman was now looking at me with eyes that blazed. She came across the road and said to me without preface:

'What saw ye then, that yer e'en looked so awed?' I did not like to tell her so I did not answer. Her great eyes were fixed keenly upon me, seeming to look me through and through. I felt that I grew quite red, whereupon she said, apparently to her-self: 'I thocht so! Even I did not see that which he saw.'

'How do you mean?' I queried. She answered ambiguously: 'Wait! Ye shall perhaps know before this hour to-morrow!'

Her answer interested me and I tried to get her to say more; but she would not. She moved away with a grand stately move-ment that seemed to become her great gaunt form.

After dinner whilst I was sitting in front of the hotel, there was a great commotion in the village; much running to and fro of men and women with sad mien. On questioning them I found that a child had been drowned in the little harbour below. Just then a woman and a man, the same that had passed the bridge earlier in the day, ran by with wild looks. One of the bystanders looked after them pityingly as he said:

'Puir souls. It's a sad home-comin' for them the nicht.'

'Who are they?' I asked. The man took off his cap reverently as he answered:

'The father and mother of the child that was drowned!' As he spoke I looked round as though someone had called me.

There stood the gaunt woman with a look of triumph on her face.

The curved shore of Cruden Bay, Aberdeenshire, is backed by a waste of sandhills in whose hollows seagrass and moss and wild violets, together with the pretty 'grass of Parnassus' form a green carpet. The surface of the hills is held together by bent-grass and is eternally shifting as the wind takes the fine sand and drifts it to and fro. All behind is green, from the meadows that mark the southern edge of the bay to the swelling uplands that stretch away and away far in the distance, till the blue mist of the mountains at Braemar sets a kind of barrier. In the centre of the bay the highest point of the land that runs downward to the sea looks like a miniature hill known as the Hawklaw; from this point onward to the extreme south the land runs high with a gentle trend downwards.

Cruden sands are wide and firm and the sea runs out a con-siderable distance. When there is a storm with the wind on shore the whole bay is a mass of leaping waves and broken water that threatens every instant to annihilate the stake-nets which stretch out here and there along the shore. More than a few vessels have been lost on these wide stretching sands, and it was perhaps the roaring of the shallow seas and the terror which they inspired which sent the crews to the spirit room and the bodies of those of them which came to shore later on, to the churchyard on the hill.

If Cruden Bay is to be taken figuratively as a mouth, with the sand hills for soft palate, and the green Hawklaw as the tongue, the rocks which mark the extremities are its teeth. To the north the rocks of red granite rise jagged and broken. To the south, a mile and a half away as the crow flies, Nature seems to have manifested its wildest forces. It is here, where the little promontory called Whinnyfold juts out, that the two great geological features of the Aberdeen coast meet. The red sienite of the north joins the black gneiss of the south. That union must have been originally a wild one; there are evidences of an upheaval which must have shaken the earth to its centre. Here and there are great masses of either species of rock hurled upwards in every conceivable variety of form, sometimes fused or pressed together so that it is impossible to say exactly where gneiss ends or sienite begins; but broadly speaking here is an irregular line of separation. This line runs seawards to the east and its strength is shown in its outcrop. For half a mile or more the rocks rise through the sea singly or in broken masses ending in a dangerous cluster known as 'The Skares' and which has had for centuries its full toll of wreck and disaster. Did the sea hold its dead where they fell, its floor around the Skares would be whitened with their bones, and new islands could build themselves with the piling wreckage. At times one may see here the ocean in her fiercest mood; for it is when the tempest drives from the south-east that the sea is fretted amongst the rugged rocks and sends its spume landwards. The rocks that at calmer times rise dark from the briny deep are lost to sight for moments in the grand onrush of the waves. The seagulls which usually whiten them, now flutter around screaming, and the sound of their shrieks comes in on the gale almost in a continuous note, for the single cries are merged in the multitudinous roar of sea and air.

The village, squatted beside the emboucher of the Water of Cruden at the northern side of the bay is simple enough; a few rows of fishermen's cottages, two or three great red-tiled drying-sheds nestled in the sand-heap behind the fishers' houses. For the rest of the place as it was when first I saw it, a little lookout beside a tall flagstaff on the northern cliff, a few scattered farms over the inland prospect, one little hotel down on the western bank of the Water of Cruden with a fringe of willows protecting its sunk garden which was always full of fruits and flowers.

From the most southern part of the beach of Cruden Bay to Whinnyfold village the distance is but a few hundred yards; first a steep pull up the face of the rock; and then an even way, beside part of which runs a tiny stream. To the left of this path, going towards Whinnyfold, the ground rises in a bold slope and then falls again all round, forming a sort of wide miniature hill of some eighteen or twenty acres. Of this the southern side is sheer, the black rock dipping into the waters of the little bay of Whinnyfold, in the centre of which is a picturesque island of rock shelving steeply from the water on the northern side, as is the tendency of all the gneiss and granite in this part. But to east and north there are irregular bays or openings, so that the furthest points of the promotory stretch out like fingers. At the tips of these are reefs of sunken rock falling down to deep water and whose existence can only be suspected in bad weather when the rush of the current beneath sends up swirling eddies or curling masses of foam. These little bays are mostly curved and are green where falling earth or drifting sand have hidden the outmost side of the rocks and given a foothold to the seagrass and clover. Here have been at some time or other great caves, now either fallen in or silted up with sand, or obliterated with the earth brought down in the rush of surface-water in times of long rain. In one of these bays, Broad Haven, facing right out to the Skares, stands an isolated pillar of rock called locally the 'Puir mon' through whose base, time and weather have worn a hole through which one may walk dryshod.

Through the masses of rocks that run down to the sea from the sides and shores of all these bays are here and there natural channels with straight edges as though cut on purpose for the taking in of the cobbles belonging to the fisher folk of Whinnyfold.

When first I saw the place I fell in love with it. Had it been possible I should have spent my summer there, in a house of my own, but the want of any place in which to live forbade such an opportunity. So I stayed in the little hotel, the Kilmarnock Arms.

The next year I came again, and the next, and the next. And then I arranged to take a feu at Whinnyfold and to build a house overlooking the Skares for myself. The details of this kept me constantly going to Whinnyfold, and my house to be was always in my thoughts.

Hitherto my life had been an uneventful one. At school I was, though secretly ambitious, dull as to results. At College I was better off, for my big body and athletic powers gave me a certain position in which I had to overcome my natural shyness. When I was about eight and twenty I found myself nominally a barrister, with no knowledge whatever of the practice of law and but little less of the theory, and with a commission in the Devil's Own — the irrelevant name given to the Inns of Court Volunteers. I had few relatives, but a comfortable, though not great, fortune; and I had been round the world, dilettante fashion.

All that night I thought of the dead child and of the peculiar vision which had come to me. Sleeping or waking it was all the same; my mind could not leave the parents in procession as seen in imagination, or their distracted mien in reality. Mingled with them was the great-eyed, aquiline-featured, gaunt old woman who had taken such an interest in the affair; and in my part of it. I asked the landlord if he knew her, since from his position as postmaster he knew almost everyone for miles around. He told me that she was a stranger to the place. Then he added:

'I can't imagine what brings her here. She has come over from Peterhead two or three times lately; but she doesn't seem to have anything at all to do. She has nothing to sell and she buys nothing. She's not a tripper, and she's not a beggar, and she's not a thief, and she's not a worker of any sort. She's a queer-looking lot anyhow. I fancy from her speech that she's from the west; probably from some of the far-out islands. I can tell that she has the Gaelic from the way she speaks.'

Later on in the day, when I was walking on the shore near the Hawklaw, she came up to speak to me. The shore was quite lonely, for in those days it was rare to see anyone on the beach except when the salmon fishers drew their nets at the ebbing tide. I was walking towards Whinnyfold when she came upon me silently from behind. She must have been hidden among the bent-grass of the sandhills for had she been anywhere in view I must have seen her on that desolate shore. She was evidently a most imperious person; she at once addressed me in a tone and manner which made me feel as though I were in some way an inferior, and in somehow to blame:

'What for did ye no tell me what ye saw yesterday?' Instinctively I answered:

'I don't know why. Perhaps because it seemed so ridiculous.' Her stern features hardened into scorn as she replied:

'Are Death and the Doom then so redeekulous that they pleasure ye intil silence?' I somehow felt that this was a little too much and was about to make a sharp answer, when suddenly it struck me as a remarkable thing that she knew already. Filled with surprise I straightway asked her:

'Why, how on earth do you know? I told no one.' I stopped for I felt all at sea; there was some mystery here which I could not fathom. She seemed to read my mind like an open book, for she went on looking at me as she spoke, searchingly and with an odd smile.

'Eh! laddie, do ye no ken that ye hae een that can see? Do ye no understand that ye hae een that can speak? Is it that one with the Gift o' Second Sight has no an understandin' o' it. Why, yer face when ye saw the mark o' the Doom, was like a printed book to een like mine.'

'Do you mean to tell me,' I asked, 'that you could tell what I saw, simply by looking at my face?'

'Na! na! laddie. Not all that, though a Seer am I; but I knew that you had seen the Doom! It's no that varied that there need be any mistake. After all Death is only one, in whatever way we may speak!' After a pause of thought I asked her:

'If you have the power of Second Sight why did you not see the vision, or whatever it was, yourself?'

'Eh! laddie,' she answered, shaking her head, "Tis little ye ken

o' the wark o' the Fates! Learn ye then that the Voice speaks only
as it listeth into chosen ears, and the Vision comes to chosen
een. None can will to hear or to see, to pleasure theirsels.'

'Then,' I said, and I felt that there was a measure of triumph
in my tone, 'if to none but the chosen is given to know, how
comes it that you, who seem not to have been chosen on this
occasion at all events, know all the same?' She answered with a
touch of impatience:

'Do ye ken, young sir, that even mortal een have power to see
much, if there be behind them the thocht, an' the knowledge
and the experience to guide them aright. How, think ye, is it
that some can see much, and learn much as they gang; while
others go blind as the mowdiwart, at the end o' the journey as
before it?'

'Then perhaps you will tell me how much you saw, and how
you saw it?'

'Ah! to them that have seen the Doom there needs but sma'
guidance to their thochts. Too lang, an' too often hae I mysen
seen the death-sark an' the watch-candle an' the dead-hole, not
to know when they are seen tae ither een. Na, na! laddie, what I
kent o' yer seein' was no by the Gift but only by the use o' my
proper een. I kent not the muckle o' what ye saw. Not whether it
was ane or ither o' the garnishins o' the dead; but weel I kent
that it was o' death.'

'Then,' I said interrogatively, 'Second Sight is altogether a
matter of chance?'

'Chance! chance!' she repeated with scorn. 'Na! young sir;
when the Voice has spoken there is no more chance than that
the nicht will follow the day.'

'You mistake me,' I said, feeling somewhat superior now that
I had caught her in an error, 'I did not for a moment mean that
the Doom − whatever it is − is not a true forerunner. What I
meant was that it seems to be a matter of chance in whose ear
the Voice − whatever it is − speaks; when once it has been
ordained that it is to sound in the ear of some one.' Again she
answered with scorn:

'Na, na! there is no chance o' ocht about the Doom. Them
that send forth the Voice and the Seein' know well to whom it is
sent and why. Can ye no comprehend that it is for no bairn-play

that such goes forth. When the Voice speaks, it is mainly followed by tears an' woe an' lamentation! Nae! nor is it only one bit manifestation that stands by its lanes, remote and isolate from all ither. Truly 'tis but a pairt o' the great scheme o' things; an' be sure that who so is chosen to see or to hear is chosen weel, an' must hae their pairt in what is to be, on to the verra end.'

'Am I to take it,' I asked, 'that Second Sight is but a little bit of some great purpose which has to be wrought out by means of many kinds; and that who so sees the Vision or hears the Voice is but the blind unconscious instrument of Fate?'

'Aye! laddie. Weel eneuch the Fates know their wishes an' their wark, no to need the help or the thocht of any human — blind or seein', sane or silly, conscious or unconscious.'

All through her speaking I had been struck by the old woman's use of the word 'Fate,' and more especially when she used it in the plural. It was evident that, Christian though she might be — and in the West they are generally devout observants of the duties of their creed — her belief in this respect came from some of the old pagan mythologies. I should have liked to question her on this point; but I feared to shut her lips against me. Instead I asked her:

'Tell me, will you, if you don't mind, of some case you have known yourself of Second Sight?'

''Tis no for them to brag or boast to whom has been given to see the wark o' the hand o' Fate. But sine ye are yerself a Seer an' would learn, then I may speak. I hae seen the sea ruffle wi'oot cause in the verra spot where later a boat was to gang doon, I hae heard on a lone moor the hammerin' o' the coffin-wright when one passed me who was soon to dee. I hae seen the death-sarli fold round the speerit o' a drowned one, in baith ma sleepin' an' ma wakin' dreams. I hae heard the settin' doom o' the spaiks, an' I hae seen the weepers on a' the crood that walked. Aye, an' in money anither way hae I seen an' heard the Coming o' the Doom.'

'But did all the seeings and hearings come true?' I asked. 'Did it ever happen that you heard queer sounds or saw strange sights and that yet nothing came of them? I gather that you do not always know to whom something is going to happen; but only that death is coming to some one!' She was not displeased at my questioning but replied at once:

'Na doot! but there are times when what is seen or heard has no manifest following. But think ye, young sir, how mony a corp, still waited for, lies in the depths o' the sea; how mony lie oot on the hillsides, or are fallen in deep places where their bones whiten unkent. Nay! more, to how many has Death come in a way that men think the wark o' nature when his hastening has come frae the hand of man, untold.' This was a difficult matter to answer so I changed or rather varied the subject.

'How long must elapse before the warning comes true?'

'Ye know yersel', for but yestreen ye hae seen, how the Death can follow hard upon the Doom; but there be times, nay mostly are they so, when days or weeks pass away ere the Doom is fulfilled.'

'Is this so?' I asked, 'when you know the person regarding whom the Doom is spoken.' She answered with an air of certainty which somehow carried conviction, secretly, with it.

'Even so! I know one who walks the airth now in all the pride o' his strength. But the Doom has been spoken of him. I saw him with these verra een lie prone on rocks, wi' the water runnin' down from his hair. An' again I heard the minute bells as he went by me on a road where is no bell for a score o' miles. Aye, an' yet again I saw him in the kirk itsel' wi' corbies flyin' round him, an' mair gatherin' from afar!'

Here was indeed a case where Second Sight might be tested; so I asked her at once, though to do so I had to overcome a strange sort of repugnance:

'Could this be proved? Would it not be a splendid case to make known; so that if the death happened it would prove beyond all doubt the existence of such a thing as Second Sight.' My suggestion was not well received. She answered with slow scorn:

'Beyon' all doot! Doot! Wha is there that doots the bein' o' the Doom? Learn ye too, young sir, that the Doom an' all thereby is no for traffickin' wi' them that only cares for curiosity and publeecity. The Voice and the Vision o' the Seer is no for fine madams and idle gentles to while away their time in play-toy make-believe!' I climbed down at once.

'Pardon me!' I said, 'I spoke without thinking. I should not have said so — to you at any rate.' She accepted my apology with a sort of regal inclination; but the moment after she showed by her words she was after all but a woman!

'I will tell ye; that so in the full time ye may hae no doot yersel'. For ye are a Seer and as Them that has the power hae gien ye the Gift it is no for the like o' me to cumber the road o' their doin'. Know ye then, and remember weel, how it was told ye by Gormala MacNiel that Lauchlane Macleod o' the Outer Isles hae been Called; tho' as yet the Voice has no sounded in his ears but only in mine. But ye will see the time—'

She stopped suddenly as though some thought had struck her, and then went on impressively:

'When I saw him lie prone on the rocks there was ane that bent ower him that I kent not in the nicht wha it was, though the licht o' the moon was around him. We shall see! We shall see!'

Without a word more she turned and left me. She would not listen to my calling after her; but with long strides passed up the beach and was lost among the sandhills.

VIII

Another Dracula?

The final Irving company tour of America, which lasted from October 1903 to April 1904, has also left us with one of the most puzzling mysteries associated with the name of Bram Stoker. In the years since Stoker's death there has been considerable discussion as to why he seemingly made no attempt to follow up the success of *Dracula* with another book featuring the same characters: a practice that has been carried out almost *ad nauseam* since the original came out of copyright. Bram did, of course, write two further novels with vampire elements in them, *The Lady of the Shroud* (1909) in which the heroine merely turns out to be posing as a vampire, and his last book, *The Lair of the White Worm* (1911) which features the Lady Arabella, a woman allegedly thousands of years old with the power of transmogrification. But neither is directly related to the immortal count.

Among some enthusiasts of Bram Stoker's works there has been a persistent rumour for years that it *was* in his mind to bring Dracula back to life in a new story, but in America this time, rather than Europe. The rumours originate from that last trip to America and a conversation Stoker had while the company was in Boston. In the first week of December 1903, Irving was appearing at the Tremont Theatre in Boston in *The Bells* and, as was customary, a number of the students from nearby Harvard University were employed for 'walk-on' parts. Among these was a 17-year-old Freshman named Roger Sherman Hoar (1887–1963) who was later to become well-known as a state senator for Wisconsin and a writer of science fiction and fantasy stories under the pseudonym of Ralph Milne Farley.

Apart from his love of the theatre which had caused him to apply for a part in *The Bells*, Roger was a keen reader of horror fiction and had not long before been absolutely mesmerised by *Dracula*. As he knew the author always travelled with Irving, he hoped that during the course of the engagement he might meet Stoker and have a chance to talk to him about the book. Stoker, for his part, liked mingling with the students as he tells us in his biography of Sir Henry Irving, and although he makes no specific reference to any such meeting, Roger Hoar later claimed that he talked with him on several occasions. Hoar says that he expressed his admiration for Dracula and 'Stoker told me he planned to bring Dracula over to America in another story.' In the years which followed, the young enthusiast waited unavailingly for the sequel he felt sure would follow. On hearing of Stoker's death in 1913, he realised sadly that the story would now never be written. However, in 1924 he began writing himself to supplement his salary as a teacher, and achieved an almost immediate success with a series of Science Fiction stories about Myles Cabot, 'The Radio Man', and his adventures on Mars and Venus, which appeared in *Argosy Magazine*.

Then in 1930 he decided to try and write the story that death had prevented his mentor from creating. The result, 'Another Dracula?', appeared as a two-part serial in the most famous of all the horror magazines, *Weird Tales*, in the September and October of that year where it was described by its author as 'based upon an idea by the late Bram Stoker'. Although the style is rather different from Stoker's, and there are elements of the story which he might well have found unacceptable, there are some things about the tale like the uncertainty concerning the victims and the unresolved identity of 'Mr Larousse', which smack of his influence. The story has long been extremely rare and it is therefore a pleasure to be including it in this collection: whether or not it solves the mystery of Bram Stoker's alleged 'sequel' to his masterpiece, I leave the reader to judge for himself.

Another Dracula?

1. The Mysterious Coffin

'I wonder who's dead?' inquired Dan Callahan, driver of Yankton's sole taxicab, pointing at a long wooden box with brass handles, which lay on a baggage-truck on the station platform.

'Search me!' replied the station agent, without interest. 'Look at the tag, if you're that curious.'

But Dan quite evidently wasn't that curious, for he slouched into a chair beside the one in which the agent sat, against the only cool wall of the freight house. It was late afternoon — or, rather, early evening — of an unusually hot June day. There never was very much doing in Yankton, Pennyslvania, and less than usual this particular afternoon.

The taxi-driver took a crumpled package from one of his blouse pockets, fished out a crushed cigarette, replaced the package, tapped the cigarette on his chair, put the cigarette in his mouth, took off his cap, ran his finger around in the sweat-band, found a match there, replaced the cap, and lit up. The station agent was already smoking a pipe. The two sat and puffed in silence, watching the coffin; not that they expected it to do anything worth watching for, but merely that it happened to be directly in the line of their vision, and hence was as easy to focus on as anything else.

The shadow of the freight house gradually lengthened in front of them, and objects in the distance took on a reddish tinge. The definiteness of the shadow became blurred, the red tinge faded out, and blue twilight began to fall. A faint warm breeze crept down the tracks. Bats fluttered in and out under the canopy of the station platform, in pursuit of flies and midges.

A clatter and a roar and a swirl of cinders, as an east-bound train swept by; then silence again, the oppressive silence of a warm summer evening. Heat-lightning played over the hills in the distance.

Dan Callahan, the taxi-driver, untilted his chair, arose slowly, and stretched his arms.

'No passengers tonight,' said he, 'so I guess I'll be going home to Maggie and the kids.'

'Say, will you look at that!' interrupted the railroad man. 'One of them bats is trying to get into the coffin.'

Dan looked, and made the sign of the cross. Clinging to the edge of the box, close to the lock, was a small brown bat, fluttering as though with suppressed excitement. As the two men stared, another bat joined the first.

'They give me the creeps,' asserted the agent, as, rising from his chair and shuddering, he switched on the platform lights.

'Hasn't it turned a bit cold?' asked Dan, shuddering too.

The squeak of automobile brakes was heard, and then a third figure rounded the corner of the freight house. The newcomer was a young man still in his twenties; erect, well dressed, with straight pointed nose, firm jaw, and pleasing smile.

'Hello, Doc,' Dan greeted him eagerly. 'How's my little boy?'

'I've just come from your house,' replied the doctor. 'You'll be glad to know that the little fellow is much better. Responding to treatment beautifully. I believe that I may safely say that he is out of danger.'

'Doctor Crane,' said Callahan fervently, 'you're a wizard and a brick. I thought sure I was going to lose little Dan. You've saved his life, and if there is anything that I can ever do for you this side of hell, just ask me. That's all, sir.'

'It's nothing — nothing,' replied Crane deprecatingly; 'merely my professional duty. And a great pleasure, I assure you. Such a manly little fellow.'

'Say, Doc,' interrupted the station agent, 'will you look at them birds trying to get into that there coffin?'

'Well, well, so they are,' replied Dr Crane, jovially. 'I wonder what's attracting them.'

'And here comes the great grand-daddy of them all,' added the agent, as a grayish bat of fully two-foot wing-spread swooped down out of the gathering dusk, hooked its wings onto the edge of the box, and snapped viciously at the two little brown bats already there. They fled squeaking, but still fluttered around in the vicinity.

'Hm,' remarked the doctor, professionally.

'Must be one of these there umpire bats I've heard tell about,' suggested the station agent.

Dr Crane strode over to the box, and brushed the huge creature aside with one hand. The bat snapped at him, and then shambled to one end of the top of the box, where it crouched menacingly. The doctor stooped and sniffed at the crack.

'Hm,' he ruminated. 'Peculiar smell, very, but not at all what I expected. No wonder it attracts these little creatures. As public health officer, I must get it to the undertaker's at once. Who does it belong to?'

'Dunno, Doc,' replied the agent, 'Look at the tag.'

By the light of the platform-lamps, Crane read aloud, 'Mr Peter Larousse, Yankton, Pa. Who is, he I wonder? There's no one of that name lives here.'

'I am he,' said a quiet voice behind them.

None of them had heard anyone approach. They turned, and saw that a fourth man had silently joined them. He was tall, well over six feet in height. Dressed entirely in black, with a short black Inverness cape across his shoulders, fastened at the neck by a single clasp of gold with jet stones. In his right hand he held a black stiff hat, rather narrowed at the top of the crown.

He was old, of an indefinable age, yet erect, and exuding power and vigour. Clean-shaved, he was, except for a drooping white moustache. His face was aquiline, with high-bridged thin nose and peculiarly arched nostrils. He had a lofty domed forehead, crowned with white hair, profuse except around the temples, where it was scanty. His eyebrows were iron-grey and massive, almost meeting over the nose, and composed of profuse bushy hairs. The mouth, so far as it showed under the heavy moustache, was fixed and rather cruel-looking, with peculiarly sharp white teeth. These protruded over the lips, whose remarkable ruddiness showed astonishingly vitality for a man of his evident years. His ears were pale, and at the tops extremely pointed; the chin was broad and strong, and the cheeks firm though thin. The general effect was one of extraordinary pallor.

His hands, at first glance, seemed white and fine, but closer scrutiny disclosed them to be rather coarse — broad, with squat fingers. In fact, most of the features of his anatomy, although appearing delicate and refined at first, nevertheless suffered by prolonged examination.

His general appearance, however, was courtly, aristocratic, and foreign in the extreme.

But the most noticeable single item about him was his eyes: small, gimlet-boring and bloodshot without being in the least bleary. The three men who had preceded him on the station platfom laid the redness of his eyes to the setting sun; but the sun had long since set, and the platform was now illumined by its electric lights.

'*I* am Peter Larousse,' he repeated, ignoring the rudeness of their stares. 'Did I hear some one mention my name?'

'Pardon us, sir,' replied the doctor. 'You startled us. I am Doctor Crane, the village health officer.'

Crane advanced, extending his right hand, but the stranger did not grasp it. Instead, he swung his hat across his breast, and made a courtly bow.

'You will excuse me, I am sure,' said he, 'for not shaking hands, as I have an unexplainable aversion to personal contacts. Well, you called for Monsieur Larousse, and here I am. What do you wish of me?'

'Is this your coffin?' asked the doctor abruptly, becoming a bit nettled.

The stranger frowned, then smiled quizzically.

'Yes and no,' he answered. 'If you mean am I inside it, the answer is no. But if you mean is it consigned to me, the answer is yes. I am not dead — yet.'

He bowed again.

'Well, it will have to get to the undertaker's at once,' asserted Crane. 'It's a menace to the health of the community.'

'In what way, may I ask?' inquired Monsieur Larousse, serenely.

'It is already attracting vermin,' replied the doctor.

The large grey bat was no longer to be seen, but the two little brown bats had returned and were clawing at the lid.

'Ah, the darlings!' exclaimed the stranger, gloatingly.

Striding over to the coffin, he shifted his pointed hat to his left hand, and scratched first one of the little creatures, and then the other, on the head.

'See,' he said turning, 'they like me. They know a friend. I love all animals, and all animals love me. I have a way with them. But now to get down to business. You wish this coffin removed, doctor? So do I. What is the next step?'

'This is Mr Daniel Callahan, of the Commonwealth Garage,' introduced the doctor. 'He can get his motor-truck at once.

The undertaker, being an undertaker, can be found at any hour. This other gentleman is Mr Bill Jones, the station agent, who can release the shipment. And I am the health officer, as I have already stated.'

'Ah, what a fortuitous conjunction of personages!' murmured Monsieur Larousse. 'The arrangements sound excellent.'

While Dan departed for his truck, and the agent unlocked the freight house and turned on the lights inside, Dr Crane asked, 'And what are your plans for the body? — that is, I assume the coffin contains a body.'

Ignoring the implied question, the stranger answered, 'It is, of course, to be buried — in your local cemetery, to be explicit. What formalities are necessary?'

'You will have to have a cemetery lot.'

'I have such a lot.'

'And a permit from the village clerk.'

'I should like to see him at once, then.'

'He will be in his office tomorrow morning.'

'He shall have to see me this evening,' asserted the foreigner imperiously. 'I suffer from a disease known as *dermatitis exfoliativa tropica*. You, as a physician, will realise that that means I must avoid the daylight as much as possible. Can not the clerk, for a fee, be induced to transact official business in the evening?'

'I am sure he can,' agreed the doctor smiling, 'when I tell him about your disease. Would you mind my offering you my professional services? The exact sort of dermatitis which you mention is a rare disease, at least among white people; and I have never had the privilege of treating, or even observing, a case.'

'Then I refuse to be experimented upon,' replied the stranger, drawing himself up haughtily.

Just then Dan Callahan returned with his truck, and the four men put the box aboard. The box was unusually heavy, which rendered all the more noticeable the effortless ease with which the stranger handled his quarter of the load.

'Gosh!' exclaimed the agent, wiping his forehead. 'It must weigh a ton.'

'Ah, my friends,' explained the stranger, 'there is a lead lining inside.'

'Then how the devil did the smell get out?' blurted Dan.

The stranger glared at him, and said nothing.

'Will you ride with me?' invited Dr Crane.

'Thank you, no,' replied Larousse with a slight inclination of his head. 'The night is beautiful. I will walk — Oh, just a moment. One more question. Need the coffin be opened by any one?'

'Not if you have the death certificate with you.'

'I have the certificate.'

So the truck and the doctor's car drove away up the street toward the center of the village. The station agent re-entered his office to put out the lights. And a large grey bat hovered around the coffin in the departing express-truck.

The centre of the village, a typical one-street Pennyslvania valley-town, was a bustle of early summer evening activity. Stores alight for the evening trade. Music issuing from the open doors of the movie-house. Couples strolling back and forth. Groups chatting at the street corners.

The grey bat did not follow the coffin into the bright lights of Yankton's gay white way.

Dr Crane and Dan Callahan found the undertaker's wife at home, and she sent one of the children out to locate her husband. When he finally arrived, the three men tried to move the coffin, and were having a terrible time at the task when a calm voice near them said, 'Permit me to assist.'

It was the tall stranger again. With his help, they moved the box with surprising ease.

Next Dr Crane and Monsieur Larousse hunted up the village clerk, got him down to his office, and secured the necessary burial permit.

When this formality was over, 'Where are you staying?' the doctor asked.

The stranger drew himself up.

'That, my dear sir,' said he frigidly, 'concerns no one but myself.'

The young doctor hastened to apologise.

'I only thought we might need to locate you, sir, if there should be any hitch in the proceedings,' said he.

'There will be no "hitch," as you call it,' replied Larousse, frigidly. 'I have made all the necessary arrangements with the undertaker, and he assures me that there can be no unexpected complications. I shall remain in this beautiful little town for a considerable while. You will find me every evening somewhere along this street.'

And bowing ceremoniously, he stalked off.

'After all that I've done for him,' said Crane to himself, 'he might have been a little more polite. A queer, queer man. My, what a spooky evening!'

The big grey bat swooped by, in spite of the bright lights, startling the doctor out of his revery.

2. *Introducing Mr Fulton*

A bit later in the evening, the tall stranger entered Morton's General Store and made a few purchases. The news of the arrival of this mysterious foreigner had spread up and down the street, and now a crowd gathered to get a good look at him.

In paying for his purchases, he lingered quite a while at the cashier's desk. Who wouldn't linger for a chat with Mary Morton? She was by far the most radiant creature and wholly desirable bit of feminity that the little village of Yankton had ever produced.

A brief description of the town will not be amiss. Yankton, Pennsylvania, boasts one thousand odd inhabitants. They are quite odd, and Yankton does not boast them very loudly.

It is a typical old-time New England village. This may seem to be a strange statement to make about a Pennsylvania community, but New England itself is now overrun by practically every nationality of Europe. The people of old English stock there have lost their control of everything, except some of the financial centres of State Street, and the social centres of Back Bay. In fact, they have been forced to recognise the Irish, most of whom came over in the 1840's to build the railroads, as allies of theirs against the later comers, whom they regard as non-American.

But years ago, in Revolutionary times, the mountains of Pennsylvania and Ohio were settled by New Englanders of the original stock. Here you will find the purest forms of New England Colonial architecture. Here the Yankee blood has remained practically uncontaminated, right down to the present day.

But they had inbred and degenerated, for all of that. Individuals of marked mentality had moved away. The result was that the inhabitants of Yankton, although superficially prosperous, well-dressed and modern, were mentally and morally in the same class with the superstitious illiterate mountaineers of other states and other parts of Pennsylvania itself. All that kept them from hexmurders and witchcraft-trials was a wholesome fear of ridicule; for they were just educated enough to know that such things were frowned upon in more cosmopolitan communities. In fact, it should be remembered that the New England forebears of these Yankton folk had had their own period of hysteria over witchcraft.

Mary Morton represented the flower of the pure old English stock. She had reverted to type, after generations of decline. She was the aspiration of all the young men of Yankton, and so she had been able to pick for herself the catch of the town, Herman Fulton.

Herman had had his eye on the main chance of his life. At an early age he had gone to work in the Yankton Bank, scorning a college career, or even the completion of high school. There were no college men in Yankton, except the two doctors. Not that Yankton men did not ever go to college, but merely that those who went to college never returned to Yankton; they went on to wider fields, where they made their long-slumbering heredity tell. Yankton could name with pride many of these distinguished sons of hers, men of national repute, who had turned their backs on their boyhood home.

But Herman Fulton had been different. He had stuck to the bank, had spent next to nothing, and had invested and reinvested his earnings to advantage. At the age of thirty-five, still a bachelor, he had worked up to the position of assistant cashier. Not that this indicated that Herman was possessed of any particular degree of intelligence. In fact, it is probable that he was subnormal mentally. Even morons are often fiendishly clever along some one line, and Herman possessed a well-developed money sense, if no other. True, he was self-educated and was an avid reader of books on all subjects, but it is to be doubted if he really understood very much of what he read, although he passed for quite a learned man in Yankton.

When the cashier had conveniently died, soon after Herman's attaining the position of assistant, Herman had demanded his place — and had been refused. At the next annual meeting he had calmly ousted the surprised board of directors, who did not realise that certain controlling blocks of stock, standing nominally in the names of old Dr Porter and others, were really Herman's; had substituted a board of his own henchmen, and had elected himself not cashier but president!

After that, whenever Herman Fulton 'requested' anything in Yankton, the request was usually granted, even if the granter couldn't quite figure out just what Herman intended to do if the request were refused. Herman was conscienceless and ruthless. Thus he speedily became the financial power of Yankton.

So all the girls, who for years had been setting their caps for him, had been intensely jealous when Mary Morton's parents had announced her engagement to Herman.

And then Dr Ralph Crane, fresh from Harvard Medical College, had come to town, just about a year before this story begins. He had picked out Yankton as a likely place to build up a country practice, and had been welcomed by old Dr Porter, who had more patients than he could handle at his advanced age.

Unfortunately, young Crane had fallen in love with the beautiful Mary, and it was evident that she liked him very much. In fact, if he had arrived on the scene before her engagement to Herman Fulton, there can be little doubt that the dashing young doctor would have speedily won her heart. But, in primitive communities such as Yankton, engagements are regarded as being almost as sacred as marriages. In fact, they are usually lived up to a lot better. Engaged girls don't even dance with, or receive calls from, young men other than their fiancés. So Ralph Crane had had to content himself with worshipping from a distance, and with such professional contacts as occasional illness in Mary's family gave him. Mary herself was always the picture of health.

Entering the Morton Emporium on the evening in question, Dr Crane observed with displeasure the quite evident regard which the courtly European was displaying for Mary, and the flattered interest which she returned. He would speak to Herman Fulton about it!

But, on second thoughts, he decided *not* to speak to Herman after all. If this old beau could make a dent in Herman's hold on Mary, so much the better. It was something that he, Crane, would have liked to do himself, if he had not been deterred both by respect for the local conventions and by fear of Herman's power.

At that, however, there was something about the performance which jarred on the young doctor's sensibilities, in spite of all his pleasurable anticipations of his rival's discomfiture. It may have been the May and December aspect of the situation. Or it may have been something else, some mere instinctive feeling. Perhaps the uncanny events, which had accompanied Monsieur Larousse's arrival, contributed to Dr Crane's uneasiness.

Had Monsieur Larousse really 'arrived'? This seems a strange question, in view of the fact that here he was. And yet, in the course of the evening, gossip developed the fact that he had not been seen to alight from any of the trains which had stopped at Yankton that day, nor had he got off the Lancaster bus, nor had he come in his own auto. Yet here he was, so he must have arrived − somehow.

The tall old gentleman lingered in the Morton store until closing time. Mostly he wandered up and down the aisles. Occasionally he would make small purchases. Whenever opportunity offered, he would chat with Mary. His attitude toward her was courtly and unexceptionable.

Morton's had many customers that evening, but Monsieur Larousse did not seem to notice that he was the centre of attraction, the cause of unwonted crowds in the usually sparsely patronised store.

When Pop Morton finally put up the shutters, no one happened to notice where the stranger went. He did not register at the Republican House, nor did he put in an appearance all the next day.

Around noon, Dr Crane ran across Dan Callahan on the street. Dan was in his cab, the doctor on foot.

'Hop in,' shouted Dan, drawing up by the curb, 'and I'll take you wherever you're going — free. I've something to tell you.'

'Not that Junior is worse, I hope?' said the young doctor, as he got in.

'Heavens, no,' replied the taxi-driver. 'Junior couldn't get worse with you tending him, Doc. No, it's about the old bird whose coffin we moved yesterday.'

'Not ill, is he?' asked Crane, professionally interested, and a bit hopefully.

'Not as I know of,' replied Dan, 'for he ain't been seen since the stores closed last night. No, it's about his coffin. They buried it this morning, without any service, and in the Wilson lot!'

'Well?'

'You know old "Aunt Hattie", the witch who lives in that little cottage just beyond the cemetery? Lives all alone except for one big black tom-cat?'

'Yes.'

'Well, she's a Wilson. And it's her who owns the Wilson lot.'

'Hm,' ruminated the young doctor. 'Bats, and coffins, and black cats, and witches, and burial without church rites. It does sound a bit spooky, doesn't it?'

'It sure does, Doc!' agreed Dan, solemnly.

But neither of them could advance any theory as to where Larousse spent his nights.

3. Eavesdropping

That evening, as soon as the sun had set and the bats were out, out came the elderly stranger as well. For some time he walked the streets, furnishing the subject of conversation for whispering groups. Then, as before, he entered Morton's store, and resumed his attentions to Mary.

His attitude was courteous and respectful. Not a word, not an action, nor even a glance, that any one could take exception to. He evidently had travelled extensively, and he talked interestingly of all the countries of the world.

To Mary Morton, cooped up all her life in this little one-horse Pennsylvania mountain town, and — since her engagement to Herman Fulton — deprived of all other male attention, this elderly stranger was a diversion, in fact almost a godsend.

Herman usually spent his evenings in his office in the bank; but tonight, due to several anonymous phone-calls in several female voices, he abruptly left the bank, dragged his fiancée out from under the very nose of the elderly stranger, and huffily took her to the movies, thus depriving her father of his cashier for the rest of the evening.

Peter Larousse promptly faded from the scene. His chauffeur had arrived in town with an expensive foreign car, and this evening drove him out into the country. The chauffeur had registered at the Republican House, and the car was kept in the hotel garage. But Larousse himself did not put up at the Republican House. His own lodging-place still remained a secret.

The next morning, as Dr Crane dropped into the Morton store to make some sort of a purchase — a collar, perhaps — he overheard heated words coming from Pop Morton's private office in the rear. The young doctor wasn't a gossip or an eaves-dropper, and accordingly would have scorned to listen in, had he not overheard the mention of Mary Morton's name. His secret infatuation for the beautiful girl now proved too much for him, and so he at once developed an unexplainable interest in some kitchen cutlery, displayed on a counter along the opaque-glass partition which shielded the proprietor's sanctum.

'Now, am I, or am I not, engaged to your daughter?' came from the other side of the wall in the unmistakable tones of Herman Fulton.

'Of course you are — of course you are,' replied Pop Morton soothingly.

'Well, then,' continued the young banker, 'haven't I a right to object to my fiancée compromising herself with that fish-eyed old French lizard?'

'But she ain't compromising herself,' objected Pop. 'That fish-eyed old French lizard, as you call him, has been perfectly polite and respectful to her. Besides, he buys lots of things at my store; and lots of people come in here every evening to take a look at him. He draws more crowds here than any advertising display I've put on in years. And if Mary draws *him*, what harm's done, at least as long as he behaves himself?'

'It's got to stop! I demand it!'

'But why? Why stop me making money? Is that a sensible way to treat your future pa-in-law?'

'The future wife of Herman Fulton has got to be discreet. If she can't be discreet, I'll break off the engagement.'

'Now, Herman,' remonstrated Morton, 'I'd hate to think you cared as little for Mary as all that. You wouldn't do anything like that, I'm sure.'

'Well, perhaps not,' admitted the banker, rather sheepishly. Then taking a new tack, 'But do I, or do I not, hold a mortgage on your store?'

'Sh! Sh! For heaven's sake, Herman, don't be so loud about it. I don't want that mortgage broadcast all over the country.'

'Why not? It's on record with the prothonotary up at the county seat, isn't it?'

The storekeeper ignored this question, and countered with: 'See here, Herman, you leave this Mooseer Larousse alone for a few weeks, and I'll be making enough off of him to pay up you d—d old mortgage.'

'Now, Pop, is that a nice way to speak of your mortgage, when I was so kind as to help you out and lend you all that money when you had to have it or go under? And it isn't a question of paying off the mortgage 'in a few weeks'; it's a question of paying off that mortgage *right now!* It's already overdue, and I demand payment. My engagement to your daughter stands, but it's the mortgage against Monsieur Larousse. Mary must stop acting as your cashier until that spooky old devil stops hanging around your store.'

'Why do you call him a spooky old devil?' asked Pop Morton artlessly, seeking to divert Fulton from his line of attack.

'Because he *is* one!' replied the latter, momentarily diverted. 'He comes here with a coffin, and all kinds of strange bats and things. Nobody knows who he is, or how he got here, or where he came from. He never shows up, except at night. He keeps under cover in the day-time, and nobody knows where or why.'

Dr Crane, listening outside, chuckled softly to himself.

'I know *why*, even if I don't know *where*. It's that confounded skin disease he told me about.'

Meanwhile Herman Fulton was continuing, on the other side of the thin partition, 'And he buried his coffin in the Wilson lot, which belongs to that old black-cat witch, Aunt Hattie. He *looks* spooky, too. He looks like — why, do you know what he looks like? It's only just occurred to me. I've been reading a book I got out of the public library, called *Dracula*, by a man named Bram Stoker. All about a he-vampire, who was dead and buried, and yet came out of his coffin every night, and sucked people's blood, until *they* died and became vampires, too. This Dracula could turn himself into a bat, or a wolf, or a shower of moonbeams, in order to get at his victims. I'll bet this old bird is Count Dracula himself, or at least another vampire of exactly the same sort. He looks just like the way Dracula was described in that story.'

'Ha, ha, ha!' exclaimed Pop Morton, with forced levity. 'Well, that's a good one. Ha, ha, ha! A *he*-vampire, eh? Why, I thought vampires were only *shes*. That's the way they always are in the movies. And they don't bite folks neither. Ha, ha, ha! A *he*-vampire! Well, that's a good one.'

'Don't laugh, Pop. I'm serious about this. I really am. This is quite a different kind of vampire. It would make your blood run cold to read that story. That man, Larousse, is a positive menace to this community!'

'Now, Herman,' remonstrated Morton in surprise. 'You don't mean to tell me that *you* take any stock in such a cock-and-bull yarn as that?'

'Yes, I do, Pop. That story is supposed to be based on mediaeval European traditions. These blood-sucking vampires were well known in the old days. I've looked up about them in the encyclopedia, too. Seriously, I believe the man's a menace. He ought to be run out of town.'

And then Pop Morton committed the tactical mistake of saying, 'But what's to prevent my making a little money off him, first?' thereby bringing the conversation back to the argument from which he had just succeeded in distracting Herman's attention.

He bit his lip, but it was too late to recall the words.

'*What's* to prevent?' snorted the banker. '*I'm* to prevent. You take Mary right out of your store and keep her out, or—'

'But it'll cost too much to hire another girl to do her work!' interposed Pop woefully. 'Entirely apart from the money I lose by losing this he-vampire's trade, you want me to lay out extra money hiring a substitute for my own daughter, who don't cost me nothing.'

'Do you talk of *money* at a time like this, with your own daughter's health, happiness, life, and even soul at stake? Pop, I'm ashamed of you! But I'll tell you what I'll do: *I'll* pay the wages of the substitute, and not put it on the mortgage either. Actually pay it out of my own pocket. And then we needn't tell Mary any of the reasons for what we're doing. No need to hurt her feelings by letting on to her what it's all about. We can tell her that I'm doing it as a special present to her, and because I object to the future Mrs Fulton occupying a menial position, even in her own father's store. *My* wife must be free of all degrading toil.'

'But think of all the trade I'll be losing,' Morton objected feebly.

'Trade be d—d!' snapped Herman. 'Think of your daughter — and your mortgage,' he added.

The two men emerged, and Dr Crane hurried away from the cutlery counter.

As he left, he heard Pop Morton whisper, 'Do you suppose he heard us?'

'Don't care if he did,' replied Herman Fulton, but not in a whisper. 'He's only a sawbones.'

That night there was a new young lady at the cashier's window of the Morton Emporium. But when Pop put up the shutters and went home at nine o'clock, he found Peter Larousse seated on the front piazza in earnest conversation with the beautiful Mary.

4. *Werewolves and Such*

So it became evident that merely relieving Mary Morton of her job as cashier of her father's store had not been enough to put a stop to the objectionable attentions of the weird old foreigner, who, Herman Fulton insisted from the depths of his reading, must be the original vampire Count Dracula, or at least his double.

Deprived of the opportunity of chatting with Mary at the cashier's wicket, Monsieur Larousse called on her at her home.

Her father felt that, of course, he ought to report the matter at once to her fiancé. But he kept putting this off, due partly to a general irresolution of character, partly the fear of facing Herman Fulton, and partly — it must be confessed — to a sort of satisfaction that he felt in the coming-to-naught of all the trouble that Herman had caused him.

As a result, it was several days before Herman discovered how the land lay. Mary could not be blamed, for no one had ever warned her against the old Frenchman. So for several evenings in succession, Peter Larousse called on her, and was welcomed. As she had been accustomed to spending her evenings at the store, time now hung heavy on her hands. Her fiancé was busy down at the bank, making money, and so she welcomed the visits of the distinguished foreigner.

Although his personality was rather chilling and revolting, yet he did bring to her the fresh outlook of the outside world. He talked entertainingly of the far countries which he had visited. All peoples and all times seemed familiar to him. And Mary rapidly began to realise what a limited, narrowing and cooped-up sort of place Yankton was, after all!

But one night, Herman called to take her to the movies, and found Peter Larousse already there.

Herman was chilled with horror at first. And then he boiled internally at the thought that all the good money he had spent in hiring Mary's substitute down at the store had been utterly wasted, for it had given 'old Dracula' an opportunity to see her even more intimately at home. Herman would have liked to make a scene then and there. In fact, he nearly did. But his long banking career had schooled him to the realisation that making oneself ridiculous has a bad effect on business. And business was always uppermost in Herman Fulton's considerations. So, although with difficulty, he steeled himself to be courteous to the older man, and politely begged him to excuse Mary for a prearranged date.

The stranger, with equal courtesy, submitted. But his eyes sized up the young banker appraisingly.

The deferred 'scene' took place in the Morton parlour later that evening, on the return from the show. Herman stormed, and Mary wept and had to be comforted. But finally, because she really did care for her fiancé, in spite of his peculiarities and his domineering manner, she agreed that she would always be 'out' thereafter, whenever Larousse called.

Larousse called regularly every night for a week, and at last gave it up. Like the drunken man who was thrown out of a party three times in succession, he knew when he wasn't wanted.

From then on, he walked the streets rather aimlessly after nightfall. Sometimes he would drop into a picture show, or would sit in the lobby of the Republican House, or even would make assorted purchases at the Morton Emporium. But by now he had become a familiar figure to the people of Yankton, and he no longer excited their attention. To no one, except Herman Fulton, old Dr Porter, and young Dr Crane, was he any longer of any moment. The interest of the two doctors was purely professional, although he would not let either of them treat his strange ailment. Herman kept his weird theories to himself, for fear of ridicule, but he read everything that he could find on the subject of vampires, even sending to Philadelphia for books, when he had exhausted the bibliography of the Yankton Carnegie Library.

And anyhow, so far as known, Larousse hadn't yet bitten any one in Yankton. But he was never seen to eat any regular food.

Even if the mystery of the mysterious stranger hadn't grown stale, there now were other matters to distract the attention of the citizens of Yankton. It was an unusually dry summer, and the drought afforded an absorbing topic of conversation.

In addition to the loss of crops and the threat against the town's water-supply, there began to be a large and unexplainable loss of chickens. Traps were set every evening, and were found sprung every morning, and still the toll of fowls continued. Several people reported having seen a lone wolf in the mountains back of the town.

Peter Larousse dropped gradually out of sight. He seldom

appeared downtown in the evening any more, but no one took particular note of this defection, so intent had they all become on the lone wolf, and the depredation of the chickens, which two phenomena were now quite generally linked together in people's minds.

More people saw the wolf. Several poultry-raisers sat up in ambush and got shots at him, but he seemed to bear a charmed life, and to be immune to their bullets.

Eventually a huge German police-dog was found dead in the hills; and from that time on, the wolf was not seen again, and no more chickens were stolen; but no one could persuade the people of Yankton that these events had anything to do with each other. They knew perfectly well, these Pennsylvania mountaineers, that the wolf had merely transferred his predatory operations elsewhere. Couldn't they tell a wolf from a dog?

As for Herman Fulton, he had his own theories on the subject, but he kept them to himself.

About the time of the end of the wolf episode, Mary Morton was taken ill, and called in Dr Crane. The young doctor didn't mind this at all, until the case began to get serious. Then he became frankly puzzled with the situation.

In spite of a good appetite and the consumption of plenty of food, Mary began to lose weight and grew pale and wan. Tonics were administered, but they seemed to be only temporarily stimulating. Finally blood-transfusions were resorted to, and these soon had to become more and more frequent. It was evident that Mary was losing blood steadily and rapidly, and yet there was no apparent cause for this loss.

Peter Larousse reappeared in his old haunts. His health seemed to have been greatly improved by the bracing air of the Pennsylvania mountains.

5. Dr Crane's Adventure

Finally the young doctor prescribed a change of scene for his patient. He recommended that she be sent to the seashore, and that specialists be called in. But her fiancé, although most solicitous, had a narrow provincial clinging to his native town.

'There is no spot in the world more healthful than the Pennsylvania mountains,' he insisted. 'Now that the wolf-scare is all over, let's put her in my cabin in the hills back of the town. I'll have the place all tidied up, and will hire Mr and Mrs Foss to take care of it. Pay for the whole performance myself, too. Mrs Foss used to be a trained nurse before she married Josh Foss, so we'll be killing two birds with one stone.'

Dr Crane reluctantly had to acquiesce. Herman Fulton was not only boss of the town; he was boss of Mary Morton, too.

Mary seemed to improve slightly under the change, and Ralph Crane soon found that the remote location of the camp gave him an opportunity to spend an undue amount of time with his patient, without attracting attention or exciting any gossip.

Then Mary began to fail again. She became paler and paler, and more and more bloodless.

Her fiancé, in accordance with his theories, made her a present of a beautiful chased gold crucifix, inlaid with (what he said were) diamonds, which he begged her to wear all the time in memory of him. He hung the cabin with bunches of garlic; but as Mary happened peculiarly to be rather partial to their acrid odour, she did not mind, especially as she thought that he knew of this strange liking of hers, and was doing it on that account.

He puttied up all the window-cracks with what appeared to be bread-crumbs, and did not mention the fact that he had procured this material at the Catholic church down the valley. Mary and he were good Methodists.

Dr Crane ascribed this puttying to the old New England superstition as to the baneful effect of night air. He remonstrated roundly on general sanitary considerations, but finally gave in when the nights turned suddenly colder with approaching autumn, especially as the cabin leaked air like a sieve, anyhow.

Ralph Crane spent long hours nearly every evening with Mary, except on the occasions when Herman Fulton was there. As a result, Ralph and Mary became very good friends. For the most part they talked of their pasts, than which there is no better way of getting well acquainted. The girl recounted all the personal details of her rather uneventful Yankton girlhood. The young doctor told of his city childhood, his boyhood on a New Hampshire farm, and his struggles to put himself through Phillips Exeter Academy, Darmouth College, and Harvard Medical School.

Herman Fulton didn't seem to mind this intimacy. In fact a sick, weak, bloodless and somewhat petulant Mary rather bored him, in spite of his regard and concern for her; and so he was glad to have someone else — provided no scandal was involved — take off his hands the task of keeping her amused.

One evening when the doctor and the girl were sitting alone together in front of the cabin, the full moon and a soft whispering mountain breeze were most suggestive of the appropriateness of ghost stories; so Crane embarked on an apt tale of his New Hampshire boyhood.

'The farm on which I worked,' said he, 'was about two miles from the lake from which we got our water supply. There was a hot-air pump down by the shore of the lake, which pumped the water up to a tank beside the barn. That sort of pump is a very simple affair: a little fire-box, holding only a shovelful or two of coal, and then a single air-cylinder and piston about a foot in diameter on top of that, and then on top of the cylinder a heavy three foot flywheel. This was the engine layout. I don't remember how the pump itself was hitched up — all we had to bother with was the engine. If that went, then the pump went too. You don't see many of that kind of pump nowadays.'

'I never heard of one,' the girl said.

Dr Crane continued, 'It would run all night on one loading of coal; that is, unless it happened to stop. When it stopped, you could tell up at the farmhouse, because the 'thump, thump, thump' in the pipes wouldn't sound any more. Then whichever of the farmhands' turn it was, would have to light up a lantern, trudge two miles through the woods down to the lake, climb up on the big flywheel, hang on to one side of it to give it a spin, and thus start the pump pumping again. Well, this particular summer, we were troubled with mountain lions.'

'Real lions?' interrupted Mary.

'Not the kind you see in circuses,' explained Ralph. 'The kind that we had up in New Hampshire looked about like a lioness, only somewhat smaller and slimmer. Both sexes look alike. The male hasn't any mane. Sometimes they call this creature a mountain lion, or a catamount, cougar, panther, painter, puma, or what have you! Well, anyhow, two of them came down out of the north woods up by Mount Chocorua, and started stealing chickens, much like this wolf they had around here last month. Only these beasts occasionally took sheep, and calves, too. A boy friend of mine, Tolly Piper, was driving the cows home from pasture one day, when one of these lions jumped out of the bushes, picked up a calf right under Tolly's nose, and jumped back into the bushes again with it.'

'Horrible!' murmured the girl.

The young doctor warmed to his story, and went on. 'One day one of them walked right into an afternoon tea of summer folks. It calmly surveyed the scene, while all the people sat frozen to stone. Then it slipped quietly back into the woods again. And at night you could hear them calling to each other from one range of hills to another. A most weird sound!'

'Did you ever see either of them?' asked the girl.

'Saw both of them,' was the reply. 'One night around midnight I was lying awake in my second-story room in the farmhouse, listening to the howls, when I noticed that the voices of the two lions came nearer and nearer together, until finally they met in the woods just between the farm and the lake. Then the sounds got louder and louder. We had some tame foxes in a wire-netting cage just back of the house, and I could hear our poor little pets whimpering with fright. Then there came an unusually fierce scream from one of the lions, followed by a crash against the wires of the cage. Then another scream and another crash, as the other beast sprang. This was repeated several times, but after a time the two animals gave it up, and came toward the house. I could see them distinctly in the moonlight, which was as bright as it is tonight. They would walk a few steps, and then sit on their haunches, throw back their heads, and howl. One time they stopped directly under my window − I could have hit them with a shoe.'

'Why didn't you?'

'Because I preferred to sit and watch them. Didn't want to scare them away!'

'But why didn't you shoot them?'

'The farmer for whom I worked didn't let any of the farm-hands keep guns. So the two lions finally trotted off again into the woods.'

'But that wasn't the adventure you were going to tell me about, was it?' asked Mary, a bit disappointedly.

'No,' replied Crane. 'The adventure happened the following night. Again I was lying awake listening to the cries of the pair, as they called to each other from range to range. And again the two animals met between the farm and the lake. But this time their cries then ceased. What silent devilment were they up to, I wondered? And then I heard the pump stop. It was my turn to down to the lake and fix it.'

'You poor dear,' murmured Mary. 'How old were you?'

'Only eleven. Naturally I was scared to death, but I had to go, for it was my turn. I begged each of the other farmhands, one by one, to go with me, but they all refused; so I lit a lantern and set off alone through the woods. Not a sound from the mountain lions. If only they would howl, so that I could tell where they were and what they were up to! But they kept absolutely silent. Somehow I reached the lake shore, got the pump going again, and started back up the road toward home. I was just beginning to recover from my stupor of abject terror, when upon rounding a curve of the path, I saw in front of me two green spots of phosphorescent light. Instantly I stopped dead in my tracks, absolutely petrified.'

'I can well believe it,' interjected the girl. 'You poor little kid!'

Dr Crane continued: 'And then the beast came toward me. At least I judged that he was coming toward me, for the two phosphorescent eyes seemed to get wider and wider apart. In an attempt at frightening him, I swung my lantern widely — and the lantern went out. I was alone in the darkness with that thing up the road. Yet still the two spots of light glowed, even though there was now no lantern for them to reflect. Instinctively I felt that this was strange, but I was too scared to do any real thinking on the subject. Wider and wider apart got the two eyes. 'What a huge beast this must be!' I thought. From a distant ridge there came the blood-curdling scream of a lion. Fascinated, I waited for the beast in front of me to answer its mate.

But the answer came from an entirely different quarter, far
away. 'Can there be *three* of them?' I wondered. And then, with
a flash of inspiration, I stepped fearlessly forward, right
between the two eyes which were facing me. They were nothing
but two glow-worms crawling on the dirt of the road.'

'Well of all the yarns!' exclaimed Mary, a bit exasperated.
'Here I have been getting up a lot of sympathy for you, and you
weren't any more in danger of being eaten alive than I am right
now.'

'But I really was frightened, terribly so,' protested the young
doctor, a bit apologetically.

There was a pause, while the two sat and watched the moonlight on the gently swaying treetops of the mountain side.

Then Mary asked, 'You have spoken of the terrifying scream
of the mountain lions. What was it like? Can you describe it to
me?'

'That's a pretty big order,' laughed the young doctor, 'for a
lion's scream is different from anything else I have ever heard.
It's just simply horrible – makes the hairs stand up on the back
of your neck, and brings out goose-pimples all over your body.
The nearest thing to it that I ever heard was a little child once,
shrieking with pain in a hospital. It's – it's–'

As he paused, groping in his mind for a smile, the calm night
air was split by one single ghostly shriek, coming from the woods
just below them on the mountainside.

Mary's pale face turned even paler, as she sat suddenly erect
in her chair and convulsively gripped the doctor's arm.

'What – what was that, Ralph?' she gasped.

'That,' replied he, 'was a mountain lion.'

Tensely the two of them awaited a repetition of the sound.
But it never came. That single fearsome howl was the only one.

Gradually they relaxed again.

'What will you do?' asked the girl solicitously. 'I can't bear to
have you go home through the woods, now that this has happened. You might meet that – that awful thing. And I'm
scared to be left here alone with only the Fosses. You must stay
with me, Ralph. Spend the night. Please do. Mrs Foss can fix
you up a cot somehow.'

So Dr Crane spent the night in Mary Morton's little mountain cabin.

6. *Bats and Other Things*

Of course, when Herman Fulton learned that the attractive young doctor had spent the night in Mary Morton's cabin, he was furious. Even the fact of the presence of Mr and Mrs Foss in the cabin, as chaperones, did not in the least mitigate his anger.

His fiancée had been compromised! He himself had been made ridiculous! To a banker or businessman there is nothing worse than ridicule. Many a man would let his business go to smash rather than run the risk of ridicule to save it; and here was ridicule to no practical end. Why, it might even result in a run on the bank!

The only way to save his face was to take some drastic action at once. Accordingly he did. He asked Dr Crane to withdraw from the case; and when the doctor refused to withdraw, Herman fired him. Herman was in a position to do this, as he was paying the bills. Old Dr Porter was placed in charge, instead.

The reason for the change, as given out to such persons as had any right to ask, was that Dr Crane had unduly terrified his patient by getting her off in a lonely shack in the mountains and then telling her ghost stories. Indeed Mary was so frightened by that single unexplained piercing scream of a mountain lion, that she insisted on being moved back to civilization the very next day. Altogether, everything fitted in to make Herman's explanation sound most plausible. And really Dr Crane was open to considerable censure for telling Mary the lion story in her condition and location.

He accepted his removal gracefully, and conferred lengthily with his successor, who brought a new viewpoint to the situation.

Old Dr Porter, after a rather cursory examination of Mary Morton and a study of the case-history, announced, 'This acute anaemia appears to me to be due to some cause which we haven't yet fathomed. You were probably taught at Harvard Medical that anaemia is a *disease*, but the more modern theory seems to be that it is a mere *symptom*, the result of one of a large number of varying causes, any of which have been run to earth, but many more of which still remain unexplained.'

The younger doctor agreed.

'I'll admit,' said he, 'that you older men are apt to be more progressive than our generation. We accept as gospel truth what we were taught at the school, whereas you have been out in practice long enough to realise how little is really known of the human body. Hence you are more open-minded to new ideas than we. Have you any theory as to the underlying cause of Miss Morton's symptoms?'

'Not yet,' replied Dr Porter judiciously, 'but I believe that I have at least discerned the group in which her ailment falls. Her bloodlessness seems to me to be due to some organism, some creature that is sapping her strength. I shouldn't wonder—'

He paused with a bit of embarrassment, and then went on, 'You know, years ago when I was a young man just out of college, I made a trip to the Argentine. One of the horses, on a ranch where I was visiting, was taken ill. It grew weak and emaciated. During the daytime it would eat ravenously and seem to pick up strength. But every morning it would be weak again. I was frankly puzzled, and was interested in the case from a medical viewpoint, although I had never felt any leanings toward veterinary practice. But my host merely shrugged his shoulders, and accepted the situation with Spanish fatalism. Also he did not seem to care to discuss the case. Whenever I broached the subject, he would avoid it with a bit of a shudder, and would make the sign of the cross. Most of the ranch-hands acted the same way about the matter. Finally one of the cowboys, not quite so superstitious as the others, led me to the horse one evening, and pointed out a huge bat — "vampire-bats" they call them — clinging to the horse's neck, sucking its life-blood.'

'There has been such a bat around Yankton all summer,' interrupted young Crane. 'Can it be—?'

'Let me go on with my story,' persisted Dr Porter. 'The bat fled before I could get my hands on it. I at once inquired why they didn't keep the bat away, but the cowboy replied, 'It is not possible, *senor*, for once a vampire marks its victim, the victim is doomed.' But I myself am not a fatalist. I insisted on putting the poor horse at once into a carefully screened shed. Nevertheless the bat got in and out, and the horse continued to fail. We blocked every hole, but we could not cope with the fiendish ingenuity of that vampire. So, as a last resort, I persuaded my friend the cowboy — by means of *'mucho dinero'* — to sit up with the horse and guard it at night; to try and shoot the bat, if he got a chance.'

'Did that work?'

'Yes, it did for a while. The cowboy didn't even see the bat again. The horse rapidly gained in strength, and I was just about to taunt the Argentinos that the vampire was not as omnipotent as they seemed to think, when one morning I found the cowboy asleep, and the horse dead, drained nearly bloodless!'

'But, doctor,' objected Crane, 'if anything like that were happening to Mary, she would know it, and there would be marks on her throat.'

'Are you sure that there aren't marks on her throat?' demanded the older man, pointedly.

'N-n-no!' admitted Crane. 'Have you observed any?'

'I haven't looked,' Dr Porter replied. 'This idea hadn't occurred to me when I first examined her. And now, frankly, I don't care to disturb her, in her present nervous condition. Nor, for the same reason, have I mentioned bats to her. But we shall keep a careful watch, from now on.'

'Well, to be equally frank with you, sir,' asserted young Crane, 'I don't place much stock in your bat theory. But there have been a great many strange carryings-on in Yankton this summer, and nothing would surprise me very much. Certainly we don't yet know what is the underlying cause of Miss Morton's illness.'

So Dr Porter, following out his hunch, next interviewed Mary's father on the subject.

'You haven't seen any vampire-bats around the house, have you?' he asked abruptly.

Pop Morton's jaw dropped, for he suddenly remembered Herman's weird theories.

'Vamp — vampire what?' he gasped.

It was Dr Porter's turn to become surprised, for Pop's confusion was clearly indicative of something.

'Why, what do you mean?' asked the doctor.

'Nothing. Nothing,' asserted Pop, much embarrassed. 'No, I haven't seen any bats at all.'

And nothing more could Dr Porter pump out of him, except the repeated assertion that he hadn't seen any bats. Nor did Pop mention the conversation to Herman Fulton until much later.

Mary continued to waste away, recovering a bit sometimes for a week or so at a stretch, only to fall still lower the next time that a relapse set in.

Meanwhile Dr Crane's patients steadily deserted him, one by one. It soon became evident to the young doctor that Herman Fulton, not content with removing him from the Morton case, was insidiously and persistently bringing to bear the bank's influence to drive him out of town, until at last the day came when the young doctor was unable to meet a payment on the mortgage on his own establishment, and was refused an extension by the banker.

Fulton then placed his cards on the table by offering a handsome settlement for the equity, if Dr Crane would move out of town; and so Dr Crane moved.

For some time past, one of the New York hospitals had been angling for Dr Crane's services, and now he accepted the offer.

Herman magnanimously permitted him to say good-bye to Mary. The farewell was touching, though brief. Not a word was said to let the girl know that Crane was the victim of her fiancé's jealousy.

'I've a splendid opening in New York,' reported the young doctor, 'and so I am reluctantly leaving Yankton to take it. But the real impelling reason is that New York will give me an opportunity to read up on anaemia, and I hope to find out some way of curing you. If I succeed, I shall be very glad that I left. In any event, please remember that I shall always be your devoted friend. Please, please call on me, if you ever need help.'

Seizing her hand, he held it tightly for a moment, and then left abruptly. There were tears in the eyes of both of them.

Immediately on his arrival at his new job, Dr Crane hunted up the member of the hospital staff who was supposed to know the most about anaemia; and through his suggestions, plunged into a line of evening reading in the medical alcove of the New York Public Library.

He wrote Mary Morton once — merely a brief note, giving her his address, and expressing a hope that she was better.

It was not long before a solution of Mary's case began to dawn on him. He found that, as old Dr Porter had stated, the modern trend of opinion is that anaemia is always secondary. He found, to his surprise, that even more of the primary causes of that disease had been worked out and pinned down than Dr Porter had intimated.

The enthusiastic young researcher compared each of the known features of the girl's case-history with the ear-marks of each of these various primary causes, one by one, until at last he hit upon what seemed to him to be unquestionably the uniquely correct solution.

Dr Porter had been very nearly right in his surmise. There was now a chance to save Mary. So Ralph Crane rushed off the following letter by special delivery:

Dr Jeremiah Porter,
Yankton, Pa.
My dear old friend,

I believe that I have at last hit upon the underlying cause of Miss Morton's condition. Her symptoms, her case-history, and the situation at Yankton seem to fit the specifications exactly. You were quite right in your hunch that she is the victim of a parasitic organism, but I do not believe that it is a vampire-bat.

The books describe a form of anaemia, very similar to hers, and often found in mining communities. It is due to a parasitic worm, the *ankylostomum duodenale*, which inhabits damp places, especially underground mines.

The symptoms are very similar to those of pernicious anaemia, for which we have been treating her; that is to say, successive remissions and relapses, with the nervous symptoms very marked.

May I suggest *santonin* for a time, in place of *blaud*?
                    Respectfully,
                    Ralph Crane, M.D.

Then anxiously he awaited an answer. It came back two days later by wire:

Diagnosis too late. Mary died Monday. Funeral three o'clock tomorrow.

J. Porter.

7. Haunted

It was already 'tomorrow' when the telegram arrived, announcing Mary Morton's death. Crane, stunned and heartbroken by the news, hailed a taxicab and rushed to the Pennsylvania station, only to find that there was no train which could possibly get him to Yankton in time for the funeral. So he sent some flowers by telegraph, and gave himself up to an afternoon of bitter recrimination.

He had failed the girl he loved. Oh, if he had but worked faster and to more purpose, and had found out the cause of her trouble before that knowledge was too late to save her! Of course, his diagnosis might not be correct; and even if correct, it might not have enabled him to cure her. But there had been a chance, and that chance was now lost forever.

Later a letter arrived from Dr Porter, but it didn't throw much more light on the situation. Marks and blood had been found on Mary's throat, but the girl had insisted that they had been due to her scratching a particularly vexatious woodtick bite, which she had acquired in the mountain cabin. A constant guard had been set over her, but no bat or other animal had approached her, except a stray black cat which had jumped over her bed on the day of her death. The huge grey bat had been seen around town occasionally, but not near the Morton house. It all sounded rather banal and silly, when set down in black and white on paper; but, in view of the previous conference between the two doctors, Dr Porter said that he felt duty-bound to state all these details. He expressed no opinion about the *ankylostomum duodenale*, except to thank Dr Crane for the suggestion, and to express an appreciation for the younger man's zeal, persistency and thoroughness at research. All of which was most unsatisfying.

Young Crane was crushed, stunned and broken-hearted. His Mary was dead! His Mary was dead!

At last he realised that what he had mistaken for merely warm affection for the girl, had really been love. Oh, if he had but realised this in time!

It was his fault! Her death was all his fault! He ought to have asserted himself, have declared his love, and have dragged her away from Yankton to New York, where she could have had adequate medical attention.

For about a week, he drove his numbed brain and weary body. During working hours, his hospital duties afforded him some measure of forgetfulness of his grief; but at night there was no relief. He walked many miles every evening. Then he would lie awake in bed, the prey of bitter recrimination, until at last sleep came, but not oblivion, for even his sleep was tortured by dreams of what might have been.

And then one night, about midnight, he suddenly awakened with a feeling that there was someone in his room. He was thoroughly frightened, even before he started to awake; and yet he could not remember any dream which could be responsible for this feeling. Merely he waked up already scared, and with no apparent cause.

The room was quite light from the reflection of an advertising sign near by, and so he could distinctly see everything in the room. By the foot of the bed there stood a young girl clad in white, smiling down on him.

It was Mary — or Mary's ghost! But it couldn't be her ghost, for there are no such things as ghosts. So it must be Mary herself. But Mary was dead. But she couldn't be dead, for here she was. What was she doing in New York City? And in his room! And at this time of night! His Mary, at last! Could it be true?

'Mary!' he gasped.

'Yes, Ralph,' the figure replied, 'it is Mary. I have come to you for help, because Herman doesn't seem to understand. Night after night I have tried to get Herman to help me; but he only cringes, and makes the sign of the cross, and says horrid things to me, which I don't understand. He calls me 'undead'. Of course I'm undead! I'm alive, as alive as you are; but somehow he says the word 'undead' as though it meant something else, something terrible and unclean. I can't understand him, and he refuses to understand me. But you will help me, won't you? You promised me, you know.'

'Of course I'll help you, Mary dear!' he exclaimed. 'But what are you doing in New York? Just step into my sittingroom for a moment, until I get some clothes on.'

She smiled wanly.

'I'm not in New York, Ralph,' she replied. 'I'm buried six feet deep in a cold dark grave in the Yankton cemetery. But I'm not dead. I'm sure of that. Sometimes I lie for hours in that awful padded coffin. Sometimes I sleep. Sometimes I lose my head, and shriek and struggle in the darkness, trying to tear the box away and get out. And sometimes I think very calmly and steadily of some place, usually Herman's room, until suddenly I find myself there. Then I plead with him to help me; but he repulses me, and drives me back into the grave again. I feel that I can't stand it much longer. Either my strength or my wits will give out, and then I shall be really dead.'

It was quite clear to Dr Crane that the poor girl was out of her mind. She had probably been in a cataleptic trance, had escaped from the coffin on the very eve of burial, and had closed and locked the box, perhaps even filling it with books so that her absence would not be noticed. Insane people are quite often diabolically clever in such ways. He remembered, from his recent extensive reading, that anaemia often results in either catalepsy or insanity, so why not both? It was the only plausible solution!

His heart went out to her in a wave of masculine protectiveness. Here was a chance for him to give to the girl he loved the expert hospital care which she had lacked in Yankton, and to restore to her both her health and her sanity. Then let Herman try and get her away from him!

As the young doctor groped in his mind for soothing words to quiet her hysteria, she spoke again, 'You will help me, won't you, Ralph? I frighten poor dear Herman so! He is beginning to get pale and anaemic just like I was. Last night he had another man sleeping with him, and so I can't go there any more. It embarrasses me.'

'Of course I'll help you,' reassured Dr Crane. 'Now if you'll just sit down for a moment in the next room, I'll be right with you.'

'Thank you, Ralph,' said she. 'Goodbye. Come quickly! Very quickly!'

He rubbed his eyes. She was no longer there! And yet he had not seen her leave the room.

Dr Crane got up and dressed, and walked the streets of New York until morning. He did not dare to go to sleep again, and thus establish the possibility that he had merely dreamed what had just happened to him.

He was standing eagerly on the steps of the Public Library when it opened at nine o'clock. As the doors were unlocked, he rushed to the medical stacks, where he plunged into a new line of reading, namely, 'cataleptic trances.'

By noon a smile of grim determination had settled over his features, and he had wired to Dan Callahan, the Yankton taxi-driver, to meet him at the Limited.

8. In the Grave

'Well, sir, you've come!' exclaimed Dan Callahan, as Dr Crane swung off the Limited late that night. 'I got your wire, and here I am, although pretty near every other man in town is up at the cemetery. But not any of the women; for it's no fit work for a woman.'

'What isn't?' asked the young doctor, with ominous foreboding.

'The gang is digging up Mary Morton's body.'

'To save her life?' asked Crane, eagerly.

'Save her life? Naw!' replied Dan. 'She's dead. But she's been haunting people all over town since she died, and so some of the men have got it figured out that she's turned vampire.'

'She's turned what?' exclaimed Crane, astonished.

'Vampire,' explained the taxi-driver. 'Not the movie kind, but the spook kind, that flies around at night and sucks blood. Herman Fulton has been reading up a lot about them in the Carnegie Library, and it seems like there really is such a thing. They reckon that that old Frenchman, Mussoo Larousse, is one too, and that his coming here had something to do with poor

Mary dying and turning into one. He's been laying low ever since Mary died. But the gang is out to get them both. It says in the book, which Herman was reading, that the only way to cure a vampire is to cut off its head and stuff its mouth full of onions.'

'Just a minute,' interrupted the young doctor, horrified; 'you don't mean to say that's what they're planning to do to Mary!'

'Why not?' replied Dan. 'She's dead, ain't she? And besides, she really has been haunting people.'

'Dan,' said Crane solemnly, seizing him by the shoulders, and staring into his eyes, 'I don't believe that Mary is dead at all. I believe that she's merely in a cataleptic trance—'

'Speaking of cats,' interrupted the Irishman, 'that's another thing. A black cat walked across Mary's body just before she died, and hasn't been seen since; and they say that that's a sure sign that both she and the cat have turned into vampires.'

'What a beastly lot of rot!' exclaimed Dr Crane, indignantly. 'It's nothing but absurd superstition! There's a very good chance that Mary is still alive, and that all this so-called 'haunting' is merely due to her efforts to communicate with her friends and loved ones, and get them to rescue her. Whereupon they go and dig her up, not to save her life, but rather to kill her. My God, while we're wasting time talking here, they may be doing it already! Come on. Are you game to help me stop them?'

'That I am!' replied Dan fervently. 'You saved little Danny's life, and I'm with you in anything this side of hell. Let's go.'

'Have you any guns?'

'One automatic pistol in my cab, and another at the garage.'

'Let's get them, then, and let's hurry. I have a revolver in my grip here.'

Soon the two allies, fully armed, were speeding over the mile of road which led from the village to the cemetery. They found the burial-place crowded with men. Cars were parked all around.

Leaving the taxicab as near to the graveyard as they could get, they hurried forward with flashlights in hand, and weapons as yet concealed.

'Thank God!' breathed Dr Crane, for the digging was still in progress.

No one paid them any attention as they joined the milling

throng. Many of the men carried lanterns, which they held high around Mary Morton's grave, while others took short turns with a spade. Little brown bats fluttered about in pursuit of the insects which the lanterns attracted.

It was evident that the digging had only just started. And every one was so excited that the hole did not make very rapid progress.

Dan Callahan had exaggerated. There were but few of Yankton's leading citizens present. Most of the mob consisted of coal-miners and others of the lower strata of the community. But there were enough of the higher strata present to make the gathering quite representative. In fact, a survey of the crowd would give a pretty good idea as to just what promissory notes, held by Herman Fulton's bank, were badly overdue.

Herman himelf was in charge of operations. He fretted and fumed and scolded and interfered, none of which helped particularly to speed up the work.

Dr Crane remarked in an undertone to the taxi-driver, 'We might just as well let *them* do the digging for us. Then we can step in at the last moment, and do the rescuing ourselves.'

So the two lay low, remained inconspicuously on the outskirts of the crowd, and waited.

Finally, well toward morning, the crunching of the shovel changed to a wooden thumping. Every one heaved a sigh of relief. Their flagging interest revived. Presently the man in the hole passed up the lid of the box which contained the coffin.

'Now to open the coffin,' said he.

'No you don't!' someone shouted. 'Haul it up, and give us all a look.'

'Yes, yes,' chorused the crowd. 'Haul it up. Give us a look.'

So ropes were attached to the handles, and the coffin was hoisted onto the ground beside the grave.

Herman Fulton bustled authoritatively forward.

'Undertaker here?' he inquired.

'Yes, sir,' a voice replied.

'Got your keys handy?'

'Yes, sir, but we haven't any permit from the Board of Health.'

'You should have thought of that earlier in the evening. The clerk will backdate a permit tomorrow, if I ask him to. A public duty, like we are doing tonight, can't wait on any formalities.'

'Yes, sir.'

And the undertaker stepped forward and unlocked the coffin. Herman started to raise the lid, and then hesitated. Dr Crane and Dan Callahan gripped their pistols tighter, and surged forward with the crowd that pressed expectantly in from all sides.

Herman said, 'Now don't be surprised if the coffin is empty, for she may be off right now on one of her vampiring trips. If so, we'll just have to wait until she returns, which she's sure to do before morning. I've been reading up a lot on the subject, and I've found out that vampires must always come back to their coffins before sunrise.'

So saying, he flung up the lid. But the coffin was not vacant. There lay the body of Mary Morton, just as when the coffin had been closed several weeks before. No ravages of decay were in evidence. A delicate pink bloom lay on her cheeks. Her lips were red. She looked almost like her old-time self of before her illness.

The crowd gasped in unison. Then some one exclaimed, 'She looks alive!'

'Why wouldn't she?' muttered the undertaker under his breath. 'I rouged her up good for the funeral.'

'Is she really dead?' asked someone.

'No,' replied Herman Fulton authoritatively. 'Haven't I explained it to all of you again and again? She is what the books call "undead." She is a vampire. This Larousse person is one, too. Vampires go on living after they die. They sneak out of their graves at night, to haunt people and to suck people's blood. And when their victims finally die, the victims become vampires in turn. Larousse sucked Mary's blood until she died and joined his band of devils. She is now haunting several of us, though she doesn't seem to have bitten any of us yet. If we don't free her, we'll become vampires when we die, and so on. It's a vicious circle. It's − it's like one of those chain-letters: once it gets well started, there's no telling where it will end up. We've got to stop it right now − nip it in the bud, as it were.'

He spoke his piece like some patent-medicine faker getting off a line of patter.

But Pop Morton blurted out, 'I dunno, Herman. I've heard all your arguments again and again. But it's contrary to nature for me to let you mutilate my daughter's body. Sacrilegious, too, after she's been given a Christian burial.'

'Mr Morton,' said Herman sternly, 'your daughter herself will be grateful. Her poor spirit doesn't enjoy being a vampire. It longs for rest. We must cut off her head, drive a stake through her heart, and fill her mouth with garlic. Then you will see a look of peace descend upon her sad face, as her spirit is released from its thraldom, and returns to God who gave it.'

'Her face do look sad,' interjected someone.

'No wonder,' murmured Dr Crane under his breath.

Herman Fulton continued sententiously, 'I was her fiancé, and so it is my right and duty to strike the blow that sets her free. I hate to mutilate the beautiful body of her whom I loved. But I know that it would be her own wish to have it so. In a few moments she shall be freed from the devil. And then we shall dig up that devil himself, over in the Wilson lot, and free him, too, though not for any love, in his case, but rather merely that his evil career may be put to an end. Mr Morton, in a few moments, loving hands will send your daughter's soul to peace.'

Herman Fulton drew a long hunting-knife from his belt.

'Stop!' shouted a voice in the crowd.

Everyone looked around, some holding their lanterns aloft and shading them to see who had caused the disturbance. They looked into the drawn revolvers of Ralph Crane and Dan Callahan.

'Stand back there from that coffin! Quick! All of you!' commanded the young doctor, clipping his words off peremptorily.

The crowd recoiled immediately and instinctively.

But Herman sneered, 'So it's little sawbones come back for his sweetie! Do you want to claim for yourself the right to save her soul?'

'I claim the right to save her *life*,' replied Crane tersely.

'Any more wise-cracks out of you, Herman Fulton,' added Dan, 'and they'll be your last remarks this side of hell.'

Herman glowered, started to say something, then thought better of it, and remained silent.

Dr Crane continued, 'You've all been listening to the most arrant lot of bosh and mediaeval superstition. Mary Morton isn't dead, she's merely in a cataleptic trance. If you idiots will keep out of the way for a few moments, I can resuscitate her, and prove it to you.'

'No you don't,' asserted Herman Fulton. 'We've got to act quick. The first thing you know, she'll vanish in a shower of sparks, or a black mist, or turn into a bat or something, and make her escape. We're wasting time talking.'

'Yeah?' remarked someone from the crowd. 'Well, you said yourself that she'd have to come back at sunrise. So what's the difference? Let's give the Doc a chance.'

'Yes, let's,' echoed several others.

Herman was nonplussed for a moment. But then, remembering that he was the banker who held most of their financial lives in the hollow of his hand, he recovered his poise. He stared imperiously round at his followers. One by one, as his glance fell upon them, they remembered some mortgage, or note, or overdrawn account, and their incipient opposition crumbled.

The crowd was angry and chagrined at Herman's power over them, but they dared not vent their anger upon him, and so they looked around for a vicarious victim, and finally centred on Dr Crane. The mob began to murmur.

The doctor sensed their growing unrest, and realised that they were rapidly working themselves into a fanatical condition, in which they would attack him and Dan, in spite of the automatics. This would mean shooting to kill. Dr Crane had no desire to kill anyone, and besides he wanted to be sure and save Mary Morton. Oh, if there were at least two men in the crowd whom he could trust to hold his revolver and one of Dan's while he himself tried to bring Mary back to life!

'What's the disturbance?' asked a quiet voice behind him.

The answer was an angry snarl from the mob, as Monsieur Larousse, in his inevitable cape-coat, stepped to the side of Dan and the doctor.

'It's the old devil himself,' snarled Herman Fulton.

'That remark appears to be addressed to me,' said Larousse with imperturbable suavity. 'Will some one please explain.'

'You don't need any explanation, you old vampire,' blurted out Herman. 'You know yourself that you are one of the undead. You sucked the blood of Mary Morton, and made a vampire out of her, too. So we've dug up her body, and are going to drive a stake through her heart, to lay her ghost. The night is nearly over, and then when you return to your own coffin with the morning light, we'll drive a stake through you, too.'

'I take it, sir,' said Larousse, ignoring Herman and addressing Dr Crane, 'that you are not in the least impressed by this tommyrot and poppycock. You and the taxi-man here appear to be opposing these gentlemen. You look sensible. Is there anything I can do to assist in preventing this sacrilege? Little Mary Morton was a dear sweet girl, whom I greatly admired.'

'We know you did,' sneered Herman Fulton.

Dr Crane felt a bit uneasy at having this suspected Dracula-person for an ally. But it was a case of any port in a storm.

'We have three guns,' said he. 'If I can get two sane individuals to help me, Dan and they can hold back the mob, while I have an opportunity to bring Mary out of her trance.'

'Doctor,' said Pop Morton, stepping forward, 'I'll take one of the guns. You're a doctor, and you ought to know what you're about.'

With a sigh of relief, Crane handed over his pistol. But instantly a crafty smile played across the features of Pop Morton.

'Stick 'em up!' he shouted. 'Crane, Larousse, Callahan! Let go your gun, Callahan!'

He had the drop on them all, even on Dan, who promptly let go the one gun which he held. His other automatic was in his pocket.

'Now do your dirty work, Herman,' exclaimed Pop, rather pleased to be usurping Fulton's centre of the stage. 'Quick, while I hold off these interferers.'

9. The Tables Turned

But, even as Pop Morton spoke, a grey arm was suddenly swung around his neck from behind, while at the same instant the other hand of his assailant seized his right wrist and elevated the muzzle of the gun. Dr Crane leaped forward and snatched away the weapon.

Meanwhile, however, Herman Fulton, taking advantage of the diversion, had sneaked up to the coffin, with drawn hunting-knife, which he now held poised aloft over Mary's breast.

'No you don't!' sang out Dan Callahan, whipping out his other gun. 'Back from that coffin, you dirty rat.'

Herman quickly obeyed.

Monsieur Larousse addressed the man who was holding Pop Morton. 'Ah, Higgins, you arrived just in time.'

The newcomer was his grey-uniformed chauffeur.

'Now, doctor,' announced Larousse, with a grin which revealed his white fangs, 'you have the two sane men for whom you wished, namely, myself and Higgins. And I have a little pistol of my own, so you are still one gun ahead. I suggest that you proceed with the resuscitation at once, before someone else tries to stop you. That old fool of a storekeeper nearly succeeded, you know.'

So saying, Larousse pulled out a pearl-handled thirty-two, and his chauffeur picked up the gat which Dan Callahan had dropped. Four well-armed and resolute men now surrounded the coffin and held the crowd at bay.

Herman Fulton felt his prestige rapidly evaporating. Something must be done to retrieve the situation!

'Just a minute,' he remonstrated, holding up his hand. 'Let's talk this thing out, like reasoning human beings. You don't look at all at ease in your own mind, Dr Crane, at having Dracula for an ally, so—'

'Dracula?' cut in Larousse. 'So *that's* what you've been reading! Bram Stoker, who wrote that infernal book as a mere bit of fiction, has a great deal of innocent blood on his head. I wonder how many superstitious mobs in back-wood communities have dug up the bodies of cataleptic sufferers and spiked their innocent lives away, since that damnable novel was written, instead of digging them up and resuscitating them!

'I speak with feeling,' he added. 'For some of the men in my club in Paris used to taunt me with the nick-name 'Dracula', because of my supposed resemblance to the hero — or rather, villain — of that story.'

'But you *are* a vampire, aren't you?' objected Herman.

'Certainly not!' replied the old man, a bit testily at last.

'Then who is buried in that coffin over in the Wilson lot, if it isn't yourself?'

'My father,' said Larousse with a touch of reverence in his voice.

'And who was your father?'

'Tom Wilson. Did any one here know him?'

There was a murmur of surprised assent from some of the older men, one of whom added the information, 'When Tommy was just a boy, he was run out of town for robbing the till at the feed store.'

'It's a lie!' shouted Larousse, his red eyes blazing in the lantern light. 'My father never robbed that till! He was falsely accused, and had to flee or go to jail. So he ran away to sea, and changed his name to Larousse — took the name of his ship captain. Finally he ended up in Paris, established a trading firm there, became very rich, and married. I was his only son. He had me educated at British and American universities. When he died — my mother having predeceased him — he left me his fortune, contingent on my burying him in his old home town, which he seemed to love in spite of the unfair way in which it had treated him — I don't know why I am telling you all this, for it certainly is none of your concern.'

Herman Fulton exclaimed under his breath, 'It's the gift of the gods! If we can keep that old bird talking until sunrise, we'll have him at our mercy.' So he asked aloud, 'But you don't live anywhere, and you come out only at night. Where do you sleep in the daytime, if not in that coffin?'

'As to my coming out only at night, it is because I suffer from tropical dermatitis—'

'I can vouch for that,' interjected Dr Crane. 'Tropical dermatitis is curable only if the sufferer keeps away from the ultra-violet rays of sunlight.'

'Aw, who cares for what the Doc says?' snorted some one in the crowd. 'He's in cahoots with Dracula, anyhow!'

'*I* care,' announced the calm voice of old Dr Porter. 'I know about that disease. If this gentleman has it, he is certainly wise to keep out of the sunlight. And, Dr Crane, I wouldn't be surprised if you were right about Mary, too. Give me your revolver, and I'll help guard the body, on my professional word of honour.'

10. The Showdown

The younger doctor handed over his gun without an instant's hesitation, and started to work on the unconscious form of Mary Morton, while Dr Porter, Larousse, Higgins and Dan Callahan guarded the coffin on four sides.

'You're licked, Herman!' asserted Dan triumphantly.

'Not yet,' muttered Fulton to himself, then aloud, 'We are willing to listen to your explanations, Mr Wilson, or Larousse, or whatever your name is. You have stated that some strange disease has made a night-prowler out of you. But where do you hole-up in the daytime? Answer me that.'

'Very simple,' replied the foreigner imperturbably. 'I stay with Miss Harriet Wilson, the old lady whom you call 'Aunt Hattie'; and she really *is* my aunt, a much younger sister of my father.'

The station agent now took a hand in the conversation.

'How do you explain all them little bats that hung around your coffin, the night we moved it for you?' he asked.

'Doubtless attracted by some of the embalming spices.'

'And that *large* bat?'

'I didn't see any large bat.'

'*You* wouldn't,' exclaimed the station agent triumphantly, 'for he was you yourself. Haw! Haw! Haw!'

'Any further questions?' inquired Larousse, ignoring this sally.

'Yes,' replied Herman Fulton, returning to the fray. 'Where have you been hiding ever since Mary Morton died?'

'Not that it's any concern of yours, but I happen to have been in Philadelphia, arranging for a fitting headstone for my father's grave,' explained the gentleman.

'That's right,' asserted the station agent; 'for, come to think of it, the waybills for a headstone came in today. That is they come in yesterday, for I suppose today is tomorrow by now.'

A few red steaks began to show in the eastern sky. Larousse at once became visibly agitated.

'Really, doctor,' he said. 'I hate to desert you at such a time. The dermatitis, you know. I must hurry away before it gets light. Here, take my revolver. You can keep it, and you can keep Higgins too, as long as you need them. I'd do anything for the sake of little Mary — except risk my damnable health.'

'I know,' sighed Dr Crane, looking up from his work, and accepting the proffered firearm.

'And *we* know, too,' sneered Herman Fulton. 'Follow him to the Wilson lot, some of you men, and watch him ooze into the grave with the first beams of the rising sun.'

'I think it would be safer, sir, for you to take your revolver with you,' asserted Dr Crane, handing back the pearl-handled thirty-two. 'When daylight comes, I am sure that Dr Porter and Dan and Higgins will be able to handle this bunch of fat-heads. Good-bye, and God bless you. I thank you for your help this night.'

'Good-bye,' replied Larousse. 'Higgins will bring me word of the little lady. Good-bye, you swine. You *chameaux!*'

It was the supreme French insult. Wrapping his cloak about him, he strode majestically away.

'To the Wilson lot! Follow him!' shouted Herman Fulton.

But that was not the path which the tall stranger took. Instead he walked resolutely down toward the road.

'Follow him!' shrieked Herman, 'Don't let him make his get-away! My God! Here we are trying to rid the world of a menace, and a nosy young doctor has to interfere and spoil it all. Come on. Never mind Mary. We must capture Dracula himself before he escapes us.'

Whereupon he and the whole crowd, with the fickleness characteristic of mobs, rushed headlong after the retreating figure.

'The master needs me!' exclaimed Higgins, and followed in the wake of the mob.

'You go too, Dan,' urged Ralph Crane. 'Dr Porter and I will be safe here, until those lynchers return.'

So Dan Callahan hurried after Higgins.

As the crowd neared Larousse, those in the lead picked up stones and began to throw them. One stone grazed the cloaked figure, now clearly discernible in the grey morning light. Instantly Larousse wheeled and faced his tormentors.

'None of that!' he shouted. 'I am a crack shot. I don't wish to fire at you, but I shall certainly do it if you make it necessary.'

'Arrr,' howled the mob, and let fly a shower of stones, several of which hit him squarely.

But he stood his ground. Instead of giving way, he raised his pearl-handled revolver and pointed it steadily at them.

'Aw, what do we care for toy pistols,' shouted one of the men, raising a stone aloft and preparing to hurl it.

'Crack!' went the tall stranger's little weapon. The stone clattered to the ground, as the man who had been about to hurl it clapped his left hand to his right wrist, from which the blood was spurting.

'I warned you that I was a crack shot,' repeated Larousse levelly, 'and I meant it. Raise another stone against me, and I swear I shall shoot to kill.'

Contemptuously he turned his back on them, and resumed his march to the road.

From a safe position in the rear of the mob, Herman Fulton urged, 'Don't let him get away! Throw a lot of rocks quick, before he can turn!'

Something hard and small and cylindrical poked Herman suddenly in the ribs from behind, and Dan Callahan's voice spoke in his ear, 'Quick! Tell them *not* to throw any rocks.'

Herman did so, promptly, in a trembling voice. Higgins dashed through the crowd to his master's side.

Said Herman, 'You'll be sorry for this, Callahan. No one ever bucks me in this town, and gets away with it. The mortgage on your garage is overdue.'

'Forget it!' exclaimed Dan jovially. 'When this gang finds out that you've made monkeys out of them tonight, I guess you won't be foreclosing any mortgages around here for quite a while. You may *control* a majority of the stock in the bank, but you don't *own* it. And Dr Porter, your largest stockholder, is on *our* side now. Put that in your pipe and smoke it!'

'Oh, Dan,' wailed Herman, 'can't you see what you're doing? We're trying to rid the world of a menace, and you and that half-witted doctor —'

The revolver bored dangerously into his ribs.

'One more wise-crack out of you, you skunk,' announced Dan, 'and I'll be making the world safe for mortgages.'

Meanwhile Larousse and his chauffeur Higgins had reached their parked car, closely followed by the threatening mob. Then, while Higgins stood them off, his employer climbed into the driver's seat, and started down the road, Higgins jumping to the running-board as he departed.

Herman Fulton was about to wail again, but a sharp jab in the ribs from Callahan's revolver kept him quiet.

Several others of the mob, however, hastened to their own cars, and soon were off down the road in pursuit of Larousse. It was now daylight, with the rim of the sun just showing above the tops of the eastern hills.

'Back to Mary's grave!' shouted someone, whereupon the rest of the mob wheeled, and started back across the cemetery.

'None of that!' shouted Callahan, standing in their path with levelled revolver.

The spirit of the mob collapsed. They gazed sheepishly at each other. It was daylight now, broad daylight. The anonymity of the night was at an end. The darkness had covered them like the mask and robe of the Ku Klux Klan, but now they stood exposed and undisguised.

It isn't exactly a dignified performance for a lot of leading businessmen, and church elders, and bank directors, and coal miners, and what-not, of a conservative Republican community, however benighted and backwoodsy it may be, to dig up a body in a churchyard in the dead of night. And being caught still at it in broad daylight is even worse. They were ashamed of themselves and of each other.

In the midst of their confusion, young Dr Crane and old Dr Porter, standing by the coffin, beckoned to them, and then advanced to meet them, Crane holding his revolver again.

'She is alive,' announced the older man, 'but she is very weak. At present she is asleep. We must carry her back to town at once, and have a blood-transfusion.'

'She called your name, Herman,' added Dr Crane, grimly. 'It was the first thing she said when she came to.'

Herman appeared visibly shaken at this announcement. Also his faith in the weird ideas gleaned from his reading was somewhat shaken as well.

'I'll call a truce,' said he. 'It's now daylight. The vampire, if she *is* a vampire, is at our mercy until sunset. We can lose nothing by giving in temporarily to the two doctors.'

'If my daughter is really alive,' began Pop Morton emphatically. And then suddenly he remembered the mortgage on his stock of goods, and became quiet again.

Ralph Crane replied to Herman Fulton's offer. Said he, toying with his gun, 'We accept your truce, but with reservations. We are armed and we intend to stay armed until we see this thing through. We've been handed treachery before by you folks, and so we are taking no chances. Mary is very weak; she must be moved immediately, but quietly. The coffin and the hearse — gruesome as it sounds — will be the best way to move her. So I want six — ah — *un*-pallbearers, one might say,' he laughed grimly, 'to assist. Fulton and Morton — the job will keep you two out of mischief — Crocker, Warren, Crosby and Banks.' He named the last four at random. 'The rest of you lunatics keep out of the way, and heaven help you if you interfere. Come on, you six, and the undertaker.'

So saying, he led the way back to the grave. It was a nerve-racking experience for the six 'un-pallbearers.' They had served at funerals before, all of them, and had thought nothing of it; had even jested, sedately, on such occasions, across the body. But never before had they spent an entire night in exhuming a corpse, only to carry it back to town with them — either alive or 'undead' — whichever it was — in the morning.

It seemed for all the world, as though their actions were actually being run backward, like a trick motion-picture film. But it was their dread of ridicule that worried them, rather than any dread of the supernatural. Broad daylight had arrived, and their antics of the preceding night now seemed preposterous to them. They felt uneasy and conspicuous.

These men, who had been game to dig up a poor girl's body, drive a stake through her heart, cut off her head, and stuff her mouth full of garlic, now balked at the mere task of carrying her back to life again! But they had no choice in the matter. Dr Crane and his supporters held the revolvers.

Without mishap, they got the coffin onto the hearse, which happened to be there merely because it was the undertaker's only means of personal conveyance. The rest of the mob rapidly and sheepishly disintegrated, all except Herman Fulton and one or two others, whose mortgages were the most hopelessly overdue.

Just as they were about to start for town, an automobile drew up, driven by one of the men who had pursued 'Dracula.'

He reported to Herman, 'We followed the old boy to Aunt Hattie's cottage. By the time we got there, he was inside, and his chauffeur was on guard at the door with a gat in his hand. Our crowd just plain got cold feet, and went home. So I came back to report to you.'

'But are you sure that Dracula is still inside Aunt Hattie's house?' asked Herman Fulton eagerly.

11. A New Victim

'N-no,' admitted the other, 'but he must be, for his chauffeur and his car are there.'

'Then he probably has a coffin at the cottage, as well as in the grave in the Wilson lot,' assured Herman positively; 'for vampires always have to sleep in coffins in the daytime. Well, he's safe for the present. Let's get Mary's body back to town, and see how *that* turns out. Then we can tend to the old boy later in the day.'

His mind still failed to grasp the fact that his little lynching-bee was over, at least for the present.

So the hearse started toward town. Dan Callahan, with drawn revolver, sat on the seat beside the undertaker. The two doctors rode in the rear with the coffin, Crane still holding his revolver. Herman Fulton followed in his own car at a safe distance. Also the six un-pallbearers.

The return to town was uneventful, and in a few minutes the hearse drew up at the Morton residence. The un-pallbearers came forward, the coffin was carried in, and the pale sleeping form of Mary Morton was lifted out and transferred to her bed. She was pale now because at the grave the two doctors had washed off her rouge, so as to be able to observe her true colour.

Then Dr Porter got the village nurse on the phone, she arrived with a lot of paraphernalia, and preparations were made for an immediate blood-transfusion.

Dr Crane, Pop Morton and Dan Callahan were each tested as a possible donor, but their bloods all gave the wrong reaction.

'Herman,' announced old Dr Porter, 'you are elected for the next test.'

Herman Fulton turned pale.

'But I read in that book,' he stammered, 'that an interchange of blood with a vampire will tie a person to the vampire forever. Oh, Dr Porter, please don't! If I give Mary some of my blood, and then she dies, it will mean that I must look forward all my life to being a vampire myself when I finally die!'

'Rubbish!' exclaimed Dr Porter, impatiently.

'Can't you use a salt and glucose solution?' Herman persisted. 'I've read somewhere that it's just as good as real blood for transfusions.'

'You read altogether too much!' snorted the old doctor. 'Saline solution is no good in anaemia. What she needs is red blood corpuscles, and she needs them in a hurry.'

'The trouble with Herman is that he's a highbrow,' added Dan. 'He's educated beyond his intelligence.'

'Herman,' said Pop Morton levelly, 'you are engaged to my daughter. Didn't you say something, up at the grave, about your having the first right to save her? Well, now's your chance, and if you don't take it, the engagement is off, mortgage or no mortgage!'

During Pop's remarks, Fulton had been getting all ready to mention the mortgage, but now Pop had got in ahead of him. Fulton squirmed visibly.

'Well,' said he finally, 'go ahead and make the test. Maybe *my* blood won't be the right kind either.'

But, alas for Herman, his blood turned out to be in exactly the same class as Mary's. He paled again.

'It's murder!' he screamed. 'It's worse than murder!'

But his captors were inexorable. While Dr Crane held a pistol to his head Dan Callahan, grinning broadly, forced him into a chair and strapped him down.

'There's one comfort, Herman,' said Dan: 'if you turn into a vampire when you die it will give me great pleasure to drive a stake through your filthy heart, and cut off your head, and stuff your mouth full of vegetables. Then think how happy you'll be! I believe you yourself got off some such pious sentiment about little Mary. We want you to be happy, Herman dear, the same as you wanted Mary to be.'

'This is no joking matter,' Fulton blubbered.

'Now, now, Herman,' soothed the Irishman, 'shall we gag you, or will you keep quiet?'

'Don't gag him,' objected Dr Crane. 'It might startle Mary. In fact we'd better even untie him. You stand out of Mary's sight, Dan, and cover him with your gun. If he let's out a yip, you shoot. I mean it, Herman, for I'm just about fed up with you.'

Then he and Dan carried their trussed-up victim, white but silent, into the sickroom, where they untied him. In another moment, two arms were antisepticised, and soon the blood was flowing from Herman Fulton's forearm through a little rubber tube into Mary Morton's.

Herman watched the performance like one hypnotised. He saw Mary's colour return, as she fed upon his life-blood. All his worst fears had come to pass. This vampire, whom he had set out to slay, the evening before, was now feasting upon him; but, instead of perching on his body with two sharp white teeth piercing his throat, she was lying luxuriously in bed, while two up-to-date doctors were doing all the work of the transfusion. What a strange modernising of mediæval superstition! Herman even felt himself under the influence of that lethargic stupor which − from his reading − he well knew that vampires are able to produce in their victims.

Meanwhile several of Herman's staunchest henchmen gathered outside.

Old Dr Porter viewed them from the window of the sickroom; then turning back, he announced, 'We're not out of the woods yet. In addition to all the trouble we're having with our patient, the mob may get up its courage again before we are through.'

'Sh,' admonished the younger doctor. 'Mary is coming out of her trance again.'

As Herman grew weaker and weaker, the flush of health gradually spread over Mary's features. She stirred in the bed, and opened her eyes.

'Herman,' she breathed, 'where am I? I had a most awful dream. I dreamed that I was dead and burried, and that you came and dug me up. What's this on my arm? And all these doctors and a nurse! What's it all about, father?'

But Dr Porter, admonishing the others to silence, said: 'You've been very sick, Mary. But we've given you a blood-transfusion, and you're all right now.'

'Herman, dear,' said the girl, as she turned a beatific smile toward her fiancé, 'you gave your blood to save my life. I remember calling for you in my dream. I left the grave, and came and stood by your bed, and begged you to help me. You seemed frightened or horrified then; I could not tell which. But you *did* come. You love me very much, dear, don't you?'

Fulton hung his head in shame, and said nothing.

Dr Porter announced bruskly, 'The patient must have absolute rest for a while. Every one, except the nurse, must go now — even the beloved Herman.'

Fulton glowered at him, but obediently left the room with the others, Mary's trusting glance lingering on him as he went.

As soon as he was outside, the old doctor whispered to him, 'You'd better get to bed, Herman. You're a very weak man, just now.'

'You can go right to bed here in our spare room,' offered Mary's father, hospitably.

To which Dr Crane added, 'Fine! Then we can keep our eyes on him.'

Herman, however, needed no surveillance. He was weak and shaken. He was through — at least for the present. So far as he was concerned, old Dracula could go to the devil! Herman himself wanted to go to bed. So he did.

But Herman Fulton was not permanently defeated. He had merely suffered a temporary setback. He was merely weak from loss of blood. But he was still president of the Yankton Bank. He still held most of the overdue mortgages in town. He was still engaged to Mary Morton. And she still adoringly regarded him as her rescuer.

12. The Denouement

By evening, Herman Fulton had completely recovered his poise. Whatever might be his future plans for combating the Dracula menace, he realised that for the present it would pay him to dissemble, and to try and make friends with the enemy.

So he warmly, and with apparent sincerity, urged Ralph Crane to return to his Yankton practice. But the young doctor declined. He could not bear to stay and see his Mary, whose life he himself had saved, happily give herself in marriage to the man who had tried to kill her.

'Herman,' said he, after refusing the other's offer, 'for once you can put your fiendish mortgage-system to a good use. Let it be known by every participant of last night's attempted outrage, that if the least hint of it ever reaches Miss Morton's ears, you will run the person responsible out of town.'

Just then Peter Larousse was announced. He had come to inquire as to the health of the patient. The two doctors reported that Mary was already greatly improved under the new line of treatment, based on Dr Crane's diagnosis.

Then Herman asked a bit apprehensively what Larousse's plans were.

'You will be relieved to know,' the old man replied with dignity, 'that I am at once shaking the dust of this town off my feet forever. How my father could ever have felt any affection for Yankton, is beyond my comprehension. But I have carried out his wishes, and have buried him here.

> Here he lies where he longed to be,
> Home is the sailor, home from the sea,
> And the hunter home from the hill.

'But, as for me,' Larousse continued, 'I am moving tonight back to civilization. Dr Crane, I am going to accept your offer, made when I first came here, to treat my dermatitis. I shall put up at your hospital in New York. You have won my respect. And there are two other people in this town who are deserving of respect, namely, Miss Morton and the taxi-man. I still mistrust you, Mr Fulton, for a dangerous idiot. So I shall instruct my solicitors to pay off the Callahan and Morton mortgages.'

'God bless you, sir; you're a brick!' exclaimed the young Irishman.

'Why — why — why,' stammered Pop Morton. 'Why, it'll put me on my feet for the first time in years! You can't realise what it means to me, Mr Dracula — uh, I mean, Mr Larousse.'

Herman Fulton looked daggers at this man who had dared to free two victims from his clutches.

Larousse continued, 'Dr Porter, I hope that you will use your bank-stock to curb Mr Fulton's impetuosity. And of course, I assume that Miss Morton has broken, or will break, her engagement?'

'Unfortunately no,' replied Dr Crane bitterly. 'She credits her fiancé with last night's rescue.'

Herman hung his head.

'And you don't propose to disillusion her?' asked Larousse in surprise.

'Why should I?' countered Crane. 'She loves Herman, so it would be best for her never to know the truth.'

'Doctor Crane,' remonstrated Dan Callahan, 'if you'll excuse my impertinence, I think you're all wet. You've got Herman by the tail now, so why not give it a twist? If I were you, sir, I'd tell Miss Morton all the facts. Begging your pardon, sir, but she loves you, and you love her, and she's only marrying that skunk out of loyalty and mistaken gratitude.'

'What?' exclaimed Herman Fulton and Pop Morton in unison.

The young doctor coloured.

'No, no, Dan,' he remonstrated, 'you are mistaken. Miss Morton and I are merely warm friends; that is all. If there is even any suspicion of anything else, it is just as well that I am leaving town for good.'

'Yes, I agree with you,' interposed Herman, a bit too enthusiastically.

Dr Crane glowered at him.

Dan Callahan snorted with disgust.

'I'm beginning to think,' he averred, 'that there's only two people in this town that ain't crazy; me and Mr Larousse. Thank you again, Mr Larousse, for fixing up my mortgage so that I can stay right in Yankton and make Herman Fulton watch his step. I'll pay you back some day, sir. And as for you, Doctor Crane, I hope you'll come to your senses before it's too late. So long, everybody.'

And he stalked out.

Pop Morton, Monsieur Larousse, Herman Fulton, and the two doctors tried to keep up conversation for a while, but at last it lagged. Every one except 'old Dracula' felt tense and embarrassed.

At last Dr Crane remarked, 'Well, it's almost time for the night train east. If Doctor Porter doesn't mind, I think I'll go upstairs and say good-bye to Mary.'

The older doctor nodded, and young Crane passed from the room.

He found the nurse standing by Miss Morton's door with an amused smile on her face. She opened the door for him, but discreetly remained outside.

Mary was sitting up in bed, pale but smiling. Crane advanced toward her eagerly.

And then he noticed that they were not alone.

'What on earth are *you* doing here, Callahan?' he demanded, coming to a halt.

But it was Mary who answered.

'He's been telling me the truth, Ralph,' said she. 'Oh, Ralph, you poor dear silly noble-minded old darling! Why did you want me to marry a superstitious moron, who tried to kill me, instead of yourself, who saved my life? Ralph, dear, I've loved you ever since you came to town, but I haven't realised it until right now.'

And she held out her arms to the astonished young doctor.

'Take it or leave it, Doc,' said Dan Callahan, with a grin, as he walked out of the room.

And Dr Crane took it.

IX

At Last

The closing years of Bram Stoker's life were a sad anti-climax after the acclaim of *Dracula*. His health continued to deteriorate, and then the sudden death of Sir Henry Irving in October 1905 left him so bereft that he suffered a stroke — another contributing factor to this no doubt being the strain his job had brought upon him. For several months he was unable to work, and then as he did recover he fell back on his writing once more. To answer the many misleading versions of Irving's life that had tumbled from the presses immediately after the famous actor's death, Bram wrote the definitive biography, *Personal Reminiscences of Henry Irving* (1906) which remains to this day the most informative and perceptive work on the man, written as it was by someone who had been close to him over all the most important years of his life.

In the time which followed, Stoker occupied himself with further books, two frankly undistinguished novels, *The Gates of Life* (1908), *Lady Athlyne* (1908), a collection of factual essays on *Famous Impostors* (1910), as well as the two novels vaguely related to the vampire theme which I have already mentioned. He also undertook the occasional assignment for newspapers and conducted interesting interviews with Sir Arthur Conan Doyle and H. G. Wells for *The Daily Chronicle*. Bram still produced the occasional short story, basing these very largely on his holidays in Scotland (*vide* 'Crooken Sands' and 'The Secret of the Growing Gold', both to be found in Florence Stoker's collection) or else based on some vivid personal experience from his working life.

In this later category can be placed 'At Last' which was inspired by events in the winter of 1903–4 while he was with Sir
Henry Irving on what was to be their final tour of America.
Much of the travelling was done by railway, and Bram had the
idea of a collection of inter-linked stories told by a group of
travellers on a train. The possibilities of this idea can be seen
from what he wrote in his biography of Irving: 'At a rough com-
putation, the railroad journeys of Irving's tours ran over fifty
thousand miles – more than twice round the Equator. The
journeys were nearly always taken in special trains running at all
sorts of hours, and almost invariably in the bad seasons of the
year. It is not to be wondered at, therefore, that we had a
certain percentage of accidents.'

On this particular American tour, in January 1904, the Irving
company was beset by a terrible snowstorm which blanketed
much of America and made their journey across the mid-West
particularly difficult. 'The cold was intense,' Bram wrote afterwards. 'There were ten feet of snow lying on the hills, and down
the serpentine valley our driving wheel got "frosted" and flew to
pieces. Fortunately, we were on a stretch of level ground. Down
the valley are, here and there, remains of train wrecks on the
bank of the river.' As Bram fretted about the delays which made
keeping to their schedule almost impossible, he found a little
relaxation in writing the following grim little story which he sold
a few weeks later to *Collier's Magazine* when he was in New
York. (Five years later, in 1908, the book which Bram had
planned finally materialised under the title, *Snowbound*.)
Though the tale is somewhat removed from the style of *Dracula*,
it does show yet again his mastery of horror, and at the same
time an insight into human emotions which makes it one of the
most moving stories ever to have come from his pen . . .

At Last

'When I was young – I'm not very old yet, but I was very young
then, and it all seems long ago – I made an ass of myself. It
wasn't very bad, not criminal; but I was pretty well ashamed of
it, for my people were of high rank and held a great position in

the county. When I came back I was afraid to tell the girl I was engaged to. She was a clever girl, and she knew by a sort of instinct that there was *something*, and asked me what it was. I denied that there was anything. That did for me, for I knew she was clean grit, and that she would have the truth or nothing, and as I didn't want to tell her I was a liar as well as an ass, I shoved for Australia. What I did there doesn't concern you much, and it was pretty tame, anyhow. I only mention this that you may understand something later. I had been a medical student, and liked the work so well that I have had a sneaking fondness for everything connected with it ever since. On the ship I went out on was a nurse, who was going out as an assistant matron to one of the Melbourne hospitals. She was a young woman, but with white hair; and she used to come down to the steerage — where I was — and try to be of service. I had become a kind of volunteer help to the doctor, who recognised that I *had been* a gentleman — you *are* not much of a gentleman in a steerage, I can tell you — and made things a little comfortable for me in several ways.

'By being about with him I met the nurse, and we became very good friends. She was very sympathetic, and knew pretty well that I was sore-hearted about something; and with the natural sweet helpfulness of a woman — God bless 'em! — soon got to know my secret. One night — I shall never forget it, a heavy, still night with the moon a blaze of gold over the silent sea — we sat out late, right over the screw, which ground away beneath us but disturbed us no more than the ticking of a clock. The mystery of the place, and the hunger for sympathy which always gnawed at my soul, got the better of me, and I opened my heart as I have never done before or since. When I stopped I saw that her great eyes were gleaming out over the sea, and the tears were rolling down her cheeks. She turned to me and took my hand between both of hers and said:

'"Oh! why didn't you tell her all? She would have forgiven all — everything, and would have loved you better for it all your life long. It is the concealment that hurts! Noble natures feel it most. I know, I know it too well, out of the bitterness of my broken heart!" I saw here a sorrow far greater than my own, and tried to comfort her. It seemed a relief to her, as it had been to me, to speak of her trouble, and I encouraged her confidence. She told me that in her youth she had run away with a man whom she thought she loved; they were married at a registry, but after a while she found out that he was married already. She wanted to leave him then at once, but he terrorised her, threatening to kill her if she tried to leave him. So she had perforce to remain with him till, happily, he met with a fatal accident and she was free. Then her baby was born dead, and she found herself alone.

'She changed her name, and after trying work of several kinds, found her way on the stage. There she fell in love, in real love, with a man she honoured; and when she found that he loved her too, she was afraid to tell him the dark chapter of her life lest she should lose him. She thought that as it was all past, and as no trace remained, no one need ever know. She was married and was ideally happy, and, after a couple of years, which had brought them a daughter, towards the end of a certain tour was on her way home where she would see her little baby daughter again, when in a time of great peril, when everyone round her was making confession of all they had ever done wrong, she was drawn into the hysterical whirlpool, and told her husband all that had been. He seemed cut to the heart, but said very little — not a word of reproach. Then she, too, felt constrained to silence, and a barrier seemed to grow up between them, so that when they reached England — home was a name only, and not a reality — they did not seem able to speak freely; and it became apparent to both that nothing remained but to separate. He had wished to take the child, and when the subject was mooted, said he wanted to take her far away where she would never know what had been. "Oh, I loved him so," she wailed, "that I felt that all I could give him was my child. The baby when she grew up would never know her mother's shame. It was a bitter atonement for my deceit; but it was all I could do. Perhaps God will account it to me and my child and the husband that I love, and somehow turn it to usefulness in His good time."

'Well, I comforted her as well as I could, though there was not much comfort to her in the world, poor soul, separated from her husband, whom she still loved, and from their child. We became fast friends, and we often wrote to each other; and in all my wanderings I kept her informed of my whereabouts.

'I went up-country herding, and after a weary, weary time on

'The bitter road the younger son must tread
Ere he win to hearth and saddle of his own,
Mid the riot of the shearers in the shed
In the silence of the herder's hut alone,'

I found my way to a lonely place on the edge of a creek. It was a lovely spot, and the man who owned it had evidently given time and care to its beautifying, for all the natural trees and flowers were used to the best advantage, and it was a delight to see growing with the added luxuriance of a new soil all the home flowers as well. My employer, Mr Macrae, was a crank in some ways, but he was a gentleman, and he made my life a very different one from what it had been in my stock-keeping apprenticeship. He, too, soon recognised that I had been a gentleman, and took me into the house instead of letting me camp outside in a rough shed, as is the usual thing with hired hands. Oh! the comfort and luxury of being in a real house with real bedding and real food, after a bunk and damper of your own making.

'Mr Macrae was very kindly, but stern on certain points. He simply idolised his little daughter, a bright, pretty child with golden hair and big grey eyes that I seemed, when I saw them, to have known all my life. The sun seemed to the father to rise and set in the child; but even to her he could be stern, even cruel, to an extent I never saw equalled.

'One night after dinner the little thing was nestling up to him and playing with him in her usual coaxing way. He asked her some little question, and she fenced with the answer. This seemed all at once to make him stern, and he asked some more questions with a fierce gravity which frightened the child. She attempted playfulness as a weapon against wrath, as a woman does; but the father would have none of it. He brushed it aside and continued his inquisition. It was quite apparent to me that the child had little or nothing to conceal, but she was frightened, and in her fear yielded to the weakness of the woman within her and lied. It was a harmless little lie at worst, one rather of not telling the truth than of speaking falsely; but it seemed to inflame the father to a white heat. His eyes glowed with the intensity of his anger. He mastered himself, however, and his cold anger was infinitely worse than his hot. He took the child very tenderly in his arms and said:

'"Little one, you know that I love you?"

'"Yes, daddy!" came the pretty voice, in a flood of tears.

'"And you know I wouldn't hurt you but for your good, darling?"

'"Yes, daddy! But, oh, daddy, daddy, don't hurt me! — don't hurt me!"

'"I must, my little one, I must! You will have to remember all your life what it is to lie; that fire on earth or in hell is the liar's portion. And it is better that you learn it now than suffer it hereafter and make others suffer!" He bent down towards the fire, holding her hand in his; her pitiful little struggles were as nothing in his powerful grasp. Seeing me instinctively draw near, for I thought to protect the child, he motioned me back gravely.

'"Do not interfere. It is necessary that my child learn a little lesson to save her a harder one later on."

'With an iron determination, and with lips set and growing white as snow, he put for a moment the rosy fingers of the child on the hot bar of the grate. Despite her shriek of pain, he held it there quite a second or two, and then drew her back almost fainting. The child loved and trusted him in spite of the cruel act, and clung to him, sobbing as if her little heart would break. He held her close to him, and then disengaged her arm very gently from his neck. He stepped closer to the fire, and saying to her: "See, little one, you have no pain that is not mine!" thrust his own right hand down into the very heart of the glowing fire. He held it there a few seconds without a quiver, whilst the child shrieked and flew to him and dragged the hand away.

'"Oh, daddy, daddy, daddy!" she wailed, "and I have by my lying made you suffer this!" As I am a living man, I saw a glad light flash into his eyes, though the pain he suffered must have been excruciating. With his other hand he stroked the child's golden locks as he said:

'"It was worth pain, my little one, that you should learn so great a truth."

'I could not but be silent in face of such a splendid heroism, and offered to use such medical knowledge as I possessed on his behalf. He accepted cheerfully, and when I had got oil and lint he made me dress the child's burn before allowing me to attend to his own. It was a bad burn, and I was in real fear that it might have an ill ending. He made light of it, however, and tried to keep up the child's spirits. I tried to help him, and she went to bed less unhappy than I expected. Macrae's strength and constitution stood to him, and, although the hand was badly scarred, he fully recovered its use.

'That night he was so feverish that I insisted on sitting up with him. I was able to give him some ease, and he was grateful for it. He talked with me more freely than he had ever done. He insisted on going several times to see how the child slept. He came back after one of these visits with his eyes wet, and as he lay down on his bed said softly:

'"Poor little mite! God forgive me if I was wrong; but I thought it best!' Then turning to me, he went on:

'"I suppose you thought me not merely brutal, but fiendish. But if you knew how deeply for her own future happiness I value truth, you would perhaps be tolerant with me. It was a lie that ruined her mother's life and my own; and I would guard her against such an evil. Her mother and I loved each other, and there seemed no flaw in our lives; but once when in danger of death as we were rushing through a seething flood, she confessed to me that the innocence which had charmed me at the first was but an acted lie; that she had loved another man before she had seen me, and had lived with him guiltily. But, there! that page of my life is closed for ever." He said no more, and, of course, I never referred to the subject again. It struck me afterwards as strange that two people whom I had met had each suffered from a similar cause − as I myself had suffered − but it never struck me to connect them.

'After that night we became better friends, for we seemed to understand each other. I grew to love the child almost as much as if she had been my own daughter. During all that time I worked hard, and had few distractions; but I promised myself a treat when I should go over to Warrow, the nearest town beyond the Creek, for I had heard from Nurse Dora that she had become matron of the hospital there. The time which I had promised myself for my holiday was at hand, when little Dora fell ill of a fever. The white woman who was with us got it at the same time, and Macrae and I had to do the nursing ourselves. The floods were out, and the Creek was like a sea; the natives, seeing a fever in the house, ran away. It was a quick fever, though a low one, and in a few days the woman died. The child got worse and worse, and her moaning was pitiful to hear. The father used to sit hour after hour with his head in his hands and groan.

'One evening I heard him say that if we had a woman to nurse her she might be saved; and this gave me an idea. I said nothing except that I was going out for a bit, for my mind was made up that I would try to fetch my friend the matron. I took my mare, Wild Meg, and swam the flooded Creek; and early in the morning, riding for all I was worth, fetched up at Warrow. I went to the hospital and asked for the matron. When she came my heart leaped, and something within me seemed to cry out. It was though two ends of an electric current were come together. Little Dora's fever-wasted face, as I had seen it the night before on the pillow, was reproduced in the pale lineaments of her who stood before me. I understood it all now. The man with the story; the woman with the story; the child parted from the mother; and mother who lied! Heaven had sent at the moment me, who, coming across the world, held in his hand the two ends of this chain of destiny. I told her of the child who was ill, dying; she wept, but said her duty held her to her post. Then I described the child and the solitary man, and a quick light leaped to her eyes. Hope had dawned in that withered heart! She said not a word, but with a gesture to me to wait, disappeared behind the hospital. In a minute she reappeared, leading by the bridle a magnificent roan horse.

'"Come!" she said, and sprang to the saddle.

'We rode all day without a word. Late in the afternoon we struck the creek, just as a thunderstorm came on, which in a moment lashed the flood into a raging torrent. But nothing daunted her. She rode boldly into the water, I following, and together we battled the watery element. Through danger and toil we won the further shore, though our two gallant steeds fell dead within sight of the house. We hurried in, she leading,

I following. When she stood in the doorway Macrae rose to his feet with a wild cry:

'"Dora, Dora, my darling, come at last! Now the child must live!' Then he fell fainting on the floor.'

Dracula's Guest

by

Bram Stoker

250TH LONDON PERFORMANCE OF "Dracula"

PRINCE OF WALES' THEATRE SOUVENIR EDITION 1927

X

In the Valley of the Shadow

As I mentioned in my Introduction, Bram Stoker spent what were to be his last days planning three collections of short stories — of which only one was to come anywhere near completion and be ultimately published posthumously by his widow. Bram was a tired and sick man as the first decade of the twentieth century drew to a close, and despite the continuing popularity of *Dracula*, he was still hard pressed financially. In the autumn of 1911 he paid another visit to Cruden Bay where his spirits were briefly restored, but a long and hard winter followed. By the spring of 1912 he was virtually bed-ridden as his remaining strength departed from his once powerful body. On the evening of 22 April 1912, as he lay in bed racked by the pain that had been slowly devouring him for the last six years, he gave a sudden start and without another word fell back against the pillows. He was sixty-four years old, and when the doctor came to write the certificate of cause of death he wrote one simple yet devastating word, 'exhaustion'.

Among the stories that lay beside his bed awaiting a place in his collections was 'In The Valley Of The Shadow' which had appeared in *The Grand Magazine*, July 1907. Ostensibly the account of a man's impressions while suffering from delirium, it was doubtless inspired by his own suffering and might well have formed the closing chapter of any biography. The end of the road had come for Bram that April evening: but for the character he had created, the vampire Count Dracula, a still greater and more enduring fame awaited. A fame that was to outshine anything he — or even the actor he had so selflessly dedicated himself to, Sir Henry Irving – might have dreamed of . . .

In the Valley of the Shadow

The rubber-tyred wheels jolt unevenly over the granite setts. Dimly I recognise the familiar grey streets and garden-centred squares.

We stop, and through the little crowd on the pavement I am carried indoors and up to the high-ceiling ward. Gently they lift me off the stretcher and put me in bed, and I say:

'What queer curtains you have! They have faces worked on the border. Are they those of your friends?'

The matron smiles, and I think what a quaint idea it is. Then suddenly it strikes me that I have said something foolish, but still the faces are there right enough. (Even when I got well I could sometimes see them in certain lights.)

One of the faces is familiar, and I am just going to ask how they know So-and-so, when I am left alone.

For hours and hours (it seems) no one comes near me. At first I am patient, but gradually a fierce anger seizes me. Did I submit to be brought here merely to die in solitude and in suffocating darkness? I will not stay in this place; far better to go back and die at home!

Suddenly I am borne in a winged machine up, up into the cool air. Far below and infinitesimally small lies the 'New Town,' half-hid beneath the fluffy smoke; yonder, clear and blue and glittering, is the Firth of Forth; and beyond the sunlit hills of Fife are the advance-guards of the Grampians. A moment only of sheer palpitating ecstasy, then a soul-shattering fall into the black abyss of oblivion. (I hold Mr H. G. Wells partially responsible for this little excursion.)

It is light again, but what is that which prevents my seeing the window? A screen? What does that betoken?

A blackness of despair grips me. It is all over, then! No more mountaineering, no more pleasant holidays. This is the end of all my little ambitions. This is, in truth, the bitterness of death.

Presently a nurse comes with a cooling drink, and, making a tremendous effort to look unconcerned, I ask for the screen to be removed. She laughs and folds it up, when I see another screen opposite partially concealing a bed. So I have company. (This was a comparatively lucid interval.)

What a queer place to have texts! Right round the cornice of the room. And they are constantly changing too. 'The Lord is my Shepherd—' 'I will arise—' Really this is most irritating. I cannot finish any of them. If the letters would only stay still for a single moment!

But what is that below? It is a wide sandy beach with the blue sea beyond. On the top of a pole in the foreground is a — what is it? — yes, a man's head, of course. (It was really a hanging electric light which by some curious means I must have seen in an inverted position.)

'Sister, I am sure that could be worked up into a splendid story. Please give me some paper and my fountain pen. If I don't write it down now I shall forget it, just as has happened before when I have thought of things during the night.' (As a matter of fact, when, I was convalescent I did want to write not only this particular tale, but a complete account of my visions. Of course, I was not permitted, and now, alas! it has gone to join that great company of magnificent — seeming but elusive ideas one has in dreams.)

'Honestly, Sister, I must go out for a few moments. The man is in great danger, and I alone can save him. There is a desperate plot against his life. He lives quite close by in one of the two houses on each side of this.'

Sister promises to see about this, and I lie back only half-satisfied.

Presently my bed begins noiselessly to move. It goes through the wall into the next house. Room after room is visited, but my doomed friend is not there. The other houses are then inspected in turn, with no result. I have a feeling that he is being spirited away just in front of me so as to be always in the *next* house. Sister is at the bottom of this trick, I am sure. (Here began that absurd hatred and suspicion of her which only left me with the delirium.)

'Oh, doctor, I *am* glad to see you! Really in a free country it is intolerable that a simple request like this cannot be granted me, and to save a man's life, too. You can see for yourself that I am quite sensible and very much in earnest. Try me.'

The doctor asks what day of the week it is. I answer, Scots fashion:

'Oh, that's easy! If I am the man who came here on Monday, then it is Wednesday, but if I came on Thursday, then it's Saturday. If you will tell me which man I am, I will tell you what day it is.'

Overcome by this logic, the doctor gives in, but suggests a compromise, to which I agree. It is that the four neighbouring houses be brought in and placed before my bed, so that I can make sure of seeing and warning my friend in distress.

'No, I will not drink whisky. Surely you know perfectly well that I am a Mussulman and forbidden to drink spirits? You cannot wish me to violate the principles of my religion?'

Sister assures me that the draught is not whisky, and puts the glass to my lips.

In horror I dash it to the floor.

'Devil in human form, you tempt me to my destruction. Begone and let me die in the true faith.' (Of course it was not whisky, but something of quite an opposite nature. Weeks later, on recounting this incident, I was reminded of having one day casually read a page or two of a novel in which a Mohammedan is tempted to drink wine. It made no impression whatever at the time, but it must have been stored up somewhere.)

Presently Sister returns with three other nurses and a fresh supply of the accursed stuff. All means are tried, from argument, in which they are signally worsted, to persuasion and gentle force.

Suddenly I resolve on flight, and actually reach the door of the room before being overpowered and brought back to bed. Then I am asked to put my finger in the dose and prove to myself that it is not whisky. In this suggestion I see Sister's malicious cunning, so I smell the wet finger, and triumphantly assert that it *is* whisky.

When they say it is twelve o'clock, and that I am keeping them all out of bed, I answer that they need not stay for me, and, anyway, what is that to the loss of my soul?

At length I am forced down, and the glass put to my clenched teeth. I pray inwardly for help in this dire extremity. Lo! a brilliant idea. I will pretend to be dead. I stiffen myself and hold my breath. (I can remember no further effort, but I was told afterwards the imitation was wonderful. Even the nurses grew alarmed, and the doctor was sent for. I have a dim recollection of his coming, and before I knew where I was he had injected something, which I thought was the whisky, into my arm.)

I sit up in bed, and glare at them all with concentrated hatred, then I fall back, heartbroken at my forced abjuration, sobbing, sobbing.

I am suffering for my sin. Sister is stabbing me in the shoulder-blade with a red-hot dagger. (It was a fly-blister, and my skin is very sensitive.) I am aching all over.

Suddenly I am alone on a flat desert plain. I am sitting with my back against one of the stone pillars of a huge closed gateway reaching to the sky. In front of me is proceeding a cinematographic entertainment on a stupendous scale. (I cannot now remember much about it, but the series was long and of an appalling character. Below each picture was a placard stating the subject of the *next* one. I had the feeling that they were not pictures at all, but real events in the process of happening; further that by answering a question put to me by a mysterious voice I could bring the series to an end, but, though I knew the answer, it was quite beyond my power to give it. Immediately following my failure to reply, from somewhere behind me a full organ pealed forth and a choir of voices broke into a mocking ditty, which embodied the proper answer, and also words of scorn directed against myself. Till recently this ditty haunted me occasionally, but I have now, I am glad to say, forgotten both air and words. All I know is that it was like a quick chant, and quite unfamiliar to me. When the horrid song was over I fell into a state of self-condemnation mixed with helpless expectancy, which was so poignant as to move me still when I think of it.)

This picture is one of wars and earthquakes and burning mountains. Underneath it are the words 'End of the World.' I have a vision of the countless myriads of mankind kneeling in agony on the other side of the gate. A multitudinous murmur swells into an awful shriek for pity.

'Who am I, O God, that this burden is laid on me? Am I the keeper of that countless host? I cannot answer.'

Even as I speak a shudder cleaves the air, a cataclysmal mirage comes into view, the organ booms and the impish choir begins its torturing refrain.

Underneath this picture there is no placard.

The dreadful music ceases, and the horrid scene before me works on in silence. It passes, and then there is neither light nor darkness. The desert disappears, the gateway is no more, the infinite host has gone like the dew of the morning, and I am left in presence of *nothing*.

The realisation is frightful; my brain is whirling; relief must come; human nature cannot bear it. Ah, thank God, I am going mad – when from somewhere, but whence I know not, comes a light scornful laugh, a Satanic voice says, 'Sold again!' the organ swells, the invisible choir sings anew, and the whole series of pictures begins again from the beginning. For a moment the tension is relaxed, 'God's in His heaven' after all, when, like the clang of steel, the Voice utters the unanswerable question. Oh, God, I must – I shall speak. The answer, the answer is—

'What time is it, Russell?' (Russell was the male night-nurse, the necessity for whose presence the reader will by this time fully understand!)

'Half-past four, sir.'

'Well, I must get up to catch the first train to Glasgow. It is a matter of life and death. Please give me my clothes.'

Russell endeavours to soothe me with promises of going to-morrow, and so forth, all of which I see through with merciless clearness. In the end, as I threaten to alarm the whole house-hold, I am wrapped up in blankets, carried to an easy-chair before the fire, and a screen put behind me.

'You can't get a train, sir, before half-past six.'

'Excuse me, there is a train at 5.55, and I am going to get it. By the way, are you sure Sister is not about? I thought I saw her round the corner of the screen. No? Then give me some soda and milk, and have you a cigarette anywhere?'

Russell naturally denied having cigarettes, whereupon, as he afterwards told me, I proceeded to curse him, his family, antecedents, and descendants together, with such copiousness and minuteness of diction that I spoke without stopping for an hour and a half! I fancy Mr Kipling is responsible for at least the Indian meticulosity of my comminations. Anyhow, the effort having exhausted me, on Russell saying that I had now missed the train, and had better go back to bed to wait for the next, I sensibly agreed.

That was the climax, and on awaking some hours later from a peaceful sleep I found that the crisis was past, and that I was as sane again as usual. The first book I asked for was the *Pilgrim's Progress*, and as soon as I was permitted to read I turned to the account of Christian's passage through the Valley of the Shadow. I had felt before that Bunyan's demons were stage demons, his quagmires and pits merely *simulacra*, the accessories generally such as Drury Lane would laugh to scorn. Now I am sure of it. The real difficulty, of course, is to do it better.

Acknowledgements

The Editor is grateful to numerous people for their help in the compiling of this book, in particular the invaluable research carried out by W. O. G. Lofts, Julia Kruk, Frank Parnell, John Bennett Shaw and David Lass. Thanks are also due to the following for their support, Bruce Wightman of The Dracula Society, London; Leslie Shepard of The Bram Stoker Society, Dublin; Dorothy Nixon of the Vampire Information Exchange, New York; and Dr Donald A. Reed of The Count Dracula Society, Los Angeles. Also the staffs of The British Museum and The London Library for their assistance.